Proud Quail
of the
San Joaquin

G·K
Hall
&Co.

*Also by Stephen Bly
in Large Print:*

Hard Winter at Broken Arrow Crossing
False Claims at the Little Stephen Mine
Last Hanging at Paradise Meadow
Standoff at Sunrise Creek
Final Justice at Adobe Wells
Son of an Arizona Legend
I'm Off to Montana for to Throw the Hoolihan
It's Your Misfortune and None of My Own
One Went to Denver and the Other Went Wrong
Where the Deer and the Antelope Play
Red Dove of Monterey
The Marquesa
Last Swan in Sacramento
The Lost Manuscript of Martin Taylor Harrison
Miss Fontenot

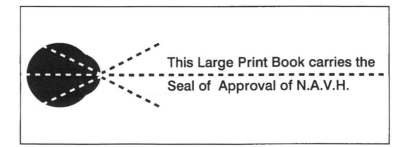

This Large Print Book carries the
Seal of Approval of N.A.V.H.

Proud Quail of the San Joaquin

Old California Series
— Book Three —

Stephen Bly

G.K. Hall & Co. • Thorndike, Maine

Published in 2000 by arrangement with Crossway Books, a division of Good News Publishers.

G.K. Hall Large Print Western Series.

The text of this Large Print edition is unabridged.
Other aspects of the book may vary from the original edition.

Set in 16 pt. Plantin by Warren S. Doersam.

Printed in the United States on permanent paper.

Library of Congress Cataloging-in-Publication Data

Bly, Stephen A., 1944–
    Proud quail of the San Joaquin / Stephen Bly.
      p. cm. (Old California series ; bk. 3)
    ISBN 0-7838-9277-2 (lg. print : hc : alk. paper)
    1. California — History — 1850–1950 — Fiction. 2. Stockton
(Calif.) — Fiction. 3. Women pioneers — Fiction. 4. Large type
books. I. Title.
PS3552.L93 P76 2000b
 813′.54—dc21
                                          00-061428

In memory of
Alice Wilson Bly
Born in the San Joaquin Valley — 1914
Died in the San Joaquin Valley — 1999
Proud of
her husband,
her children,
her Lord

I will open rivers in high places, and fountains in the midst of the valleys: I will make the wilderness a pool of water, and the dry land springs of water.

ISAIAH 41:18 (*KJV*)

One

Seven miles west of Stockton, California. April 1888.

At the first muted knock on the distant wooden door Christina's eyes opened.

Twelve feet above her a pounded tin ceiling square dangled on one side like the last leaf of autumn. A well-marked copy of *Evangeline* lay opened on her chest. The rows and rows of tiny blue flowers on her long flannel gown raced down toward the foot of the lumpy bed.

She stared across the room, sighting in on the brass knob of the schoolroom door between her green-sock-clad feet. Between that door and the one that echoed from the persistent knock were forty-one empty school desks.

Go away. I'm not home.

The knocking was firm, persistent.

Okay, I am home, but it's late.

Like heavy hooves of a Percheron on a cobblestone street, the knocking's rhythmic pattern persisted.

All right, it's not late, but it's after dark.

She thought she heard a voice call out, "Christina!" But the sound was so muffled it sounded more like a crow squawking in the poplar grove.

She glanced through the side window. A dull

evening light, long past sunset, glowed around a tattered beige window shade. *Okay, so it's not quite dark. But I'm already in bed.*

This time the voice was distinct, more forceful. "Christina!"

I'm not exactly in bed. Not even little children are in bed at this hour. I'm on top of the comforter. But I do have on my flannel gown . . . because Raymond Bill Knuteson threw up all over my dress, and it's soaking in the basin.

"Christina, are you in there?" The voice now reminded her of a coyote's plaintive yelp.

Of course, I have my flannel gown on over my petticoats and corset, and I haven't let my hair down . . . or taken off my earrings. I do have my shoes off. I'm certainly not going to the door with no shoes.

"Christina, open up please. I need to talk to you."

It's definitely not one of my students. They all call me Miss Swan. Except for Leonard. The image of the six-foot, 200-pound fifteen-year-old boy lumbered through her mind. *He insists on calling me "Little Missy."*

Christina swung her feet to the floor and laid the book on the dusty chairless school desk that served as a nightstand. Hanging on a rusty nail behind the desk, a twenty-four-inch, circular stained-glass window read "Swan's, since 1849."

The knocking and the calling ceased.

Thank You, Lord Jesus. I'm sure whoever that was will wait until tomorrow. There is nothing in my life that couldn't wait another day! If it weren't for those forty-one mostly clean faces every morning, I would have little to look forward to.

She shuffled across the bare wooden floor toward the chipped porcelain basin on top of a bookcase against the far wall. *I might as well clean up and get ready for bed. Nothing personal, Henry Wadsworth, but you are not a very exciting companion tonight. I took this remote teaching job, Mr. Longfellow, because I wanted the quiet, meditative life. I just don't remember why I wanted that.*

A rap of knuckles on the window of her backroom bedroom caused the thick auburn hair on the back of her neck to bristle. She clutched her flannel gown at the collar even though it was fastened up under her chin.

"Christina, I need to talk to you!" a man called out.

She glanced over at a short double-barreled shotgun that leaned against the desk by the bed.

I ought to shove it in his face — that's what I should do. "Christina, the mark of a Merced woman is graciousness..." Yes, Grandma Alena, but I'm a Swan, remember? Of course, I look exactly like you — not like my mother.

"Christina, open up." The voice became high-pitched, whiny. "I know you're there. I can see your silhouette on the window shade."

He can see my what? I ought to shoot him for sure!

She marched to the window and tugged on the patched shade until it finally lurched upward. In

9

the evening shadows stood a five-foot-seven, 140-pound man with slick dark hair parted on the right. He sported a worn three-button corduroy jacket buttoned up over a black and gray striped tie. The top button on his white shirt was missing, and the tie hung to one side.

"Open the window, Christina!"

In the twilight she couldn't see the pleading in his eyes, but she could remember it from the last time they had talked. She unlocked the sash and lifted the window about an inch. A splash of fresh spring air charged into the room. As the man stood on the bare dirt next to the side of the white clapboard schoolhouse, his clean-shaven face was about even with the open slot of the window.

"Can't you open it wider?" he urged. "I can't see anything."

Christina folded her arms across her chest and stared down at the man. "There's nothing to see. Harvey Jackson, what are you doing here? I thought you were in Missouri."

He jammed his hands into his coat pockets and rocked back on his heels. "I came back."

The words darted from her mouth. "So I see." *This reminds me of how you used to climb the poplar tree next to my house and throw pebbles at my window.*

"We have to talk." His voice was still a whine, but Christina knew that it was as assertive as Harvey Jackson ever got.

She brushed her curly auburn bangs out of her

eyes. "Why don't you come back tomorrow at about 4:00 P.M.? We could sit out in the school-yard and visit."

He put his mouth near the narrow opening of the window. "This is important. I didn't even know you were teaching at Willow Bend School until yesterday."

Christina inched back from the window but continued to stand tall. "This is my third year, Harvey."

He placed his fingers on the sill underneath the open window. "I've been gone almost five years."

Harvey, I have never in my life known you to have clean fingernails. "It seems like only weeks," she murmured.

"Yeah, doesn't it? Eh, Christina, can I come in and sit a spell?"

"No."

His fingers rapped on the windowsill. "Why not?"

The thought of slamming down the window danced in her head, but she chased it off. "Because I have on my nightgown."

"I've seen you in a nightgown before." His voice took on added excitement.

"Not since I was ten." With her right hand she clutched the collar of her flannel gown.

"But we were next-door neighbors over twelve years."

"Harvey, that doesn't give you the right to barge in here. Now go away. I'll talk to you

11

tomorrow." *I should have left on that foul-smelling dress. That would send him away him in a hurry.*

His fingers slid back out of sight. His voice softened. "Mama's sick, Christina."

"She is? I didn't know that. What ails her?"

"She's got pneumonia. Didn't your mother tell you?"

"A schoolteacher has papers to correct, lessons to plan, and students to tutor. I've been very busy." *Except at nights and on weekends when I'm as bored as a pumpkin in January.* "I haven't had much time to visit."

"But they are only seven miles down the road. That isn't very far."

It was now dark enough that the lantern light reflected off the inside of the window and glared back into the room, making it impossible to see Harvey Jackson. "I'm glad it's only a short distance, because then I'm sure you won't mind going home tonight and coming back to Willow Bend tomorrow afternoon. Please tell your mother that I will pray for her healing."

"Thank the Lord, she is getting better."

"Is that why you came home? To see your mother?"

"I got tired of that drafting job in Kansas City. I decided to come home and find something new."

I wish you would find someone *new.* "You should check with Loop. He might know of a position for a draftsman."

"It's boring work, Christina. I'm too adventurous a fellow to be stuck with that all my life."

You are, without doubt, the most boring man I have ever known in my life. "We can discuss all of this tomorrow, Harvey."

"But, Christina, we need to talk about you and me . . . and our future together."

Our future together? We do not have a future . . . nor a present together! "Good night, Harvey. A schoolteacher can't be having gentlemen visitors at this hour. What would the neighbors think?"

He stuck his face so close she could see his pleading pink lips in the opening of the window. "There aren't any neighbors within a mile."

"The Knutesons live one-half mile to the north. I'm going to close the window now. I'll visit with you tomorrow. Please give your dear mother my kindest regards. I'll look in on her the next time I'm in town." She shoved the window down, locked it, and then pulled the shade.

"Christina!" came a muffled plea. "You can't treat me this way."

She sauntered across the room toward the lantern. Even with the thick wool socks her feet felt cold. *So he could see my silhouette on the shade? Perhaps I need wooden shutters. . . . I'll ask the school board for . . . No, they insisted that a woman cannot live out here alone, that it's a man's job. I will not ask for shutters. I will not give them that satisfaction.*

There was a tapping on the glass and another summons: "Christina, you have to talk to me.

13

I'm still your beau."

Harvey, you haven't been my beau since I was four and you tossed my favorite doll into the privy. She scooted to the bedside and plucked up the shotgun. She raised the weapon to her shoulder and stared at the shadows temporarily tattooed on the inside of the window shade.

The rapping and the beckoning finally ceased.

Maybe I'll just paint that shadow permanently on the shade. Every time it's pulled, it'd look as if I'm standing here with a shotgun!

Christina shoved the shotgun behind the nightstand and then moved the lantern to the top of the old dresser with the cracked mirror and missing bottom drawer. A shipping crate turned on end and covered with a thin, quilted green pillow served as a seat. She pulled off the dangly silver heart earrings and rubbed her earlobes as she stared into the mirror.

Lord, I didn't mean to be harsh with Harvey. I just don't honestly know how to keep him from pestering me. He's been gone for years and then begins right where he left off. Why do I attract such strange men?

Perhaps You shouldn't answer that.

She glanced down at the gold-filigree-framed photo on the dresser. She saw the images of three women — her mother, herself wearing her black graduation robe, and Grandma Alena.

Well, Christina Swan, you said you could do it, and you did it. You graduated with a degree in mathematics from the University of California and finished sixth in your class.

Christina stroked her hair with an abalone-handled brush.

I would have finished higher if I hadn't slapped Dr. Ledbetter. Professor or not, no man accidentally brushes against my chest three times during the same hour.

She unpinned her auburn hair, and it curled down to the collar on her flannel nightgown. *I should let it grow out like Grandma Alena's. Lord, may I be as beautiful as she is when I'm sixty.*

In the mirror she surveyed the small spartan room behind her.

Well, you made it big, Christina Swan. Now you have this challenging position as schoolteacher in a one-room schoolhouse at Willow Bend. You could have landed this same job after two years of Normal College. Probably could have been hired without any college.

"You are overeducated, my dear."

"Thank you, Mother."

"Big companies won't hire a woman, and the schools will be afraid you'll be easily bored and want to move on."

Christina looked at her image.

You look exactly the same as you did three years ago. The nightgown is three years old, the earrings ten years old. The smile is . . . the same wearisome one you've had for years. The unmarried Willow Bend schoolteacher. Lord, I know You have more for me.

I just don't know what.
Or where.
Or with whom.
I have never really been sure.

The crash at the front door of the schoolhouse brought her to her feet and scurrying to the shotgun.

Harvey Jackson, if you broke my front door, I'll have you arrested; I swear I will, no matter how sick your mama is. Lord, why doesn't he just go away? I don't want to get mad at Harvey. I don't want to get mad at any man. Well, perhaps one or two, but Harvey's not one of them.

She looped the shotgun over her right forearm, plucked up the lantern with her left, and marched out into the dark shadows of the twenty-four-by-thirty-six-foot classroom where rows of oak and black iron desks loomed as silent sentinels of emptiness. In the darkness near the front door, a man in a boiled white shirt and suspendered jeans knelt by the barely open door.

"Turn off that lantern, Christina darlin'." It was the voice of one used to giving orders.

"Cole Travis, you get out of my schoolhouse right now." She replied with the voice of one who did not take orders well.

"The lantern!" he hollered and then pulled his revolver. She could hear the hammer click twice, and he pointed the barrel out the crack of the doorway.

Lord, this is ludicrous. Is every derelict from my past showing up at my door tonight?

"Cole, I don't know who's chasin' you, but if I pull the trigger on this shotgun, you won't have to worry about who's out there. Now please leave."

"You can't shoot me, darlin'." Even across the room she could see the sly smile under the thick mustache and feel the tickle in his words.

"If you think two and a half years of a miserable relationship gives you the right to . . ." she blurted.

"It wasn't all miserable," he murmured.

". . . bust up a schoolhouse door and barge in here, you've got another think coming. No, it wasn't all miserable. Just the last two years." The chalkboard on the side wall caught her eye. In perfect cursive she could read, "Every good boy does fine."

Travis continued to kneel and peer out into the darkness. "That's not why you won't shoot me."

She pulled her gaze from the chalkboard. *But what do the bad boys do?* "You don't think I could hit you from here?"

"I know you could; that's the problem. I've seen you blast a glass ball from 300 feet. You won't shoot me because it would hit me and make a bloody mess all over your front door. You'd have to explain that to the children in the morning. That is something Miss Swan does not wish to do."

"I'm certainly going to report this to the sheriff in the morning."

"At the moment that's the least of my worries. By morning I could be in the Sierras or in the grave. For the sake of mercy, Christina, turn off the lantern."

Perhaps I should just go to my room, pull the covers over my head, and wait for all of this to go away. "Who's chasing you this time, Cole?"

"I couldn't tell. It must be a Pinkerton or a railroad detective. I haven't seen him before."

She watched him hunker down at the door like a cat preparing to pounce. "You have some explaining to do."

He waved an arm back at her but stared out into the night. "In the dark," he insisted.

"Are you going to stay over there by the door?" she demanded.

"I promise."

The smell of chalk dust hung in the air and blended with her violet perfume. "How do I know you'll keep your promise this time?"

"You never let up on that, do you?" he grumbled.

Her answer came like a heavy boulder dropped into the mud. "No."

"Turn off the lantern so I can focus on the poplar grove. I'm not leaving this doorway," Travis demanded.

Christina edged to the back of the classroom, plopped the lantern on the desk, and slammed the gun next to it. She sat in the oak swivel chair and turned the lantern down but not out. "That's the best you get."

"You don't trust me?"

"I have no earthly reason to. What did you do? Is there a nice reward out I can collect?"

"That isn't funny, Christina."

"I didn't intend it to be. If you are uncomfortable with this conversation, you may leave," she announced. *This is like a bad dream. I'm sitting in my classroom in my flannel nightgown about to witness a shooting. I hope I wake up soon.*

He pulled off his drooping hat and wiped his short brown hair and high forehead on his shirt sleeve. Then he jammed the hat back on his head. "We got even with them, Christina. Not that the score is settled, but at least we announced our presence."

She rapped her fingers on the brown ink blotter that stretched across the oak desk. "Who did you get even with?"

Cole Travis turned and sat with his back against the door. "The railroad, that's who."

Christina stiffened. "Got even for what?"

"For Mussel Slough, of course." His voice was hushed.

"Cole, that tragedy was eight years ago."

"It doesn't matter. They cheated good folks out of the land and then shot 'em down like dogs," he justified himself.

"But that was over 100 miles south of here."

"Yep. That's why I figured they wouldn't follow me this far north. Guess I was wrong. You ever heard of Pixley, Christina?"

She glanced toward the north wall where a

map hung in the shadows. She could not read anything other than "Alta California." "No."

"You will soon. A train engine blew up about a mile south of there. Took twenty-four sticks of dynamite."

She picked up the shotgun and laid it across her lap. "Cole, what did you do?"

"I did just what you and me said should be done when we sat out on your mama's porch years ago."

"I never ever said anything about violence. You know how I feel about that. I just said the railroad should be held accountable for their actions."

"And that's what we're doing. We've waited years for justice from the state and got none."

"So you're saying there's a railroad posse out after you?"

"Not a posse. Not yet. That's the thing. I thought we'd made a clean escape. But there was someone waitin' in the trees out front of your school when I rode up."

Christina rubbed her hands along the polished walnut stock of the shotgun. It felt slick and cold. "In the schoolyard?"

"No, he's in the trees by the creek."

"What did he look like?"

"How would I know? He was lurkin' behind a tree, tryin' to keep out of sight."

"It could have been anyone. Maybe just a drifter passing through. They camp down there all the time."

Travis stuck his nose back into the crack of the door. "And it could have been a Pinkerton man. They sneak around in the dark like that. He was waiting for me to show up."

"California is a big state," she added. "How would he know that you would come here, of all places?"

"Because you're my girl."

"I am not your girl," she snapped.

"You used to belong to me." His voice was more a plea than a declaration.

She leaped up and waved a long, narrow finger. "I never belonged to you, Cole Travis. That was the problem, remember? You treated me like an object to be possessed or disposed of."

"This is not the time to relive this discussion. Why doesn't he make a move?" Travis kept his eyes fixed on the blackness of the night.

"What is he doing?"

"He's just standing out in the trees watching the schoolhouse. Maybe he's waiting for others."

"In that case, this might be a good time for you to make a break for the mountains," Christina suggested.

"Course, you might be right. Maybe he's just a drifter. I think I'll wait for him to make a play. He's probably trying to determine if I have the gold."

The words fell like an anchor in shallow water. "What gold?"

21

"From the train robbery, of course," he mumbled.

"Gold? You stole gold?"

"Everyone has to eat. But I don't have it. I sent Billy to the mountains with it."

"I don't want you here, Cole. I will not have an outlaw and thief in the schoolhouse." Christina stalked toward the door, the shotgun in her hand.

"I'm not an outlaw and a thief. I'm a promoter of justice. The railroad forfeited its title to the land when they decided not to follow the surveyed route. Crocker said they'd sell the land for $2.50 an acre and invited folks to move in, but by the time people took formal title, the railroad wanted to make them pay $25 an acre after they had already improved the land. That's deceit and robbery, and you know it."

"Yes, but the courts upheld it." She could feel her forehead bead with perspiration.

"Then the courts are rigged. And that's a crime."

"So is blowing up a train and stealing someone's gold." *I want this man to leave, Lord, and I want him to leave right now!*

"Your kin wasn't there. It was my Uncle Dan that was shot in the back by Walter Crow."

"And I believe Mr. Crow likewise was killed with a bullet in the back."

"It don't matter. The railroad has to pay."

"It matters to me. The sinfulness of man can never accomplish the righteousness of God."

22

There were no soft edges to her words. "Get out, Cole."

"You can't throw me out!" He stood and stormed right at her. "And it's a cinch you won't pull that trigger!"

With the butt of the shotgun tucked against her flannel-robed shoulder, she raised the gun to the ceiling. She could feel the cold case-hardened triggers under her finger. She slid them to the side and squeezed tight on the right trigger.

The explosion slammed the stock of the gun into her shoulder. She felt as if she had been struck with a big wooden mallet. She staggered back; her ears rang from the explosion, and the thick acrid cloud of gun smoke circled the room.

Cole Travis froze in place, his revolver still clutched in his drooping hand.

"I do believe the Pinkerton man will be at the door any second now," Christina shouted. "And no telling how many neighbors will come running."

Travis took one more step toward her.

Her finger slid to the trigger on the left. "This is a double-barrel."

"I never thought you'd treat me this way," Cole grumbled.

"Why would you expect anything else?"

The front door swung open, and a winded Harvey Jackson sprinted into the room. He halted when he saw Travis and the guns.

Cole Travis pointed the revolver at Jackson. "You're a dead man, Pinkerton," he shouted.

Harvey raised his hands and hurdled backward. His round hat tumbled to the floor, revealing slicked-down dark hair. "Pinkerton?"

"You thought Harvey was a Pinkerton man?" Christina called out, her shotgun still pointed at Travis.

"I'm no Pinkerton," Harvey pleaded, shielding his face with his hands.

Travis took a step toward the cowering man. "Who are you?"

Harvey Jackson inched back toward the empty coat rack. "I'm . . . I'm . . . Christina's . . ."

"You're her beau?" Travis growled. "I should have known."

"What does it matter if he is or isn't?" Christina challenged, as she kept the shotgun sighted on Travis. "Get out of here, Cole."

The outlaw surveyed Harvey Jackson from head to toe and then shoved his revolver into his holster. "He's the one who's been standing out in the trees. You have a boyfriend who's a peeping Tom?"

"I didn't say he was my boyfriend."

"I wasn't peepin' at anything." Harvey lowered his hands. "Christina and I go way back."

Travis kept his eyes trained on Harvey Jackson as he shuffled toward the door. "I can't believe you'd choose a mouse over a — a —"

"Is *polecat* the word you're searching for? Get out, Cole, or I'll shoot more than shingles."

"I hope you two have a wonderfully dull life together." Cole Travis trotted down the row of desks, scooting past Jackson as if he weren't there.

Harvey Jackson reached into his coat pocket and pulled out a small revolver. He quickly pointed it toward the back of Cole Travis's head.

"No!" Christina screamed as she lunged toward the men.

Travis dropped to the floor, rolled toward a desk, and drew his revolver.

Harvey Jackson blasted two shots wildly toward the front door.

Christina pounced on Harvey and slammed the shotgun barrel into the back of the man's head. Like a sack of oats tumbling out of the hayloft, Jackson crumpled to the floor.

"I knew you were on my side." Travis's brown eyes danced in the shadowy flicker of the distant lantern.

"You're wrong. I just didn't want you to kill Harvey! Get out of here, Cole."

"Come with me."

"Never!"

"You didn't used to say that."

"You didn't used to be a cutthroat and an outlaw."

"I haven't changed."

"Then I have."

"I don't intend to come back."

"I'm sorry for you, Cole."

"That I'm not coming back?"

"That you're using your enthusiasm and drive in such a destructive way. I fear it will lead to an early, violent death."

"Miss Swan! What's going on here?" a deep voice rang out. At the schoolhouse door loomed Myron Knuteson and L. D. Traver. "We heard gunshots."

"Mr. Travis was just leaving." She lowered the shotgun and clutched the collar of her still-buttoned flannel gown.

Cole Travis jammed his revolver in its holster. "That's right, fellas, I've got to get moving. Give my regards to your mother, Christina. I suppose she'll be delighted to know that she was right about me."

"But w-what . . ." the school board president stuttered. "What is this all about? This is highly irregular!"

"Just a lover's quarrel," Travis announced as he stood in the open doorway.

"That's ludicrous," Christina replied.

"Who's that on the floor?" Mr. Traver challenged.

"He's the lover that won!" Cole said and then sprinted out into the night.

Christina paced the floor of her schoolhouse bedroom. Her brown dress hung to the floor, the lace collar stiff on her neck. Her lace-up black shoes tapped along with her stride. Dangling silver earrings danced beneath her lobes.

The woman in the straight-back rocking chair brushed down her blue skirt. Her dark brown hair tumbled down her back to her waist. Two light blue ribbons circled her head like a stylish hat. Several rings decorated her strong, pale fingers.

"Mother, you didn't have to come," Christina insisted.

Martina Swan Hackett brushed a wisp of hair out of her eyes and tucked it behind her ear. "Honey, I didn't want you to face the school board all by yourself."

"I'm never by myself. The Lord is with me always."

"I know, I know." Martina watched her daughter wring her smooth, long white ringless fingers. "I also know what it's like to have to struggle against very unjust circumstances."

Christina stopped pacing and rested her hand on her mother's shoulder. She pointed at the stained-glass sign that hung on the wall. "You mean when you had all the trouble at the store when I was a baby?"

Martina patted her daughter's hand. "You've heard the story often, honey."

"Yes, and you were married at the time." She ran her fingers through her mother's silky long hair. "At least you had Daddy on your side."

"He was there at the end. But he was busy for a while in Nevada, remember? I couldn't count the nights when it was just you and me and a pillow full of tears. I know the Lord will lead you, Christina. But I don't know how this will turn out. You may not need me, but I need to be

27

here. You have been the center of my life for twenty-four years. I don't think I can be any other way. I want to be here to rejoice with you in good news and . . ."

Christina gently rubbed her mother's shoulders. "And watch me cry if they fire me?"

"I can guarantee you, if that's the end of this matter, I will be crying, too. Loop wanted to be here, but a bridge washed out up on the Tuolumne, and they couldn't get along without his engineering expertise. But he did offer to hold a gun on the school board until they treated you right."

Christina studied her mother's veined fingers. "He would have done it."

"Yes, he would have."

"If I had him and Uncle Joey —," Christina began.

"Loop and Uncle Joey? Those two would take on the host of Hades for their redheaded angel."

"I know, Mama. But there are some things I've just got to go through on my own." Christina paced the room again. "Mother, did you ever wonder why the Lord would give you two good men, Daddy and Loop Hackett, while some women have no one at all?"

Martina bit her lip and paused. She stared off in the distance. Finally she turned to her daughter. "Are you speaking from personal experience, darling?"

"Maybe. Look at the two men in my life — a

next-door neighbor who pursues me like a hound stalking a quail and a misguided political zealot turned outlaw. It's depressing."

Martina stopped rocking and rapped her fingers on the arms of the chair. "Have you talked to Harvey Jackson recently?"

"Not since I flattened him out last week."

"His bruise is that sort of sickly yellow color. But he can cover it with his hat now."

"He tried to shoot Cole in the back, Mother. I had to bushwhack him, or I would have had a killing right here in my schoolroom. I don't think there is an ounce of wisdom in those two men combined."

"Loop said you did the right thing. He's proud of you. In fact, he was bragging about you to the mayor the other night."

Christina paused in front of the mirror to straighten the lace yoke on her dress. "How about you, Mother? Are you proud of me?"

"Darling, as I said, you have been my delight and my pride since the day you were born."

Christina watched her mother's reflection. "Will you be proud of me if I get fired from teaching school, and no one else wants to hire me?"

The answer drifted back across the room like a blown kiss. "Yes, of course I will."

Christina spun around. "You didn't hesitate."

"Why should I? I know you acted with honesty and integrity in what you did. I have no reason not to be proud of you."

Christina marched over toward the door to the classroom. "That's not exactly the way the school board sees it."

"Well, they are distracted by the shingles that were blasted off the roof, a schoolteacher parading in front of men in her flannel nightgown, a man unconscious on the schoolroom floor, and a notorious train robber waving a gun and claiming to be your lover. It must be somewhat confusing."

"I wish they'd hurry up." Christina leaned against the door. "Either they believe me, or they don't believe me. What's the delay?"

Martina glanced away from her daughter. "I would say they have a difference of opinion . . . or perhaps they're waiting for more character references."

"What do you mean, character references? I've taught school here for three years. Every parent in the district knows me."

"Perhaps they are waiting for . . ." Martina bit her lip again. "Listen, punkin' —"

"Why am I still called punkin'? I'm twenty-four, Mother."

Martina's brown eyes stared straight into Christina's green ones. "You're my only child."

Christina stared out the curtainless window to the poplar grove beyond the unpainted picket fence. "A fact I have often regretted, as you know."

"By the time I finally married Loop Hackett, I

thought I was too old to begin again. You were twelve."

"Why didn't you marry him sooner?" Christina rambled with no mystery in her tone of voice.

"Darling, we've been all through this before. I wanted to wait so you wouldn't forget your father."

"I was only a year old when he was murdered while saving our lives. I can't remember anything but what you've told me."

"I know, dear. That, too, is the loving-kindness of the Lord."

Christina suddenly leaned her head back against the door. "Who's that?"

Martina stood but didn't move any closer. "Who?"

"I heard someone else come into the school-room," Christina replied, her ear still to the door. "I wonder if one of the parents came to the meeting after all."

"I believe they said it's a closed session," Martina cautioned.

"I think I'll peek out there."

"Do you think that would be wise?"

"They said we could wait in here. Obviously, they must suppose that we can hear what's going on."

"But we can't hear."

"But we can peek." Christina slipped her hand to the cold brass door handle.

"Wait, dear, I don't really think . . ."

Christina nudged the wooden door with chipped white paint open about half an inch and surveyed the schoolroom. She focused on the half-dozen men seated at the far side of the room near the chalkboard. She spun around and shut the door with a bang. "I can't believe it!" she moaned.

"What is it?"

"They brought in Dr. Ledbetter to speak against me."

"Against you? Oh no, dear, he's here to speak on your behalf."

Christina marched over to the narrow bed and flopped down on her back. "You expect me to believe that Dr. Ledbetter came all the way down from Berkeley to defend me? Why would the school board bring him in for that?"

"Maybe the school board didn't send for him," Martina murmured.

Christina sat straight up on the bed. "What?"

Martina took a deep breath and then let each word out slowly. "I summoned him."

"Why on earth did you do that?"

"Well, he always wrote you those glowing letters about what a wonderful student you were. I thought a word or two from such a learned man would be appreciated. He wired back and said he would be delighted to take your side."

Christina collapsed back on the comforter and stared at the tin ceiling. *Dr. Ledbetter was always interested in more than just my side!* She closed her eyes. "Why didn't you ask me if I wanted him to come?"

"Because I assumed you would not want anyone to fuss over you like that."

Still lying on the bed, Christina turned her head so she could see her mother. "Mama, you have no idea what you have done. Did it ever occur to you why Dr. Ledbetter sent me all those flowery letters?"

Martina Swan squinted her eyes. "You don't mean . . ."

"Yes, I do mean . . ."

"But he's a married man," Martina objected.

"That doesn't seem to slow his pursuits."

"You rejected his advances, no doubt."

"On more than one occasion."

"Oh, dear, what will he tell the school board?"

"That I'm headstrong, insubordinate, and won't listen to reason. That was in the last letter he sent to me."

Martina held her cheeks in the palms of her hands. "I do believe I have rather muddied the waters. Darling, I'm very sorry."

The only sound was muffled male voices. A knock on the door brought both women to their feet.

Christina reached out for her mother's hand. "I'm really glad you came out to be with me."

"No matter what?"

"No matter what. I can't even imagine not having you around for any important event in my life." She turned to the door. "You may come in," she called out.

Mr. Traver stuck his head in the doorway. "We're ready for you, Miss Swan." His eyes looked as gray and tired as his hair.

"I presume my mother is allowed to be with me."

"Eh, certainly," Traver mumbled. His thick sideburns seemed to slip lower with each word.

Christina laced her arm in her mother's as they proceeded toward the door.

Martina leaned close to Christina's ear. "Would this be a good time for me to challenge the professor's inappropriate behavior toward my daughter?" she whispered.

A smile broke across Christina's face. "I don't think so."

"Then I'll just have to take him out behind the woodshed after the meeting," Martina added.

"Perhaps I'll help you." She squeezed her mother's hand.

Christina and her mother waited at the front gate of the schoolyard while the men packed the final crates out of the backroom and loaded them into the carriage.

"Inappropriate social relationships in school facilities!" Christina fumed. "It sounds like I set up a brothel."

"When you are persecuted for doing the right thing, we can only assume it is the Lord's directing."

"I won't even get to see the children again. That seems really cruel."

Dr. Drew Ledbetter, French silk suit still carefully buttoned, carried out the final box of personal belongings and stacked it behind the carriage seat. He stepped over to the women and then looked straight at Martina. His starched white collar showed little sign of perspiration. "They seemed to have had their minds made up before I arrived. I did what I could for your daughter." He leaned close to Christina. "If I can do anything for you in the future, please contact me. I do have school connections all over the state. I'm sure that under the right conditions, there's another position for you. I'm terrible sorry, Christina."

Martina's eyes narrowed, smoothing the wrinkles. "Are you sorry for inappropriate behavior and advances toward my daughter over the past six years or just for the fact that she was unfairly fired?"

He jumped back as if stabbed with a hat pin. He frantically searched Christina's eyes.

She slipped her arm into her mother's. "Mother and I are very close. I tell her everything."

His face flushed.

"I was quite shocked about that time you called her into your office and —," Martina began.

"Mother!"

"Well, you're right. There's no reason to repeat what all of us already know," Martina said.

"But . . . but . . . I can explain that. It was merely an accident. . . . Surely you don't believe . . ."

"Dr. Ledbetter, my daughter is as pigheaded and stubborn as her mother and her grandmother. When she sets her mind to it, there is nothing, and I do mean nothing, that she can't do. But Christina never ever lies to me. I believe every last word she tells me."

The professor seemed to be searching for a school board member to rescue him. "Well," he huffed, "I think it's time for me to go. I will write to you and send you my bill for my time and boat passage."

"Very well," Martina added, "I will send it promptly back. I've been meaning to write to your wife."

Suddenly his pink face turned pale. "You what?"

"Yes, what is your home address?" Martina pressed.

"You can just send it to the university. I'll see that my wife gets your letter," he said.

"I think not, Dr. Ledbetter. If you send me a bill for this trip, then I shall find a way to send your wife a note. That's the way it goes."

"That's — that's blackmail."

"No," Martina replied. "It's called getting what you deserve. I believe that's the definition of justice."

The tall professor with the thick dark mustache stomped over to his waiting carriage.

"I believe we whipped him good, Mama."

"Yes, and we needed one victory today. Now I must apologize to the Lord for how self-satisfied I felt."

Unassisted, the women climbed up into the carriage.

"Shall we leave the woodshed?" Christina said.

"Whenever you're ready, punkin'."

Christina slipped her arm into her mother's. "Take me home, Mama."

Martina brushed a kiss on her daughter's cheek. "Only if you tell me what really happened in Dr. Ledbetter's office!"

Two

Christina strolled under the huge oak tree whose massive branches and blanket of green leaves provided an umbrella of shade. Her right hand clutched the strong left arm of the middle-aged man with identical auburn hair. "Maybe in the long run it's best, Uncle Joey."

His shoulders stiffened. His graying thick mustache bristled with the rumble from his deep voice. "Nobody treats my Christina that way. I should have been there. I would have reminded them that there were Merceds in this land before gold was ever found. Why, we tamed it, we did. Who do they think they're dealing with?"

Christina brushed her bangs out of her eyes. "My name is Swan, Uncle Joey. Remember?"

"Hah! Look at you — red hair, green eyes." He patted her hand. His fingers felt like rough granite. "You're Merced to the soul. They needed a history lesson."

Acorns mashed under the heel of her black lace-up boots and planted themselves in the dark alluvial soil. "Now you're sounding like Grandpa."

Joseph Merced stared into the sunlight of a patch of bright orange poppies that spread up the hill past the oaks. "I reckon you're right about that. All us boys get more like him every year."

She tugged at the high collar of her dress, trying to fan a little air on her chest. "I truly miss him. Don't you, Uncle Joey?"

He let his big hands slip into the pockets of his ducking trousers. "Ever' day of my life."

She tugged on his arm until they started walking again. "Perhaps it was good you weren't there at the school board meeting." Christina smiled. "They were in a bind, Uncle Joey. It did look very suspicious."

"Merced women are above suspicion," he grumbled.

She leaned over and kissed his tanned cheek. "Only to Merced men. Anyway, it was Cole Travis who caused all the grief. If he hadn't shown up, none of this would have happened."

The rumble of a stagecoach on the road beneath the hill caused them both to stop and gaze to the east. A cloud of dust followed the coach like a posse.

"I don't know what got into Cole. He worked for me for six months. A fine worker, too. Then he just up and quit one day. I figured he wanted to move back north to be near you, but he went south and got into trouble. Now that I'm opening up that land in Tulare County south of the King's River, I could use some good hands. I should never have bought something so far away from the home place."

"Well, I'm unemployed, Uncle Joey. Maybe

you ought to hire me to work on your ranch. Grandpa taught me how to work cattle, and Grandma taught me how to ride like the wind."

"I'd hire you on the spot, darlin', and you know it, but that land is primitive. Besides, it isn't any place for someone as smart and talented as you."

Christina untied her straw hat and held it in her hands. "Being smart and talented doesn't seem to be all that advantageous."

"In what way?"

She shook her hair out and then fanned herself with her hat. "Look at the kind of men I attract. They all seem to be totally devoid of any sense."

The white teeth of his smile contrasted with the dark tan of his face. "Why do you think that is?"

"Because normal men don't like a woman who is college educated and challenges their way of thinking."

"It's not that simple." He scratched the back of his neck. "Look over at that cedar fence post, and what do you see sittin' on it?"

"A valley quail."

"Male or female?"

"Male, of course. I can see his topknot from here."

"And what do you see down there in the green grass?"

"Is this going somewhere, Uncle Joey?"

"Answer my question."

"There's another quail and six little ones following her."

"How do you know it's a female?"

"Because of the babies, and there's no marking, no topknot."

"Now what do you think would happen if one day mama quail jumped up on the fence post and said, 'You take the kids to breakfast'?"

"I don't know, but I have a feeling you're going to tell me."

"I think papa quail wouldn't know what to do. He'd just walk around the post squawkin' in bewilderment."

"Uncle Joey, are you saying I'm a quail?"

"A proud quail."

"And I should know my place and be like everyone else and never hop up on top of the post?"

He pulled off his felt hat, wiped his brow, and then replaced it. "Nope. You're already up there, darlin'. What I'm sayin' is, if you want to stand on top of the post, you better get used to havin' men strut around squawkin' in bewilderment. The higher the post, the more bewildered they will be."

"Why, land-a-goshen, Uncle Joey," she drawled as she dropped her chin and batted her long eyelashes. "You ain't sayin' I ought to jist pretend like I'm some simple, little, naive farm girl who goes barefoot and wears her one tattered dress while she slops the hogs and milks the cows, waitin' for some fella with the muscles of an ox and the brain of a chicken to come carry me off to the corn crib, are you?"

He grinned and shook his head. "I ought to just pick you up and toss you in the creek for that mocking."

"It wouldn't be the first time," Christina giggled. "Remember when you, Uncle Walt, and Uncle Eddie tossed me in Cow Creek?"

"Your mother pitched a fit."

"Well, it did cure me of throwing pinecones at the ponies. I've always been a pill, haven't I?"

"Spoiled rotten, restless, and stubborn to the core." His laugher rolled in waves. "But I wouldn't call you a pill."

"Loop and Mama spoiled me. The Lord created me with a strong will, but I don't know where I get the restlessness."

He led her out into the sunlight as they hiked toward an unpainted corral. "You probably got that from your daddy."

She retied her hat, then trotted to catch up with his long strides. "Was Daddy the restless type, Uncle Joey?"

"What does your mama tell you about him?"

When she reached him, she slipped her arm into his. "That he saved our lives, and it cost him his own."

"That's true enough. Anything else?"

"When I was young, she would often tell me that when she first met him, she was afraid her heart would stop beating. And later on she just couldn't believe that a man so handsome actually wanted to marry her. I used to think she was afraid I'd forget, but looking back, I think maybe she was afraid she would forget. After she and Loop married, she didn't mention Daddy too often. But that's all right. It was painful for her."

He marched them over to the corral and leaned against the top rail. "How about the time between their getting married and the tragedy at the store? Did she tell you anything about what happened during those months?"

"Not much — other than that they tried to make a go of it in the store after Grandpa Swan died, and Daddy went to the Comstock, but was unsuccessful in starting a store over there. What else was there, Uncle Joey?"

"Oh, I reckon that about covers it."

"Why did you say I inherit restlessness from my father?"

"He was always . . . one of those men with grand schemes — you know, starting a store here or a business there. . . . Not that he always did it, mind you. But he always seemed to be lookin' for something else. I guess some folks are that way — never really satisfied with what they have."

"Except for Mama. He was always satisfied with Mama. Right, Uncle Joey?"

He seemed to be studying the horses that milled about in the corral. "I reckon givin' your life for your wife and daughter kind of says it all, doesn't it?"

"Yes, it does. And maybe you're right. Perhaps I have some of his wandering spirit. It's not that I want to leave family; it's just that I . . ."

He kept his eyes focused on the horses. "You keep wonderin' what's on down the trail, and is there an adventure where you can prove your worth on your own?"

She climbed up on the bottom rail of the corral and surveyed the horses. "How did you know that?"

"Because I've seen it in you since the day you were born. That's why you went to the university and majored in mathematics. Everyone advised you not to do it. No woman had ever marched down that trail, but you were determined to see if you could make it."

A gray stallion with long thin legs paced nervously on the other side of the remuda.

"I would like to think of myself as more mysterious than that. It's kind of disheartening that even my Uncle Joey can read my mind."

He put his hand on her shoulder. "Well, darlin', I never thought you would want to keep teaching school your whole life. I really didn't think you'd last this long."

"Grandma Alena says all I need to do is find a good man and get married, and I'll be perfectly content after that."

"Mama isn't exactly the 'stay at home and be content with your knitting' kind herself. She still rides eight miles every morning of the year. She found her man in old San Juan . . . and she found her place . . . Rancho Alazan. Then she squeezes every ounce of life out of it that she can. Your mama's the same way."

"She found two men."

"Yes, she did. I first met Loop when you weren't more than a year old. I pestered her for eleven years to grab onto that man. Your Uncle Walt, Uncle Ed, and me figured that if Loop had red hair, we would just adopt him into the family."

She slipped her arm around his waist. "Uncle Joey, other than Mama and Loop, you're the best friend I ever had."

"There's eight horses in this pen. How many of 'em would you buy?" he probed.

"For ranching or for kids to ride?"

"Ranching."

"You mean, after I check their hooves and their mouths?"

"All things being equal, how many would you buy?"

"One or two, depending on whether I had time to train up the gray stallion."

"What's the other one?"

"The bay mare, of course."

"That's my girl. There aren't six men in California who know horses better than you, Christina."

"And most of them are named Merced."

"Perhaps."

She climbed down off the rail and leaned her back against the corral. "Should we walk back to town? Francine will be getting jealous."

"Now that's something you won't have to worry about. What with Faith, Fannie, Flora, Felicia, Frances, and little Frank running through your mama's house, she won't have time to think about her husband."

Christina started back down the road, her hands swinging at her side. "Grandma calls your gang the Merced flood."

"That's not a bad description. And every one of those girls wants to grow up to be like her Cousin Christina."

"And Frankie?"

"He told his mama that when he grew up, he was going to marry you."

"My goodness, that's precocious for a four-year-old."

"Before you get too worried, he did say he could hardly decide between marrying you or Bravo, his horse."

Christina giggled and clapped her hands. "I won out over Bravo! That might be the highest compliment any boy has ever given me. What did Francine tell him?"

"She told him that you might just be married by then, but that the Lord would provide someone just as wonderful and beautiful as Christina."

"I hope she's right."

"About who he finds to marry when he grows up?"

"About me being married by then. Much to my mother's amazement, I really wouldn't mind being married, Uncle Joey. I like what you said. I want to find the right man and the right place . . . and then get all the life out of it that I can."

"Which are you going to start with?"

"Finding the right place seems almost impossible, but highly more likely than finding the right man."

"I do believe you'll be surprised how quickly the Lord can act when the time is right."

"Uncle Joey, would you really hire me to work that new property of yours?"

He looped his thumbs in his trouser pockets. "You're teasing me."

"No. I want to do it."

"That's no place for someone who's —"

"Joseph Merced, you said you'd hire me."

"Of course, but I didn't —"

"You didn't think I'd call your bluff."

"It's just that it sounds easier than it is. You have no idea what you'd be getting into."

"I want a chance to go accomplish something that people don't think I can do. I failed at doing something everyone said would be easy."

"It's not a pleasant situation down there, Christina. There's problems with the ditch company and the railroad. I'm not even sure *I* can pull it off."

"That's the thing. You have your beautiful place at Mariposa. You don't want to spend all that time separated from Francine and the children. Let *me* develop the Tulare County land."

"Develop it? You mean you want to be in charge?"

"I want to be foreman."

"You don't know the first thing about developing a ranch."

"I can learn."

"You've never even seen the soil. It's one foot of hog wallows on top of eighteen inches of hardpan."

"You're raising hogs?"

"No, I'm going to raise barley, wheat, and hay. But the soil is difficult. What makes you think you can do it?"

"I'm a Merced, remember? You said so yourself."

"Might be some cattlemen that don't want crops down there," he warned.

"I'll have them crying for mercy," she replied.

"You have a cabin full of squatters near the road that don't want to leave."

She scooted up ahead of him, then turned around, and walked backwards. "I'll talk them into moving to Willow Bend and running for the school board."

He chuckled and shook his head. "There are no delta breezes down there in the summer. It gets over 100 degrees for weeks and months at a time and doesn't cool off much at night."

"I'll sleep out on the veranda under a wet sheet."

"There is no veranda. In fact there's no house. Just a barn."

"I'll build an apartment in the loft."

He stopped his stroll. "Hold out your hands."

"What?" She stopped and came back to where he stood.

"Hold out your hands, Christina Swan," he demanded.

Christina stretched her hands out straight in front of her.

"You have beautiful hands. Turn them over."

Christina turned her palms up.

"Now look at my hands." He put his alongside hers. "Mine are scarred, callused, gnarled, sun-baked, and chapped. Do you want your hands looking like this?"

"If that's what it takes, I'll do it. Uncle Joey, I really do want to find my place. Maybe my place is in Tulare County."

He slipped his arm around her waist and hugged her. "Well, darlin', maybe it is. Course, it will take a month just to get things ready to ship south."

"I've got plenty of time. I could come down to Mariposa with you and Francine, and you could show me what you want me to do."

"I suppose you'd want to go down there without me?" he asked.

"Oh, yes!" Christina could feel her own eyes widen. "You mean, you'll let me do it? I really get to develop the new ranch?"

He pulled off his hat and ran his fingers through his gray-sprinkled auburn hair. "Provided your mama don't up and skin me first."

Christina's carriage ride from the train station at Goshen to the Tulare County Courthouse had been eight miles of hot, miserable dust. Visalia reminded her of how her grandmother had described the early years of Sacramento. Through the June heat she had seen farmland and fenced cattle ranches as she approached the city. Traveling down Main Street to the east, she spotted horseback cowboys straddling famous Visalia saddles, red-dirt farmers in Mr. Strauss's coveralls, and prospectors loading up pack strings for Mineral King in the high Sierras. Silk-tied promoters lounged in the doorways of land speculation offices, and hard-working Orientals scurried to some important task.

One block north of Main Street, the Tulare County Courthouse stretched from Court and Church Streets, dwarfing the trees and buildings near it. Somewhere in the distant east Christina knew the massive Sierras hunkered under the blazing summer sun. But at the moment the dust was too thick to see much beyond the court-house.

She hiked up twenty-two wide sandstone steps to the front door and then tried to brush herself clean in the vestibule. She wandered nearly empty halls until she spotted the Office of Surveyor and Records. There was a small hand-printed sign on the oak-and-opaque-glass door that read, "Open. Come in."

The door was locked.

Christina tugged off her dusty gloves and rapped on the glass. There was no answer.

Finally a broad-shouldered man with crumpled dark blue suit and a tie dangling loose around his neck stuck his head out of a neighboring office. His voice sounded distracted. "Lady, no one is there."

She pointed to the door. "The sign says, 'Open.' "

He stepped out into the hallway. Christina thought he looked about thirty-five or forty. "Yeah, and they call June spring, but it's already hotter than Hades. So what else is new?"

"When will they return?"

He tugged at the silver watch chain in his vest pocket but didn't bother pulling the watch out. "Probably right before quittin' time but maybe not until tomorrow."

She glanced down at the brown envelope she held in her hand. "But I have business to take care of today. I need copies of some legal descriptions, and I want to pick up a copy of some water rights."

The man yawned, stretched his arms, and then wandered down the hallway toward her. He stood an inch or two taller than Christina. "They're all at the trial."

"What trial?"

"Lady, have you been hiding in a haystack? The 76 Land and Water Company is being sued by the railroad over rights to lieu lands just south of the King's River."

She clutched the big brown envelope with both hands. "Lieu lands?"

The man refused to look her in the eyes, but instead he stared at a cobweb in the corner of the twelve-foot ceiling. "About ten years ago, Fowler, Baker, and them at the 76 Land and Water Company went in and bought up great sections of land to build their canal and ditch company. But when the eastside railroad was completed, the railroad informed the ditch company that some of that property was lieu land."

She paused for a moment and then gave up trying to catch his eye. "Explain that term, would you?"

Still gazing at the light green ceiling, he continued, "It's a ten-mile buffer outside the railroad land grant that's exchanged for private claims already approved within the grant."

She cleared her throat and threw her shoulders back. The man dropped his eyes to look at her. "So there are two big companies fighting each other?"

He gazed at her from boots to hat. "It's more like one medium company and one monopoly. 76 Land and Water sold all their property except for the canals and ditches so that folks could farm — and buy their water."

Christina watched the man appraise her. *Perhaps it was better when he stared at the ceiling.* "And the railroad claims it's their property and wants it back. It's Mussel Slough all over again," she observed.

"Only this time they don't want the farms back. They just want what they consider just compensation from 76 Land and Water Company."

The air in the courthouse hallway smelled old, musty. "How much money are they asking for?" she asked.

"More money than the company is worth."

"If they win, the railroad owns 76 Land and Water?"

"That's about it. Unless they figure out some other settlement." His eyes bounced back up to the ceiling sanctuary.

"I wonder if the outcome will affect my property?"

"You have property?"

"You seem surprised. Why is that?"

"No offense. I guess I get used to mainly men coming in here. Unless you have a lot out at Traver, you're probably all right."

"Are you assuming I don't have acreage?" she snapped.

This time his eyes glanced down at the top of his scuffed dark brown boots. "Just a deduction, I reckon. A purdy young woman like yourself surely ain't going to farm. I can't see you dirtying yourself on a ten-acre plot."

She folded her arms across her chest. "You're right about that. I wouldn't dirty myself on a ten-acre plot."

He rocked back on his heels as if in triumph. "I figured as much."

"I have three sections of land running down from the springs on the south slope of Stokes Mountain to the hog wallows on the flatland below. I expect to farm about 600 acres of it and graze the other 1,200," she announced.

The man let out a big whistle. "Three sections!" He looked across at her ringless left hand. "Eh . . . you going into farmin' with your, eh, daddy?"

The hallway seemed narrow, stuffy. "Are you insinuating that I can't handle such a project by myself?"

He stepped back and scratched his head, leaving a wisp of dark brown hair sticking out comically over his ear. "No, ma'am . . . more power to you. Of course, that is rotten land up there. It's a red gumbo that turns to concrete about this time of the year. Under it all is hardpan so thick the water won't drain, and everything you plant will sour. It's common knowledge that it isn't good for anything, but the government is smart enough not to take it back. . . . No, ma'am, I don't want to discourage you at all. At least the taxes aren't much on it."

She stepped toward the wall as a well-dressed black man with a polished cane strolled by, tipping his hat. Then she turned back to the man in the crumpled blue suit. "You have not been a beacon of hope."

"Just giving you an honest report."

She stepped back out to the center of the hallway and tried to read the name on the door of the man's office. "Exactly what is your position with Tulare County?"

"I'm Frank Briggs, a member of the Horticultural Commission," he reported.

"Then you have knowledge of my property?"

"Oh, yes. At one time it belonged to old Hiram Willoughby. He thought he could find a silver mine up on Stokes. John Cutler wanted to buy it, but Hiram didn't like the old man, so he willed it to his sister in Ohio. She kept it for a while and tried to lease it out, but no one ever stayed the summer. After that she donated it to Oberlin College. They sent a man out to inspect the property, but he got lost in Antelope Valley, and no one ever heard from him again. So they just up and sold it at an auction in San Francisco. I hear that some Mariposa County cattleman bought it. Probably thought he got a good deal, but it's not a bargain at any price."

"That was my uncle, Joseph Merced. I'm going to develop the property for him."

"Good luck, lady, 'cause there isn't any development on it now."

"According to the County Assessor's papers, there is a barn."

"Probably up by the springs. I've never been up there. Hiram used to have a cabin, but it slid down the hill." A strange grin broke across his face.

"How does a cabin slide down a hill?"

"Hiram built it on skids so he could drag it around to wherever he was diggin' that week.

55

One spring after he passed on, we had a torrential rain, and his cabin slid down to hog wallows out by the road. I guess it just kept oozing forward day after day. I reckon it isn't worth dragging back up to the springs."

Christina glanced up at a pendulum clock at the end of the hall.

"Lady, you'd better go down and attend that trial. Your property is part of that lieu land."

"I thought you said it was a matter between the water company and the railroad," she challenged. "Either way, the property still belongs to my uncle."

"Maybe." He strolled back toward his office. "Maybe not."

"Mr. Briggs, I don't have time to watch a trial. I have an appointment to meet a Mr. Joshua Slashpipe at the Mill Creek Livery."

The man turned in the doorway and leaned his hand against the frame. "Is he out of jail?"

The man who slept on top of the dark gray canvas tarp tied over the heavily loaded farm wagon looked so thin that Christina was amazed he didn't blow away with the swirling, dusty breeze. His dark brown skin was shriveled like a prune, and his short white hair was neatly trimmed. The week-long white beard wasn't. His cheeks looked sunken, shallow. The long-sleeved white shirt was buttoned high at the neck. One collar was turned down, the other creased upwards. His gnarled hands were folded across his stomach. They clutched a silver-trimmed Mexican sombrero that looked as if it had been run over by stampeding buffalo.

Christina adjusted her white straw hat, loosening its wide yellow chin ribbon, and glanced back at the livery boy. "Is that Joshua Slashpipe?"

"Yes, ma'am." The boy grinned, showing two silver front teeth. "You was expectin' a little bit more of somethin'?"

"I was expecting a little bit more of everything."

The young man turned back to the barn. "If you want to wake him, just put your hand on General Grant's nose."

"Put my hand where?"

"The black horse on the left is General Grant. The gray one on the right is General Lee. You touch either of those horses, and Slashpipe will pop up like a gopher out of a flooded tunnel."

The young man disappeared back into the barn.

Uncle Joey, this is the man you hired? He should be at a poor farm or an old soldiers' home or in a hammock in the shade. She glanced around the yard but saw no one else. Christina stepped toward the black horse. *Perhaps the Slashpipe Uncle Joey hired is the son. Maybe he is just allowing his aged father to . . .*

She reached up to rub the horse's neck. When her ungloved fingers stroked the stiff, sun-warmed horse hair, the old man leaped to his feet and stood straight up on the wagon seat. He slapped his sombrero and waved a bony fist.

"*Este caballo negro es el mío y es poco bronco!*" He was completely toothless.

She shaded her eyes and looked back up at the old man. "Your black horse doesn't look wild to me."

"Ay!" The old man leaped to the ground with such decisiveness that Christina was afraid he would break a leg. "*¡La Paloma Roja de Monterey! ¿Es verdad?*"

"Mr. Slashpipe, my Spanish is nowhere as good as my grandmother's. You speak English?"

A wide grin broke across the man's face, and he shrugged. "Spanish is not my best language either. You say the Red Dove of Monterey was your grandmother?"

"She still is," Christina said. "She lives up at Rancho Alazan, north of Sacramento."

The old man shook his head. "It is like I have lived an entire lifetime and now get to start it all over. You look just like your grandmother did forty years ago."

"The hair is the same color, but hers was longer then, and she was thinner."

"But there is no mistake. I trust next time you see your grandmother, you will mention my name." The old man danced from one foot to the next. "I knew her in Monterey when her father, Mr. Tipton, was buying hides and tallow."

Christina stared down at bony toes that

peeked through the top of the man's left boot. "You knew my great-grandfather?"

"I was only a young man, a lad, but I knew him, yes."

There is nowhere I can go in the entire state that my grandmother's reputation does not precede me. "Does my Uncle Joey know that you were an acquaintance of Great-grandfather Tipton?"

The wide brim of the dark sombrero cast shade on the man's face, and his skin seemed even darker. "I have never met Mr. Merced."

"But Uncle Joey said that when he came down to buy the property, he hired you to start work this month."

"Oh, no, he hired my son."

"Oh, your son is Joshua Slashpipe?"

"Yes, and so am I. He is Joshua Slashpipe, Jr."

"That explains things." Christina surveyed the livery corrals. "Where is your son?"

"In Arizona."

"In Arizona? How can he go to work at the ranch if he's in Arizona?"

"I am the one working for Mr. Merced."

"Wait . . . wait . . . I'm confused."

"Mr. Merced met with my son and hired him last March to be caretaker of the ranch until June. But my son moved his family to Arizona in May and left me the job."

"But he hired the younger Joshua Slashpipe."

"My son knows very little about horses and nothing at all about tomatoes."

"What do tomatoes have to do with any-

59

thing?" she pressed.

"I like tomatoes. Perhaps we could grow some at the ranch."

I haven't even seen the place, and I'm having a management problem. Lord, I have had this day completely planned out for weeks, and this is not on the agenda. This man makes Harvey Jackson sound sane.

"Mr. Slashpipe, perhaps you did not know, but I will be in charge of the ranch — not my uncle. So to assist me I'll need to hire someone who —"

"Someone who knows the animals, the land, and the water. Plus you will need someone who can help you build a cabin and chase off the 'wolves.' "

She wiped the perspiration off her forehead and then examined the tracks of grime on the fingertips of her gloves. "Yes, something like that."

"I am just the man you need." It was a toothless, comical smile. "I have done it all, Señorita Merced."

"Swan. My name is Christina Swan."

"Are you ready to go to the ranch?"

Christina's eyes searched the livery stable corrals.

"Are you looking for a young, strong, handsome man to work for you?" He reached out his hand to assist her up onto the wagon seat.

A slight smile broke across her face. "All right . . . I *was* looking for someone younger."

"And more handsome, no? You can tell me the truth. I know I merely possess average good looks." His dark brown, almost black eyes locked onto hers and seemed to dance with the dust in the breeze.

She stared right back at him. "Well, Joshua, to be honest, I did expect to find someone with teeth."

He pushed his sombrero back until it dropped to his back, looped to his neck by a woven horsehair stampede string. "I have teeth!" he triumphed.

"You do?"

"Certainly. I use them when I eat."

"Why aren't you wearing them now?"

"I'm not eating."

The trip north of Visalia was straight and level once the loaded wagon crossed the St. John's River. The fruit trees and grapevines gave way to several dairies, then to fenced pasture.

Mile after mile of fenced pasture.

"Ten years ago there were no fences in here at all," Slashpipe explained. "But now look at this. Fences are never friendly. In the old days California was friendly."

"Mr. Slashpipe, I have a personal question for you."

"I was wondering how long it would take you to ask," he replied. "Here's the answer, Señorita Swan. No, I am not married, and, no, I'm sorry to report, I'm not interested."

The jostling of the wagon seemed to fade as Christina froze in place. "What?"

The old man slapped his knee and laughed. "Señorita Swan, you will be fun to have around for a while. You are very easy to tease."

She ground her teeth. "I intend to stay a very long time."

"Yes, I'm sure that is your intention. But you did not ask me the personal question. After you do, I have one for you."

"I was curious about the origin of the name Slashpipe. It doesn't sound like a Mexican name."

"I'm not Mexican. Slashpipe is Scottish."

"Scottish! . . . You don't . . ."

"I don't look Scottish? Well, my father was from the old country. He came into California with Jed Smith in '26. They hiked up in this very valley when no one lived here but the Yokuts. I was born in '27."

"He had a — a wife?" she asked.

"My mother was Yokut, as you can plainly see by my skin."

"But you seem so . . ."

"Mexican?"

"Yes."

"Well, it's easier to survive in this valley as Mexican than as an Indian. And I have a very difficult time passing for a Scotsman."

"You speak Spanish fluently."

"Yes, and I speak Yokut fluently as well. But as far as you are concerned, Señorita Swan, I'm strictly a Scotsman!"

Christina laughed. "Joshua, you look no more like a Scotsman than I do an Oriental. But I accept that story, and I promise that I will never speak to you in Spanish or Yokut."

"Now, lassie . . ."

Christina continued to laugh. "No, no, Joshua. You are right. . . . You can't impersonate your father."

"*Sí.*" He shrugged. "But I want to ask you a personal question also."

Christina laced her hands on her lap. "No, I'm not married, and, no, I'm not looking for a husband at the present time, but thank you very much for the offer."

A wide grin broke across the old man's startled face. He pulled his sombrero back to the top of his white hair. "I'm easy to tease as well. But my question is, why are you doing this?"

Christina licked her chapped lips. "My uncle purchased the property and was going to hire someone to develop it. I wanted the challenge."

"Yes, but why do it alone?" Slashpipe waved both hands as he spoke. "It's a job for a young family. A beautiful young lady should have no problem finding a good man to marry."

"Thank you for the compliment, but I know I possess merely average beauty."

The old man roared. "I like you, Miss Swan. Perhaps I was hasty in turning down your marriage proposal. But go on."

"I have absolutely no problem finding men.

It's extremely more difficult to find a good one — who is young and has teeth!"

"That's your problem. You are too choosy. But now you have come to look in a new location?"

She brushed down the front of her dress. *I do not believe this dress will ever be clean again.* "My purpose here is to develop this property into a self-supporting ranch and farm — not to find a husband."

"That is good. Because on the south slope of Stokes Mountain, you will be lucky to find a four-legged deer, let alone a two-legged one."

They bounced along without talking for several more miles on the perfectly straight course.

"Joshua, I have another question for you. A man at the courthouse said he thought you spent last night in jail. Is that true?"

"Yes."

"I'm from the old Californio school. I know it's impolite to ask, and please forgive me if I offend you . . . but what were you in jail for?"

"Miss Swan, those old days of gallantry and privacy are long gone. You do not offend me. I was jailed for dancing the fandango."

She stared at his small brown eyes, forcing herself not to look at his toothless mouth. She bit her lip to suppress a grin.

"What?" he exploded. "You have doubts that I can still dance the fandango?"

"Oh, no. My grandmother still dances the fandango. But I do have doubts that a man would be jailed for such action. I believe you are teasing me again."

"They said I was dancing it on another man's head. In Visalia they call that disorderly conduct."

She lowered her chin and raised her thick auburn eyebrows. "You were in a fight?"

"It was a minor skirmish, Señorita. Look at me. There is no dried blood. Look at my hands — the knuckles are not damaged."

"What did you get in a fight over?"

"A woman, of course."

Christina stared straight ahead. "Are you teasing me again?"

"No. But the woman was my niece, not my *amor*. I was staying at her house, and a former friend came over drunk and behaved rather poorly, so I persuaded him to leave."

"By dancing on his head?"

"It's very effective."

"A person gets arrested for that?"

"He was white. I am . . . dark-skinned. I got arrested. Don't worry. It won't happen often. I only get arrested when I win."

Lord, Uncle Joey was right, of course. This is a different kind of land. More primitive. And I don't have any idea what I'm doing. But You promised, "I will open rivers in high places, and fountains in the midst of the valleys: I will make the wilderness a pool of water, and the dry lands springs of water." That's what I want, Lord. And not just on the ranch . . . but also in my soul.

65

As the dust began to settle, a large, brown, grass-covered, treeless mountain loomed ahead of them on the horizon. "Is that Stokes Mountain?" she asked.

"Yes, it is."

"It's bigger than I expected."

"Your ranch starts at the crest on the western end and then falls off this south side to the hog wallows," he announced.

"I've heard that term several times. Just what exactly are hog wallows?"

"Look at that land over on the right. What do you see?"

"Clay soil that is undulated like small waves."

"Yes, but they are not even. There are little pockets."

"Like a hog pen where the pigs have been rooting."

"Yes, but out here no one but the Lord knows how those were made."

"And what is hardpan?"

"It's like dirt concrete," he explained. "But you will not believe it until I show it to you."

Stokes Mountain slowly crept toward them. The wind seemed to stop completely; the sun was hotter. Christina's arms warmed under the long sleeves of her dress. "I understand there is a spring on the ranch."

"There are two of them," he said. "But only one runs all year long."

She pulled a white linen handkerchief from her brown leather purse and dabbed her neck. "I do trust I'll be able to bathe tonight."

"Do we have a bathtub?" When he spoke, his bright pink tongue seemed to dart all over his mouth.

"No bathtub," she admitted. "But we do have a stock tank."

"That is for the cattle," he reminded her.

"We will not have any cattle until fall."

"That's not completely true." He waved toward the top of the mountain. "There are a few wild cows on the ranch even now."

"How can that be? I was told the entire ranch is fenced with barbed wire."

"Yes, that's why the cows are there. They can't get out."

They came to a small, treeless creek where the only water stood in pools.

"What is this called?" she asked.

"Cottonwood Creek."

"But there aren't any cottonwoods."

"Nor much water. Even this will be dry soon. But we will water the horses here. It will be a steep climb up to the springs." He stood up and stretched as he allowed General Grant and General Lee to drink from the pool of water at the bottom of the creek. "Can you see that tiny building about a mile up there?"

Christina stood alongside the old man. "What is it?"

"That cabin is on your ranch."

"Is that the one that slid down the mountain?"

"The very same."

"Let's proceed, Joshua. I'm anxious to get to the ranch."

He kept the team at a steady pace until they crossed an east-west running road that was empty in both directions. He pulled across the road and jumped down to swing open the sagging wooden gate. "We are home, Miss Swan."

"It's different than I had imagined."

"It's different than anyone imagines. Would you drive the rig through the gate?"

She slid over, plucked up the lead lines, and slapped them on General Grant's rump. The wagon rumbled and squeaked past the gate. She waited for Slashpipe to close the gate and climb up on the wagon. Christina pointed toward the ramshackle building. "Can we repair the cabin? Perhaps we could use it for storage."

"No, it's damaged beyond repair."

"Then we will tear it down."

"Not until she moves out."

"Someone lives in there?"

"Señora Mofeta Diablo."

Christina stared at the building several hundred feet away. Even from that distance, it looked as if a giant had stepped on the roof and squashed it sideways. "I thought you said it was uninhabitable?"

Slashpipe waved his hand toward the pale blue June sky. "For us mere mortals. But not for her and her brood."

"My word," Christina gasped. "She keeps children in that little cabin?"

"Children . . . grandchildren . . . relatives of all sorts."

"But it's such a tiny cabin."

"I suppose it's very crowded."

As the wagon rolled closer, Christina studied the building. "But there are no windows, and the door has fallen off the hinges."

"Señora Mofeta Diablo is not very discriminating."

Christina tried to stare into his dark, perfectly round eyes. "Are you teasing me again?"

Even with no teeth, his demeanor was extremely serious. "I will tell you the truth — many a good man has tried to evict Señora Mofeta Diablo, and no one has ever succeeded. And not one of them has ever come back to try again."

He stopped the wagon. "The ranch stretches from this fence to that one. It's a distance of one mile. Then it goes three miles right up the mountain. Do you see that small patch of green grass?"

Christina gazed to the north. "Is that the springs?"

"And the barn."

"I don't see any barn."

"It's hard to see from the road. But that's good. It gives you privacy."

"I will be sitting in the middle of 1,800 acres of fenced land. I think I will have a lot of privacy. How do we get up there? I don't see a driveway," she asked.

"It's June. The land is baked dry. . . . From

now to November we can drive up any path we choose."

"And after November?"

"The clay soil will be so sticky, you could not get in with a dozen team of oxen."

"Then we must build a drive before November," she announced.

"That would be a very good idea," he said. "Would you like to ride up the west side or the east side of the ranch?"

"Why don't we go over to the cabin first. I will tell the Señora she has to move."

"She does not like to visit."

"That's too bad. But I won't throw her out right away. She can certainly take a few weeks to find a new place. I understand that. That place is not safe. Even if I wanted to, I could not in good Christian conscience allow her to live in such primitive conditions."

"You'll have to walk over there on your own. Last time I was near there, she tried to shoot me," Slashpipe cautioned. "She only missed me by a little bit."

"Uncle Joey told me there were some squatters to deal with. I really must speak with her. If she won't leave, I'll have to contact the sheriff."

"He won't do a thing. He's scared to death of her, too."

"I can't believe this!" Christina exclaimed. "Is everyone in the county frightened of this woman?"

A wide grin broke across the old man's toothless face. "Woman? She is no woman. She is Señora Mofeta Diablo, *la madre de todas las mofetas malas.*"

"The devil what?"

"Mrs. Devil Skunk, the mother of all evil skunks." Slashpipe's open-mouth smile almost made the rest of his face disappear.

Christina broke out in laughter. She clutched her sides and continued to chuckle until tears slid down from her eyes. "A skunk! Joshua . . . you had me fooled all the time. I can't believe you teased me like that!"

The smile dropped off his face. "I was not teasing about this skunk. She really is a devil skunk. That's all I will say about that. And we are not going to drive the wagon by the cabin."

The heavily laden wagon squeaked, rattled, and jostled its way up the gradual incline of the lower 640 acres of land.

"Joshua, will this lower section irrigate from the bottom of the mountain out to the road?"

"Yes, if it's leveled and plowed correctly."

"Where is the 76 Water Company canal?" she asked.

"Three miles that way!" He pointed to the west.

"Three miles? I thought we had water to the property. Uncle Joey said by June first we would —"

"It's the trial, Miss Swan. Until the matter is settled, the water company will not dig any more canals and ditches."

She stared at the barren land in the east. "Then we will have to dig it ourselves."

He pushed his big sombrero to the back of his head. "Do you know how to dig a ditch, Señorita?"

"No, but I can learn."

Joshua Slashpipe pointed to a slight column of dust to the east. "I believe that man might help you."

"Who is it? I didn't think there were any neighbors."

"He moved into that section last month."

"He? Just a single man?" she inquired.

"I don't know his marital status, but I can ask if you wish."

"I didn't ask if he was married," Christina muttered. "That doesn't concern me. I wanted to know if he has a family or a crew with him to help him, or is he developing that ground by himself?"

"He is not alone. He has a partner — a black-and-white cow dog."

"A dog is hardly a partner."

"You have never met this dog, Miss Swan."

"I plan on meeting them both in the near future."

"I can arrange that if you would like."

"I don't need you to arrange my meeting of men."

"No, ma'am, I'm sure you don't."

"What is his name?"

"Mr. Kern Yager. The dog's name is

Buscadero, but everyone calls him Busca."

"What does everyone call Mr. Yager?"

"They call him Mr. Yager."

"Is he old?"

A grin broke across Slashpipe's face. "The dog or the man?"

Christina scowled.

"He is middle aged." He shrugged.

"The dog or the man?" she countered.

"The dog. Mr. Yager is not much older than you."

She stared over at the distant column of dust.

"He is very, very smart," the old man continued.

"The dog?" she pressed.

"Yes. And the man also. He graduated from college, you know."

So did I, Mr. Slashpipe, but I'm not sure this is the time to announce it. "What is he doing now?"

"He's getting a few acres ready to plant, but I believe he's a little touched in the head."

"Why is that?"

"He only has a hand-dug well that barely supplies water for himself and the dog. He will not be able to irrigate tomatoes."

Christina surveyed the barren land surrounding them and stared to the east. "There are no neighbors in that direction until the post office and store at Churchill. Is that right?"

"Further than that. The store and the post office are closed."

"What do you mean, closed? I have had all my

73

mail sent to Churchill."

"Everything is in Visalia now."

"I have to go ten miles to get my mail?"

"In the spring it's much longer," he announced. "The creeks run high, and there is often much flooding."

She stared at a small green meadow on the hillside ahead of them. "Is that our springs?"

"Yes. We must fence it off and clean it up. It's very sweet water when it's clean."

"I trust there are no skunks in that old shed. It looks ready to topple over also."

"There are no skunks. But that is not the shed."

"What is it?"

"It's the barn."

"That's the barn I'm planning on sleeping in? I can look right through the cracks in the boards and see the mountainside behind it."

"Perhaps you will have a nice breeze during the summer nights."

"Where are you going to stay, Mr. Slashpipe? There is no bunkhouse."

"I will sleep under the wagon, Señorita."

"That doesn't sound very comfortable," she protested.

"Perhaps not, but at least I'm assured that it will not collapse on my head during the night. That's more than can be said for the barn."

Three

The bed was no more than scattered straw in a breezy hayloft in a barn that slanted downhill. She slept in clothes that she had worn for three days, removing only her dusty gold jewelry and her black lace-up boots. For covers she had two dark green, rough wool blankets, and both reeked of campfire smoke. Her dresser was a black leather suitcase, left open, with various garments peeking out, her pillow a rolled-up old ducking coat that had been a last-minute present from Uncle Joey.

Somewhere, by one of the massive, rough twelve-by-twelve wooden pillars, was her shotgun. Her mother had said it must always be at her side when she slept. Below her, on the ground level, she knew there was no lock on the barn door.

There was no barn door.

It was not her room at her mother's house, with its white four-poster bed and seven-foot-tall wardrobe crammed with dresses.

It was not the storeroom at the back of the schoolhouse, with its homey smell and sagging featherbed.

But it was the best night's sleep Christina had had in months.

Perhaps years.

She lay on her dark green blanket and stared out the cracks of the barn loft at the morning sun just breaking over the top of the Sierras.

Lord, this is it, isn't it?

It's my place, and I know it.

It's home.

I went to college four grueling years to sleep in a barn?

Yes, I did. I proved that I can compete with any person.

Now I just want my home.

This is the place where I want to grow old.

Grandma has Rancho Alazan.

Mama has her Victorian house in Stockton.

This is mine.

I love it. Raw, undeveloped acreage in a land that's changing from open range to fenced farms and ranches. "I will open rivers in high places, and fountains in the midst of the valleys!" That's Your promise to me . . . and this is where I'm going to find its fulfillment.

Christina sat on the floor beside the straw bed and plucked up her heavy lace-up black boots. She carefully turned each over and shook it out before pulling it on her stockinged feet. She glanced up at the ceiling. "Did you see that, Grandpa? I checked my boots before I pulled them on, just like you taught me." Christina brushed a tear back from her eyes.

"Was this how you felt, Grandpa, when you and Great-uncle Echo Jack first settled at Rancho Alazan?" This time she let the tears roll.

Lord, I really, really miss my grandpa. I never knew my father. I don't know how to miss him. But, oh, how Grandpa would hold me so tenderly with his big, old, callused hands. Even at the last, when he was sick in bed and hurt too much to talk, he would insist on holding my hands . . . and the tears would flow from his tired, tired eyes.

"Oh, my, Christina, you are getting melancholy. That was eight years ago. You really must move on."

She carefully washed her face from a large tin can of clean water and patted herself dry with a clean tea towel. Then she strolled across the loft, stretching her arms, surprised to find no major aches and pains.

I will have to eventually build myself a bed. Joshua told me he has spent most of his life sleeping on the ground. I suppose a person gets used to it.

She took a big, deep breath and let it out slowly. The loft smelled of stale hay, dried manure, suspended dust, and the aroma of the earth warming in the hot June sun.

Lord, Francine told me that each of her children has a different smell. She knew at first whiff that they belonged to her. This ranch isn't a real baby, but it's my baby. And it smells like it belongs to me. If I make a go of it, I mean, when I make a go of it, Uncle Joey will sell it to me.

She stood at the edge of the loft and glanced down at the dirt floor of the barn below. She could hear Joshua Slashpipe humming to himself around the oven in the middle of the yard.

Christina strolled back to her suitcase and retrieved a brown leather-bound journal. She retreated to the edge of the loft and backed down the ladder.

"Well, boss lady, what are your orders today?"

She grinned at her own question.

"I have my lesson plan for today, students . . ."

She hiked out of the barn into the yard next to the springs. Joshua Slashpipe was hunched over a large beehive-shaped earth oven. His long-sleeved flannel shirt was buttoned to his neck, and his ducking trousers showed excessive wear in the pockets and knees. The big black sombrero was pushed to the back of his head.

"Joshua, you look very handsome with teeth," she snickered.

He held up a tortilla and grinned, showing the straight, white false teeth. "Yes, I'm eating! Are you ready for breakfast?"

Her feet encased in the boots felt gritty as she approached the adobe oven. He pointed toward a black iron frying pan, still steaming with food. "I like to cook."

She peeked into the skillet. "I don't."

Still squatting on his haunches, he wiped his mouth on his sleeve. "Then I'm the official cook of the Mofeta Ranch," he beamed.

She spun on her heels, digging a slight hole in the dirt. "Oh, no, this is not going to be the Skunk Ranch."

The old man shrugged. "That's what all our neighbors call it."

"What neighbors?"

"Mr. Yager."

"Who else?"

"He's our only neighbor."

"Well, Mr. Kern Yager is greatly mistaken. From this moment on, and for a hundred years to come, this is going to be known as the Proud Quail Ranch."

Joshua looked up so quickly that his sombrero tumbled off the back of his head. "Proud Quail Ranch? I like that." He punctuated his approval with a large bite from a rolled-up corn tortilla. "I can hear them ask, 'Hey, old *vaquero*, what outfit do you ride for?' And I will answer them with dignity, 'I ride for the Proud Quail of the San Joaquin on the slopes of Stokes Mountain.' "

Christina chuckled. "Joshua, you are a very eloquent man."

"Yes, and I have a way with words, too."

She plucked up a stick and drew in the dirt. "The next time we are in town we will register our brand. I thought about it last night and decided on a design. It will look like this — a PQ, only it will have a small topknot, like a quail, on the Q."

He rubbed his clean-shaven chin. "To start with, I can do that with a ring and a running iron. I will make us a branding iron when I get a chance."

Christina glanced east at the sun rising above the Sierras. "Are you also a blacksmith?"

"I build saddles, engrave silver, braid horsehair, break broncos, throw a hoolihan, trip wild horses, and I blacksmith. I worked for Mr. Miller for years."

"Miller and Lux?"

"*Sí.*"

"My Uncle Ed married one of his daughters."

"He's got himself some good outfits, but I just got too old to keep up with the younger boys."

"Is there anything you can't do, Joshua?"

"I'm a dally man. I can't tie hard and fast."

"All right, but I don't intend for us to dally around the barn all morning."

He stared at her.

"I know perfectly well what dally means, Mr. Slashpipe. I was just teasing you."

He grinned broadly. "This is going to be a very enjoyable summer."

"Oh? Do you plan on quitting me in the fall?"

"No, ma'am . . . I will stay at this ranch as long as I am needed."

"Then you better select your gravesite while there are many available. I plan on spending my life here."

"That is good. Then I will also stay. I want to be buried in the poplar grove."

"We don't have a tree on the ranch."

"Then I will have to plant them. When they are big and shady, I will have a place to be buried."

"That will take decades."

"I will wait."

She looked around for a place to sit. "Well,

one thing we need right away is a table and bench for meals."

"Yes," Slashpipe concurred. "But we don't even have a kitchen."

"That doesn't matter. When the lumber gets here, we'll build a table and benches. Will they deliver the boards today?"

"Today . . . tomorrow . . . next week. . . . They deliver whenever Ol' Sy needs a few more dollars."

"Ol' Sy?"

"He has the freight wagons, and his place is over there by Twin Buttes. Whenever he's runnin' low on cash, he drives up to Antelope Valley and makes deliveries for the mill. You never know when you'll get your lumber."

"That doesn't sound very efficient." She rolled a one-foot round of oak toward the oven and sat on it. He handed her a tortilla.

"What's inside?"

"Refried beans and chilies."

"This is quite a breakfast."

"It's an old Scottish recipe. But I don't have any tomatoes. I can cook you something different."

"No, this is fine. I will eat what you eat. Do you have coffee in that pot?"

"Yes. I don't care for tea, and chocolate has become too expensive," he explained. Slashpipe dipped his tortilla in a small jar of thin red sauce and took a big bite. The liquid streamed down his chin.

81

"Is that your private hot sauce?"

"Yes, and it makes an excellent dewormer."

"For man or beast?"

"Both," he laughed.

She stared down at the stuffed tortilla in her hands. "Have you said grace yet, Mr. Slashpipe?"

He chewed the rest of his bite and then swallowed hard. "No, miss. I'm not a very religious man. I have never had much use for it."

"Well, Mr. Slashpipe, I do. My relationship with the Lord Jesus is extremely important." She lowered her head. "Lord, please bless this food and give me strength for the work of this day. I'd ask You to bless Joshua's food too, but he's not much for religious stuff and doesn't have any use for You. So not to offend him, please, Lord, don't bother blessing his food. In Jesus' name, amen."

When she looked up, Slashpipe's eyes were as big as silver dollars. "Why did you go and do that?" he gasped.

"Do what, Mr. Slashpipe?" She cocked her head sideways and then took a long, slow bite from her tortilla.

"Ask the Almighty not to bless my food," he huffed.

She wiggled her toes inside her boots and could tell they were already starting to sweat. "Isn't that what you wanted?"

"Señorita, I, personally, do not need to pray for my food, but if you want to include me in your prayers, I give you permission."

"Thank you. That's very generous, Mr. Slashpipe."

"But I don't want you to try to convert me."

She brushed her hair behind her ear. "I wouldn't think of it."

He leaned closer. "You wouldn't?"

She leaned close enough to smell the garlic in his hot sauce. "Of course not. That's the Lord's business, not mine."

Finally, he backed away. "That's good."

The old white cotton blouse was covered with dust and sweat-streaked. The two collar buttons were unfastened, but the big red bandanna around Christina's neck hid the collar from view. Her long, brown ducking skirt swished with every step, and the heels of the black boots crunched into the hillside. The floppy felt hat hung heavy with perspiration but shaded her face. Slick leather work gloves covered pale, blistered hands.

"La Dueña, perhaps we should have ridden the horses along the fence line," Slashpipe suggested, as he twisted the barbed wire with a heavy pair of pliers.

"You call me La Dueña?"

"The lady who owns the place — the one who gives orders," he replied.

Three miles up on the flank of Stokes Mountain, Christina stopped and stared down the descending hillside. There were no trees and few boulders from the upper fence all the way to the abandoned cabin and the road far below.

"How many wild cattle have we counted?"

"Eighteen."

"I didn't know we had that many."

"There are only eleven, but some of them we counted more than once." He pointed west toward several distant grazing animals. "We have six cows and five calves. And no bull."

"There has to be a bull somewhere."

"Perhaps he's visiting the neighbors."

Christina glanced down at her blouse and tried tucking it back into her skirt. "Joshua, at this time yesterday this blouse was as white as snow."

"If you keep this work up, by this time tomorrow it will be as black as sin."

She held the top of the tilting split cedar fence post while he tamped around its base with the handle of a shovel. "I wanted a firsthand inspection of the entire fence line."

They moved on to the next post, and he handed her a leather canteen of water. She started to wipe the spigot on her blouse sleeve, then hesitated. She took a large gulp of the tepid water and handed the canteen back to Slashpipe.

"What is your opinion of the fence so far?" he asked her.

She wiggled the next post. "I'm amazed that those cows haven't run away."

A broad grin broke across his face. "I told

you, they like it here."

"When Uncle Joey sends down 100 cows this fall, they are going to want to run all the way back to Mariposa. Did we bring enough wire to fix the fence?"

"It depends on the east side." He took off his sombrero, then shaded his eyes with his hand. "La Dueña, it's getting quite hot. Perhaps you would like to go back to the barn and rest in the shade."

She put her hands on her hips. "What on earth for? We are going to inspect the entire fence line today. That's what's on my list, and that's what we're going to do."

"You are getting a little flushed."

"That's to be expected. I've spent the last three years in a classroom. But it *is* quite warm." She held the post straight. "I don't see how you can stand wearing that flannel shirt and have it buttoned up like that. Aren't you sweating to death?"

"It's like wearing a cool, wet sheet," Slashpipe reported. "As long as I drink plenty of water, the shirt keeps me cool."

When they reached the northeast corner of the highest section, she discovered a pile of granite boulders, each about the size of a hog shed. "Perhaps we should take a rest here," she suggested.

"I don't believe that's a good idea," Joshua objected. "I heard that old man Willoughby called these Snake Rocks."

Christina scampered away from the rocks.

Slashpipe studied the sky above them. "The sun is straight above. It's time for lunch."

"Let's eat out here."

"Why?"

"Because it seems rugged, more frontier-like, to eat out on the mountainside while one is inspecting fence," she explained.

"You may take your lunch wherever you want, but I'm going to the shade. There are two things I demand from this job."

"What is that?"

"That we try to grow tomatoes."

"And the other?"

"That I'm allowed to have a noon siesta in the shade."

She waved him off with the flip of her hand. "Just leave me my lunch. I'll eat it up here."

He slung the shovel over his shoulder. "I didn't bring our lunches."

"But I saw you make them," she insisted.

"I made them, but I didn't bring them. I left them in the shade of the barn."

"Why did you do that?"

"I didn't know anyone would be so rash as to eat lunch in the summer sun when the shade is only a mile away."

"You will find, Mr. Slashpipe, that I do many things that you aren't used to."

"Yes, ma'am. Do you want me to bring your lunch when I come back out after my siesta?"

"That will be fine."

"You keep the water," he instructed.

"Thank you."

"Do you want me to bring General Grant and General Lee when I come back?"

"I told you, I'm going to walk the fence line."

"Yes, ma'am, but you do look a little flushed."

"I assure you, I'm doing fine."

"You need to get out of the sun."

"I need the freedom to do what I want," she snapped.

Joshua pulled off his black sombrero, wiped his forehead on his shirt, and then jammed the hat back on. He turned to hike through the dead grass toward the barn and the springs.

Christina watched him for a moment. Then she plodded down the grade. She could feel the toes of her stockings rub because of their wetness.

I must powder my feet tonight. I must wash my feet tonight!

I must wash everything . . . somehow.

She recorded and numbered each fence post in her journal, with a sentence describing its condition. Most of the four lines of wires were Decker '84 double-strand with spread dual barbs. But they were patched with whatever was available at the time. The posts were set anywhere between eight and sixteen feet apart, with no pattern that she could discern.

After hiking half a mile of the upper section, Christina stopped to stare across at the barn. She couldn't see Joshua Slashpipe anywhere.

I didn't ask him how long his siesta is. I should have gone back with him. I'm not in that much of a hurry. But, of course, I'd be embarrassed to go in now. You're much too prideful, Christina Swan.

The hot water in the leather-wrapped canteen felt as if it almost scalded her tender, cracked lips. She washed her fingertips clean and brushed her lips.

This is your very first day, Christina. You don't have one dry stitch of clothing on your body. Even with gloves and a hat, your fingernails are dirty, your lips chapped, your face sunburned. And to think you used to spend most of your entire day inside a classroom.

She pulled off her floppy hat, wiped her forehead, and used the hat for a fan. A brown-and-white-splotched cow grazed up the hill about a hundred yards below her.

She doesn't look all that wild. In fact, she looks a lot like Uncle Joey's cow Muley. I could probably grab her by the ear and lead her over to the corral at the springs. Now that, Christina Swan, would impress even old Joshua. And I'd have a reason for sneaking back to the shade.

The cow munched on the short, thick dead grass closer to her. "Are you coming up here to get a closer look at me?" she asked the cow.

The cow turned her tail toward Christina and continued to graze.

Perhaps this is a good time to make my acquaintance. I think I'll just lead you right over to the corral.

Christina stacked her journal, canteen, leather gloves, and hat by the last fence post she had inspected. Then she started slowly toward the cow. She took long, slow strides and could feel her sore leg and hip muscles begin to stretch.

The cow grazed and ignored her. Christina moved farther and farther down the hill, always keeping a good distance between herself and the cow.

How does she do that? She doesn't even look this direction, and yet she knows how close I'm getting.

Christina halted, then started up, then halted again. Each time the cow paused in tandem with her.

Well, Mrs. Cow, this is an interesting relationship we have. Close . . . but not too close. We keep our distance, respect each other's privacy. Lord, this sounds like some of the men in my life. Why do the men I want to get close to keep their distance? And the ones I want to keep away from burst through my door? There's a lesson here with this cow; I just can't figure out what it is.

She picked up her pace, and the cow broke into a trot. *Mrs. Cow, you are not going to get away from me. And I can't keep calling you Mrs. Cow. There are other Mrs. Cows on the ranch. So I will call you Señora Manchada . . . Mrs. Spotted. . . . At least, I think that's what it means. Perhaps I should not call her that until I talk to Joshua. I don't want to embarrass myself. Of course, there is no one in front of whom I can embarrass myself at the moment.*

That's what I like about this setup, Lord. No one

is inspecting me. Except for Joshua Slashpipe per-
haps, and it's difficult to worry much about a tooth-
less old man.

She had trailed the cow about half a mile when
a medium-sized black-and-white dog sniffed his
way across plowed ground toward the eastern
fence. Christina shaded her eyes from the blazing sun with her hand and glanced over at the
property next to hers.

He's plowing it too dry. Look at the size of those
clods. He'll need to drag a log over them in the next
couple days, or they will be so hard he won't break
them up until winter. What kind of college graduate
is he?

She stared across the plowed ground to a small
whitewashed corral and shed. There were two
horses in the corral, but she couldn't judge their
quality from a distance. Next to the shed was a
large white tent.

He's a college graduate who lives in a tent. Not
exactly a monument to success. Of course, I live in a
barn loft . . . for the time being. But I've been here for
one night, and he's been here a couple months.
Doesn't he have any ambition? He could have built
a cabin by now. I will certainly begin building my
cabin the day the lumber arrives.

The dog stood silently watching her from
behind the fence, his head tilted to one side.

"You look lonely, boy. Did your master take
off and leave you all alone?" The dog wagged his
tail but didn't bark. "What's your name? Bubba?
Buster? No, it was Buscadero . . . the lawman,

the gunman." The dog anxiously paced along the fence. "Busca — that's it. You're Busca!"

On hearing his name, the dog dropped his stomach to the dirt and scooted under the lower wire on the fence.

"No, I didn't mean you have to come over here. You just stay there . . . Busca."

The dog sprang to his feet and sprinted to her. His tail dragged the ground as he approached.

Christina put her left hand on her hip and waved her other hand at him. "Now you listen to me, Busca — you are not supposed to be over here."

He bellied his way up to her dusty boots and licked them.

She squatted down. "Now, Busca . . ." She held out her fingers. He sniffed them, then licked. She stroked his head. "You are a very warm dog. It's too hot for a fur coat. Perhaps it acts like Joshua's flannel shirt. At least it keeps you from getting sunburned."

His tail thumped a response in the packed dirt of the hillside.

"You are a very polite dog."

He cocked his head.

"You haven't said one word. Perhaps you are not allowed to speak to strangers. Not that I'm a stranger. I'm your neighbor." The dog's long pink tongue almost dragged in the dirt. "Okay, I may be a little strange."

The dog, still on his stomach, scooted around to lie in her shade.

"You are a very smart dog, Busca. If I were smart, I would not have left my hat way back up the mountain."

He panted as she rubbed his head.

"You really do remind me of some men I have known. How about you — do you have a girl-friend? I suppose not. Not way out here anyway. Perhaps I should buy myself a nice cow dog like you. Then you would have a buddy to visit with. I could get a lady dog and then . . . eh, no . . . never mind."

She patted him one more time, then stood. The horizon blurred and rotated. "Well, Busca, I stood up too fast, and now I'm dizzy. Does that ever happen to you? I always wondered how dizzy a dog gets chasing his tail."

She took several deep breaths. Her head cleared. She started to walk down the hill, and the dog strolled beside her. "I am definitely going to get a dog, especially one like you who is a good listener and doesn't talk very much. You see, I'm walking down this mountain because I want to herd Mrs. Manchada over to my corral. Oh, I haven't introduced you two." She stopped hiking, and so did the dog. "Busca?" The dog pointed his nose down the hill. She waved her hand at Mrs. Manchada. "Busca, do you see that cow? Her name —"

The minute she waved her hand and said "cow," the dog took off on a furious sprint toward the brown-and-white cow.

"No! . . . No! I didn't want you to chase her!

Come back. . . . Come back here right now," she hollered.

The dog slunk low in the weeds toward the back of the cow, dove in and nipped at its hind leg, and then started barking wildly.

"No!" Christina called out. "Don't!" She sprinted down the hillside. She could feel the veins in her neck throb from the heat and strain. "No! I didn't mean for you to corral her!" she screamed.

With the word "corral," Busca turned the cow toward the distant corral by the white tent. He ran the cow straight toward the barbed-wire fence.

"No, Busca! No!" she hollered.

The dog stopped barking and dropped to his stomach.

Mrs. Manchada, however, did not stop running. She stampeded straight into the four-wire fence, which snapped like a popcorn string at Christmas in a room full of hungry children.

"No! Busca, see what you have done! I'll never get that cow back." Christina waved at the bovine, and the dog bolted after the cow again with a string of decisive yelps.

Christina followed the dog through the broken fence. As she trotted into the plowed ground, her boot toe caught the bottom strand of wire. Her face and nose ground into the dirt. For a minute, she couldn't breathe. Christina rolled over to her back, gasping, holding her stomach with dirty hands.

A shout from the direction of the white tent brought her to her knees. The panicked cow trampled right over the tent. A barefoot, shirtless man ran around the corral, shouting at the cow and the dog.

Everything seemed to blur as she squinted her eyes. *I have no idea why I'm so dizzy today.*

When her vision settled, she ambled across the plowed ground toward the demolished tent and the screaming man. As she approached, she noticed the swelling muscles on the man's chest and upper arms.

Mr. Yager, you must have studied wrestling in college! I can't imagine you in an intellectual major.

Christina was totally out of breath when she reached the corrals. The sweat on her forehead felt cold and clammy.

Barefoot, the man squatted down next to the dog, holding him back. "Woman, is this your cow?" he screamed.

Mrs. Manchada seemed content to rest on top of the white tent, now mashed flat on the ground.

Bent over at the waist, her hands on her thighs, she tried brushing her curly bangs from her eyes. She could feel the grime on her forehead. "Mr. Yager, I presume. My name is not 'woman.' It's Swan."

"Well, Mrs. Swan," he yelled, "get your cow off my home!"

"It's not Mrs. Swan; it's Miss Swan. But as far as you are concerned, you may think of me as

Mr. Swan," she fumed.

"Oh, no!" he shouted, staring at the cow. "Get her off there!"

Mrs. Manchada raised her tail high in the air and deposited her morning leftovers on top of the torn tent.

"Lady," he yelled, "if you don't get your cow off my tent, I will shoot her!" He stepped over to the corral gate and retrieved a '73 Winchester carbine and checked the lever. The dog remained at his side.

"What do you think you're doing?" she screamed.

He lifted the carbine to his shoulder. "I'm protecting my property."

Christina ran over between him and the cow. "And I'm protecting mine." She could feel her temples begin to throb. "I will not let you shoot Mrs. Manchada."

"Who?" he hollered.

"That's this cow's name," she explained.

"You name them?"

"What's wrong with that?" she snapped.

"You're daffy!" The muscles across his chest and arms rippled with each word.

"Me daffy? I'm not the one running around in public half-dressed."

"This is not public. This is my farm. And I was taking a siesta. I didn't intend to have a 900-pound cow sitting on my head," he screamed.

"You don't need to yell at me, Mr. Yager. I can hear you fine."

95

"I'm not yelling so that you can hear. I happen to like to yell!"

"You are a very strange man."

"Me? Look at you. You're covered with dirt from chasing cows through fences."

Her eyes narrowed. "It was your dog that chased her through the fence."

"That's a lie."

The blood rushed to her face. She bit her chapped lip and could taste blood and salt. "You dare call me a liar?"

"Busca won't go past the wire unless someone calls him," he yelled.

"I visited with him for a moment, but I didn't imagine he would chase my cow."

"What do you think cow dogs do, woman? Knit?"

She ground her teeth. "I told you, my name is —"

"Your name is Christina Alena Swan, and you once stood up in advanced algebra and told Dr. Ledbetter the equation he wrote on the blackboard was incorrect, and he asked you to stay after class and prove it. After which you always sat in the front row and seemed to have the inside track on every quiz and test."

It was like a kerosene lamp that runs out of fuel and slowly fades into night. First his voice dimmed; then the edges of her vision began to blur and darken. Her knees buckled.

She collapsed onto something hard and dirty. Then nothing but darkness.

"Christina, you are a very special young woman. I think it was divine Providence that brought you into my classroom."

She sat on the hard wooden chair in the small, book-lined office and refused to look at the man in the bow tie and three-piece brown suit who sat on the edge of the desk only two feet from her.

"I needed this class for my major, Dr. Ledbetter. I'm not sure there is any special significance to it," she explained.

"Perhaps not to you. But it's an answer to my prayers. Your inquisitive mind and your quite attractive, eh, smile . . . are truly the highlight of my day."

She glanced up at the brown eyes of the man twice her age. "I do believe you exaggerate, Professor."

"No, no. But I wouldn't expect you to understand. Most students think of professors as machines of some sort that give out countless pages of data and then heartlessly correct papers, looking for any way to humiliate students."

"That's not true."

"Christina?"

"Okay." She broke out in a slight grin. "That's the way some students see college, but not me."

"Precisely. That's why God sent you to me. I needed someone who sees me differently."

She glanced over at the door that led to the

hallway. "What do you mean, differently?"

"Well, there's a little tension in the department . . . and sometimes I have to carry that load into class. Your smile eases the burden. The Lord must know I needed you as a friend, a personal friend."

I do not like the direction this conversation is taking. Loop warned me to watch out for city boys, but he didn't mention city professors. "What kind of department tension, Dr. Ledbetter?"

"Call me Drew. But I will not burden you with it. No matter what they say, you have every right in the world to study mathematics."

She raised her head and could feel her neck stiffen. "Do you mean that my being in this major causes you trouble?"

"Some of the professors are terribly old-fashioned and shortsighted — that's all. Most of the time I can keep them contained. Don't you worry your very pretty head over it. I will never cease to defend you!" He reached over and put his hand on her shoulder. "I will always be on your side."

Not if I can help it. "I do not like to be touched," she warned.

"Now, now, Christina . . ." His hand continued to massage her shoulder. All of a sudden he shook her shoulder so firmly that her head bobbled back and forth.

She reached up and grabbed his thin, bare wrist and yanked it away. "Don't touch me," she snapped.

She opened her eyes.

The hand belonged to Joshua Slashpipe. His furrowed brown face showed toothless concern. "I think, La Dueña, you will be all right now."

Her head was propped on a leather harness, but she was lying on a rough wooden floor. "Where am I?" she mumbled.

He rubbed his flat nose with the back of his hand. "In the loft of your barn."

Her head felt so heavy she couldn't lift it. "Why are my clothes soaking wet? Did I sweat that much?"

He leaned back on his heels as he squatted beside her. "That is my fault, La Dueña. You were suffering from the heat. I poured two buckets of spring water over you. I wanted to bring your temperature down."

Her wet skirt felt so heavy it pinned her to the floor. "And that's the only way you could do it?"

"No, there is another way. But I am of the old Californio school. I am a gentleman, and it's the only way my spirit would allow me."

"I understand. Thank you, Joshua. I believe you are right. I did get too hot."

"Hot, bothered, tired, dirty, blistered — you had a very busy day." He tugged his sombrero back onto his gray head.

She turned her head and studied the daylight beaming through the cracks in the barn wall.

"What time is it?"

Slashpipe glanced out the open barn door at the shadows near the springs. "I suppose it's near five, but what difference does it make? I see no reason to count the hours."

"Would you help me sit up?"

"Be careful. . . . You need to rest."

He tugged on her hand, and Christina struggled to sit up on the barn floor. She scooted over to lean her back on a rough wooden post. She gasped for breath.

"It hurts to breathe. It feels like a side cramp is about to seize me, and I'm afraid to move."

"You rest. Can I bring you anything?"

She brushed her hair back out of her eyes. "I look horrible, don't I?"

He nodded.

"Right at the moment, I don't seem to care."

"Even a rare jewel is always discovered covered with dirt."

"That's very poetic, Mr. Slashpipe."

"I have a way with women — I mean, with words."

"I'm sure you do quite well with both." Christina tried to shift her shoulders to a more comfortable position. "How did I get up here in the loft?"

"Señor Yager carried you up here."

"Up that rickety ladder?"

Slashpipe glanced behind him in the loft. "Yes. He is a strong man."

"But how did I get from his place to the barn?"

"Mr. Yager carried you."

"All the way? It's over a mile."

"Like I said, Mr. Yager is a strong man."

"Mr. Slashpipe . . . did . . . did Mr. Yager . . ."

"Did he tell me what happened? He said you chased a cow without a hat on a day when the temperature is higher than 100 degrees. He said he hopes you learn prudence soon."

"And he has a lot to learn about manners! Prudence? Who does he think he is?"

"He thinks he's the man who carried you for a mile."

"Joshua, did Mr. Yager carry me over his shoulder like a sack of barley or in his arms like a sick calf?"

"You were the sick calf, but I don't think it matters how he carried you."

It matters to me! "Joshua, I left my hat and —"

"He went out and got your things and brought them back."

"He walked another two miles to retrieve my things?"

"I didn't want to leave you." Slashpipe glanced down at his boots. "I was afraid you might die."

"A person doesn't die from fainting," she scoffed.

"The summers in the San Joaquin are not forgiving. People die every year from the heat."

Christina leaned her head against the post and then brushed her bangs off her forehead. "The cow . . . what about my cow?"

"Busca brought Mrs. Manchada home to our corral."

"He told you that I named her?"

"Busca didn't say a word, but Señor Yager told me that. I think it is very good. But there is a problem, La Dueña, with naming your cattle."

"What's that?"

"It is sometimes difficult to eat animals you know by name."

"We'll keep Mrs. Manchada and raise her calves."

"Mrs. Manchada is barren. She did not calve this year."

"How do you know that?"

"There is no calf following her around."

"Yes, well, we'll have to consider that. What else did Mr. Yager tell you?"

"He said he knew you from college. I think it's quite amazing that you attended the same class. Was he a good student?"

"I have no idea. I don't remember him at all. I must talk to him about that sometime."

"You might want to wait until he repairs his tent and belongings. I don't think he wants to visit right at the moment."

"Did he tell you that Mrs. Manchada not only stomped it flat but then stood on it and . . . and, you know, plopped on it as well?"

A wide grin broke across Slashpipe's face. His toothless smile made Christina laugh. When she did, her side locked up in a tight cramp. "Oh, no . . . oh, my side."

"Give me your right arm," he commanded.

"What?"

"Your arm!"

In agony she sheepishly held out her arm. He yanked it straight forward, then took two fingers and jabbed her side halfway down to her waist.

The pain instantly stopped.

"Oh, my, I don't know what you did, but it worked. Is that an old Yokut remedy?" She lifted her hair off the back of her neck and could feel water and sweat rolling down it.

"No." He paused, then winked. "It's an old Scottish remedy."

"Well, I'm not going to laugh anymore — it's too painful." She rubbed her chapped lips. "Could you bring me a little water? I think I'd like a drink and to clean up a bit. I'll be all right if you need to go fix that fence."

"Mr. Yager fixed it."

"He's quite a busy man."

"He said he didn't want his home destroyed again."

"It was his dog that chased the cow. Did he tell you that?"

"He told me you called the dog and sent him after the cow."

"I most certainly did not!" She glanced away from Slashpipe. "Well . . . I didn't mean to. . . . Anyway, how did Mr. Yager know that?"

"Busca told him."

"The dog tells him things?"

"They have been good friends for a long, long

time, I think. The dog tells him everything. I will go get your water."

"Thank you."

"You're welcome. Please don't try to stand. I don't want you falling out of the loft."

She watched him climb down the ladder to the barn floor.

"Well, Christina Swan, this has been an eventful first day," she mumbled. "I trust you have done the full requirement of foolish actions and will be wiser from now on."

"Yes . . . Mama."

Her lips hurt when she spoke, and she reached up to touch them with her fingertips. There were traces of blood when she removed her hand.

Uncle Joey . . . you told me it would be this way. . . . But it's much more adventuresome from a distance. Which could also be said about most of the men I know.

Christina heard Joshua talking to some man with a deep, soft voice. She tried to pull herself to her feet. Her upper body felt so heavy she could not get any further than her hands and knees. She pulled her long, wet dress up and crawled over to where she could look out the barn door.

It must be Mr. Yager, but I can't hear what they are discussing. And I can't see them. I wish I could see them . . . but then they could see me. Lord, I don't want anyone to have to look at me right now. Even You. If You want to just glance over at the cows while we talk, I'll understand.

She crawled on her hands and knees over to the leather suitcase next to the bed of straw and stared at the clothing. *At this rate, I'll run out of something to wear by tomorrow evening.*

She turned around and sat down as she heard Joshua climb the ladder.

"Was that Mr. Yager?" she inquired even before he came into view.

"Yes, he came back."

"What did he want?"

Slashpipe set the wooden water bucket on the loft floor and then climbed back up carrying a plant growing in a one-gallon tomato can. "He wanted to bring you a present."

"That is the ugliest plant I have ever seen. I trust it has beautiful blooms, because it looks like just a bunch of big deformed succulent stems," she ranted.

"It's not for its beauty that he gave it to you."

"What is it?" she asked.

Joshua set the succulent on the floor, took out his folding knife, and sliced off a six-inch sprig.

"Hold out your hand," he said.

She hesitated. "What are you going to do?"

"Hold out your hand," he commanded.

Slowly she extended her hand. He squeezed the stem, and a dollop of thick, light green, cloudy liquid plopped into her palm.

"What is that?"

Slashpipe's voice was firm. "Medicine."

Her voice was a whine. "What kind of medicine?"

"For sunburn, dry skin, but especially for chapped lips. It's an aloe plant. Put it on your lips."

"Does it hurt?" she whimpered.

"Do your lips hurt now?"

"They're killing me."

"Then what do you have to lose?"

Christina gingerly dabbed some on her lips, and it instantly brought relief. "Oh, this does work. This is wonderful. Maybe now I can talk without them bleeding."

"Aloe is good for the blisters on your hands as well."

"Cut me off another sprig." She motioned with her hand.

"Yes, and I will leave my knife with you. You might wake in the night and need another dose."

She tried to brush the wrinkles out of her damp, dirty skirt. "I know I behaved foolishly today."

"You were zealous. We all have to learn the land. Every region demands respect."

"But I've lived all my life in the valley . . . in Sacramento and Stockton."

"But you have the delta fog to cool the nights, and an occasional breeze blows in from Benicia. This is the south San Joaquin. It's a different land."

"I will learn. I should have taken a siesta. I will not make that mistake again. Tomorrow we will both come in and take a rest in the heat of the day."

"You will not leave this barn during daylight hours for three days," he announced.

She bristled. "Are you telling me what I can and cannot do?"

"Yes, and I will tell you what I cannot do." His voice got louder. "I cannot ride 100 miles to Mariposa to take your body back to your uncle. It would be too sad. It would break my heart." He brushed his callused finger along sun-baked eyes.

She looked away. "Do I really have to stay out of the sun?"

"Yes. When I agreed to work for you, I volunteered to protect you from wild animals, dangerous men, and this savage land."

"I see." She unfastened the top button on her collar and rubbed aloe on her neck. "Is this stuff an old Scottish remedy also?"

"Oh, no, it is a Yokut remedy." The toothless grin was back.

"Thank you for looking after me, Joshua. I will try not to be such a nuisance in the future."

"You are the boss. It's your privilege to be an aggravation every day of the year."

"I will try to keep it to a minimum."

He turned toward the ladder. "I will go cook some supper now."

"I don't think I can eat."

"I will bring you something anyway. Perhaps later you will wake up hungry."

"Are we having tortillas and beans?"

"No, I thought I would try something different. We are having beans and tortillas."

This time the giggle did not hurt her lips.

"And pork and tomatoes and apple cake."

"Apple cake? You had time to make an apple cake?"

"I traded with Mr. Yager — apple cake for a jar of my special hot sauce."

He shuffled to the ladder.

"Mr. Slashpipe, I have another question about Mr. Yager. When he carried me all the way across the pasture, was he wearing shoes?"

"No."

"Did he carry me barefoot?"

"No, La Dueña. He was wearing boots."

She watched him descend out of view.

"Mr. Slashpipe!" she yelled. "I have one more question."

Slowly he climbed back up the rungs of the wooden ladder. His head appeared above the loft floor. "Yes?"

"When Mr. Yager carried me here all the way from his tent . . ." She chewed on her tongue and glanced up at the rafter above the loft. ". . . was he wearing a shirt?"

"What did you say?"

She looked straight at him. "I said, was Mr. Yager wearing a shirt when he carried me here to the barn?"

"He was wearing boots, shirt, pants, suspenders, and a hat. More than that, I could not tell, nor did I ask. You were unconscious. It doesn't make any difference if he was wearing a shirt or not." He slowly descended back out of sight.

It makes a world of difference to me, Mr. Slashpipe.

Four

Christina spent four days quarantined from direct sunlight. It didn't seem much different from teaching school, except that there were no students.

She had breakfast outside with Joshua before the sun broke above the Sierras. And took her supper an hour after the sun dropped below the western valley horizon. He fastened the wagon tailgate to two empty nail kegs to make a long, narrow table. Two cottonwood log rounds, lined with straw and covered with tanned deer hide, served as padded stools.

On the morning of the fifth day she lingered by the table as the sun peeked above the towering, snowcapped Sierras to the east.

"Daddy, may I stay outside and play today?" she asked.

Slashpipe's shining white teeth glistened as he grinned. "I'm sorry to boss you around, La Dueña. How do you feel this morning?"

"Like a mushroom growing in the dark! My face is peeling. The blisters on my hands are still a little sore. My joints are stiff. But I didn't think this would be an easy job." She pulled her old hat down to shade her face. "I want to finish inspecting the fence line. I intend to spend about two hours on it this morning and three this evening before sundown. In between I will stay in the shade and take a siesta."

Joshua sat drinking his coffee and rocking back and forth. "You are very wise, La Dueña."

Christina wiggled her nose and tried to suppress a smile. "I have had much experience in this land and many fine *vaquero* teachers."

Joshua plucked his teeth from his mouth and plopped them in a leather pouch. "And handsome, too. You forgot to say many fine and handsome *vaquero* teachers."

She stretched her arms straight out and slowly rotated her neck. "Not all have been as handsome as Joshua Slashpipe."

"Oh, well, that is to be expected, La Dueña." He set down his coffee cup and pulled a yank of horsehair from a small basket near his feet.

"What are you braiding today?"

"A new *mecate* — if I have enough hair. Maybe we need more horses."

"Will you use the McCarty with the hackamore?"

"Not McCarty . . . *mecate*. You will never make *vaquero* until you learn the terms," he grinned.

"I do want to know enough that you won't be ashamed of your La Dueña." Christina opened up her journal.

"Is that my chore list?" he asked.

"It's your purchase list."

"We are going to Visalia?"

"You are going to Visalia," she corrected. "I just don't want to spend that many hours in the sun."

"Will you be all right by yourself?" he asked.

"Will you?" she countered.

Slashpipe laughed. "You are right, La Dueña. I have more talent for trouble. I will behave myself as if you were by my side all the time."

"And I will do likewise," she added.

He pushed his sombrero to the back of his head and laid the braids back in the basket. "Carry your shotgun if you stroll along the fence."

"Why should I do that? There is absolutely no one around. I will be safe on my own ranch."

He rubbed the dirt from the crevices around his small, narrow eyes. "You will be down by the cabin, and Mrs. Mofeta Diablo thinks it's her ranch. She and her brood will sometimes run right at you. It is well to be prepared."

She took up her pencil and wrote "shotgun" in her journal. "That will be a strange sight, me parading along the fence line with a gun."

"But who will see you? Like you said, there is absolutely no one around."

She glanced to the east in the direction of the plowed field. "There is one neighbor."

"Señor Yager and Busca went to Antelope Valley to check on the lumber. He is still waiting for his delivery, too. He left yesterday and said he will not return until tonight or tomorrow."

She forced herself not to look at his toothless

smile. "Does it take that long to go to the mill and back?"

He scratched his short gray hair, plucked something out of it, examined it in his fingers, pinched it tight, and then dropped it to the dirt. "No, but I do not ask a man what he does with his spare time."

"There you have it. No one's within shouting distance today."

"There is no one to hear the report of a rifle either. Take your shotgun so that I can rest easy on the trip."

"Sometimes, Mr. Slashpipe, it's difficult to know who is running this ranch."

He rubbed the one-week stubble of white whiskers on his chin. "That's not a problem on payday, is it?"

"Oh, do you need some pay? Tomorrow is Saturday, but I can pay you today so you can have money for town. Uncle Joey said the wage is $2.00 per day."

"That's fine."

"Is it fair?"

"I have not earned much money this week. I have branded eleven cows and repaired a little fence."

"You have done everything I asked," she countered. "I'll go get your money."

When she returned from the loft, Joshua was shaving with a pan of steaming water and a straight razor. A neatly tied bundle wrapped in brown paper lay on the table.

She handed him a ten-dollar bill and four silver dollars.

He stared at the money for a moment.

"The greenback is good. Any store will cash it," she assured him.

"It's strange to have something made out of paper counted as valuable. But you gave me fourteen. I don't work Sundays."

"I know. I would not allow it — unless it was an emergency. But you will be paid for Sunday, too."

"You pay me to rest?" He took the money and shoved it into the pocket of his leather vest.

"Do you cook on Sundays?"

"Yes, of course."

"And do you wash the dishes?"

"Most definitely."

"And feed the horses?"

He nodded his gray head.

"Then you will certainly get paid." She glanced at the bundle. "Now you must tell me what you're taking to town in that bundle."

"I'm not taking it to town. I'm giving it to you. It's a present."

"For me?" She slowly untied the strings. She found a neatly folded red-plaid flannel shirt inside.

"It's not new, La Dueña, but I had it cleaned at the Chinese laundry and have not worn it. You need to wear it when you work today."

"Oh, yes, I intend to do so. I have on my list for you to buy me two such shirts."

He dried his clean-shaven face on a scrap of burlap bag. "Now I have another surprise for you."

"You have been busy."

He jammed his sombrero back onto his head. "You have been in the barn many days."

They hiked around the four-rail corral to the southern slope of the mountain. A three-by-six-foot tub, three feet high, was propped off the ground a few inches on flat rocks. "You installed our stock tank!"

He waved at the large object. "This is not a stock tank."

Christina put her hands on her hips. "Of course it is. I purchased it."

"The wild cattle find their own water as usual. The horses have their trough. We do not need a tank like this until fall." He pulled his old ducking trousers up and adjusted his leather suspenders. "This tank is our fresh water supply."

"What do you mean?"

"Now that we have the springs fenced off, the water is clean and sweet for a little while before it rolls down the hill and disappears in the sandpit. So I ran a small trough over here. You see, when you raise this gate, water flows into the tank. When it's full, you shut the gate. When you pull the wooden peg out of the bung, it all drains to the pasture. If we want, we can leave both gates partially open and have a constant pool of fresh, flowing water." He was as proud as Michelangelo admiring the completed Sistine Chapel.

"That's wonderful, Joshua."

"It will be more wonderful when I bring back some wire screen for a lid to keep the bugs out. It's like a big bathtub, no?"

"It's a little too exposed for a bathtub, I'm afraid."

"Exposed to what? I will be in Visalia. You may do whatever you want."

I will bathe from a bucket as long as I have to, and I refuse to take an open-air bath. "It will be wonderful to have fresh, clean water to wash my face when I come in from the field."

"You use it however you wish. I will harness the team."

"And I will change into my new work shirt."

Christina knew she had squandered the coolest part of the morning seeing Joshua off and getting prepared for the day. She wore her dirty ducking skirt, the newly acquired flannel shirt, Uncle Joey's old floppy hat, and leather work gloves. She threw the worn saddlebags over her shoulder like a pack and carried the shotgun in her hand.

Christina Alena Swan, if only the class of '82 could see you now. What a character you have become. Maybe you always were, but you didn't have the arena in which to perform. This is my arena, Lord — a big, old, empty ranch with no one but You around.

It's like I'm playing a game, like I'm trying to be Grandma and Grandpa Merced.

116

Maybe I am. But in my heart, I love it. I love playing the part. I really want to make this work, Lord.

It's my place.

My time.

And I'm going to squeeze all the life out of it I can.

The saddlebags began to feel heavy on her shoulder. She switched them to the other side. She toted a full canteen, her journal, fence pliers and hammer, a stalk of aloe, three bean tortillas, and two shotgun shells.

She examined the fence line carefully, walked slowly, kept her face shaded with the hat brim, drank small sips of water often, and sweated profusely.

She took another sip from the leather-wrapped canteen and then tugged at the buttons on the front of the flannel shirt. *I don't think I'm doing this right. This shirt is very hot. Perhaps I should not tuck it in.* "It is never Christian nor even proper to be slovenly dressed, Christina Alena." "Yes, Mama." *Never once in your life did I ever see you slovenly dressed. There were years when we didn't have very much, but your dress was starched and pressed, the ribbons in your beautiful, long hair perfectly placed.*

Grandma was the natural beauty who turned every Californio's head.

Mama worked at hers, and she became the queen of every social event in Stockton.

And me? Lord, they just sat me in the center of the room and told me how cute my chubby little cheeks were. And I believed them. At least, for the first six-teen years.

But Mama can't see me now, and I'm wearing my shirt out.

With the tail hanging down over her skirt, she used it to fan air up inside. *That's much better. Of course, a larger shirt would probably let more air in. Joshua is a rather small-chested man, and I am . . . eh, I'm not a small-chested man.*

Christina had almost finished the east side fence line when she paused to look across the plowed ground at Kern Yager's tent and corrals.

I'm glad you could repair your tent, Mr. Yager. Of course, it does have a rather large brown splotch on the side. Joshua said he was to keep an eye on your place; however, Joshua is gone to town. Per-haps I should keep an eye on it . . . a little closer.

Christina studied the barbed-wire fence that separated her from the plowed field.

This is much easier to cross if a cow runs through it first.

She tossed the saddlebag over the top wire of the fence and propped the shotgun against a post. With the leather gloves she pushed down a wire and held up the top one with the other hand. But she found she couldn't lift her leg high enough. She let the wires down.

"We need a gate between us, Kern Yager. I mean, if we are neighbors and plan to visit once in a while, we need a gate," she mumbled. "Not that I will come visit you, but Joshua might . . . and he's getting older. He will need a gate."

118

This time she surveyed the entire landscape of the southern flank of Stokes Mountain for any signs of human existence. Then she hiked her skirt up to her waist. This time, by prying the wires apart, she could step across to the plowed field. She let the wires and her skirt drop.

As Christina went to retrieve her saddlebags and shotgun, something tugged at her skirt. She heard a decisive rip. Unfastening the hem of her dress from one of the barbs, she discovered a tear up the right side to the lower part of her calf.

Christina hiked across the plowed ground, trying to break up the bigger clods as she went.

Mr. Yager, these clods are too hard already. I told you what would happen if you didn't . . . Well, actually I didn't tell you, but I thought about telling you.

She climbed up on the bottom rail and peered into his round fifty-foot corral.

"You took both horses but not the wagon, Mr. Yager. . . . Why did you take two horses? Does Busca sit a horse?"

Christina propped the shotgun against the small shed and let the saddlebags slip to the ground. She approached the six-foot-tall white canvas tent.

She cleared her throat. "Mr. Yager, are you here?" She eased toward the neatly tied tent flap.

Christina Alena Swan, don't you dare open that tent and look inside.

No, of course I won't. Yet I'm supposed to live life to the fullest . . . squeeze every bit of adventure out of it I can.

Without sinning.

Oh, yeah, I forgot that part.

She took her hand off the tent flap and turned around. "Okay, Christina, time to head back to the Proud Quail Ranch."

She glanced around. *As soon as I peek at the shed. We need to build a shed also. I'll just see how it's constructed.*

When she reached the eastern side of the shed, she discovered a porch roof extending over the dirt at least ten feet beyond. In the shade of the roof stood a wide, hand-hewn wooden rocking chair.

"Mr. Yager, what a nice thing to own!"

She sat down in the rocker and leaned back. "And there's enough room here for a friend . . . eh, a dog friend." Finally she pulled herself to her feet as her legs cramped. She turned and slowly opened the door of the shed. The only light came through the open door.

Shovels, picks, pry bars, planters, harnesses, seed, several cases of dynamite, horseshoes, nails . . . dynamite?

She stepped into the small shed and looked closer at the wooden cases. "Mr. Yager, since when did anyone ever farm with dynamite? There isn't one stump on your entire place . . . or mine for that matter. That is a lot of dynamite! You'd better have a good explanation for this. Which I will never ask for, of course."

She looked down at a full burlap sack beside the dynamite. "And that is a lot of tomato seed! Forty pounds?"

Christina exited the shed and felt a nice drift of breeze blow through the little covered porch.

"Mr. Yager, you have a very nice and compact operation here. If you made this chair, I will order one for myself."

She hiked over to retrieve her saddlebags and shotgun. "Now, if you'll excuse me, I'll rip my way back through the fence and go take a little siesta. If I had a chair like yours, I'd park in the shade and siesta right there."

She turned and stared at the big rocking chair. *Of course, I do have three tortillas and water with me. . . . And this is very cool and shady. Perhaps I'll just . . . Even a man as hot-tempered as Yager won't begrudge a woman a short siesta. It's not as if I'm eating up his porridge.*

She plopped down in the chair and opened the saddlebags. She munched on one of the bean tortillas as she rocked. *There's just enough breeze when you rock to keep it feeling cooler.*

She was halfway into her third tortilla when the chair stopped rocking. Her hand dropped to her lap. Her chin sagged to her chest.

Christina stood in the shade of a big oak tree and watched the younger children swim in a shallow pool at the edge of the river.

I miss being young enough to swim. But when a girl is my age, she must be discreet.

She surveyed the people at the picnic — uncles, aunts, cousins, grandparents, friends.

Her mother and Loop seemed to be in charge. The banks of the wide river were lined with golden poppies and green grass. The breeze was just barely cool. Everyone looked younger. Except Grandma Alena. She always looked the same.

This is absolutely the most perfect kind of a day!

She strolled among the people, listening to each conversation. They kept talking as if they didn't see her.

Loop was telling Uncle Walt how to build a flood-proof bridge.

Great-uncle Echo Jack had all the young men spellbound with a Californio tale about escaping the clutches of the *comandante* of Yerba Buena.

Grandma Alena had a cluster of older men engrossed in a story about a bear-and-bull fight in old San Juan.

Christina breezed up to her mother.

"There you are." Martina Swan smiled. "I thought you completely disappeared on us."

"I went for a walk. Can I help?"

"I'm serving the pie. You can take it around for me."

Sitting on the grass by himself, his back against the trunk of an oak tree, was a young man with big ears that stuck out beyond his wild hair and the gray Confederate cap pulled down almost over his eyes. What she could see of the dark, sweeping eyebrows made her stare more closely. His pointed jaw was set tight, and his narrow lips sported an I-don't-want-to-be-here frown.

I don't know him. He looks so out of place. Perhaps he works for Uncle Ed or Uncle Joey.

Her mother handed her two pieces of gooseberry pie. "Take this smaller one to Grandpa and the big one to your brother."

Right in the back of her head between her ears, a cold chill hit and then slid down her back, like a cramp she couldn't break free of.

"Christina?"

"Mother, what did you just tell me?"

"Take the pie to Grandpa and your brother."

"Eh . . . Uncle Joey?"

"Not *my* brother," Martina insisted. "*Your* brother."

"What do you mean, my brother?"

"I mean Willie." She pointed to the tree. "He's sitting over against the oak. My word, Christina, are you off daydreaming again?"

Christina found it hard to catch her breath. "Mother, I don't have a brother."

"That's ridiculous! Of course you do."

"Mother, I'm an only child. Daddy died when I was only one. You had no more children. Remember?" She could feel tears welling up in her eyes.

Martina brushed her brown bangs out of her eyes, accenting her irritation. "I don't know where you come up with such stories, young lady. I do not appreciate your little charade. Take your brother the pie."

Christina fought to hold back the tears. "Mother . . . I can't. . . . That isn't my brother.

I've never seen him before in my life!"

Grandmother Alena strolled up to the table. Christina was surprised that she was wearing a different dress than she had on just a few minutes earlier. Now it was her red fandango dress. "My, my, you two, what seems to be the problem?"

"Grandma," Christina wailed, "Mother told me to give this pie to my brother. I don't even have a brother!"

Alena glanced at Martina. Mother and daughter shook their heads. "Has she been in the sun?"

"Christina Swan, I've had enough of this!" her mother huffed.

"My dear *Palomita Roja*," Grandmother Alena cooed. "Your brother Willie is right over there under the oak."

"He's my brother? He can't be!"

"And why not?" Grandma asked.

"H-He — he — doesn't even have red hair," Christina whimpered.

"Neither do I," her mother reminded her. "Now go on; give him the pie."

"But . . . no one ever told me I had a brother. Why didn't someone tell me?"

Her mother began to cut another piece of pie. "You must have forgotten."

"How could I forget? A person doesn't forget her own brother!"

"Now look what you've done." Her mother waved her hand toward the oak tree. "You've made him disappear."

Christina glanced at the oak. The young man was gone.

Where did he go? What did she mean, disappear? I can't see him, but I can hear his horse.

"Well, there you are, darlin', waitin' for me in the rocker. I can't tell you how happy I am to see you."

Christina leaped to her feet, clutched her shotgun and saddlebags, and stumbled out into the direct sunlight of a June afternoon. Her eyes were so dilated she could not focus on anything.

"I was taking a siesta," she mumbled. She heard the hoofbeats of more than one horse and thought she heard the squeak of a wagon wheel. She tried to squint the sun out of her eyes.

Something wet licked her fingers.

"Busca! I'm very glad you came home." She knelt down and patted the dog's head as she pulled the floppy-brimmed hat lower so she could identify those on horseback.

Kern Yager slid down out of the saddle. Behind him was another horse loaded with a sack of oats. And behind it came a carriage with a woman wearing a hat with a long peacock feather.

"I'm sorry . . . I, eh, Joshua asked me to . . . I was tired —"

"I really missed you!" He grinned, his back now to the carriage. He threw his arms around her so rapidly she couldn't resist. He plucked her off her feet as if she were merely a pillow, her shotgun still dangling in her hand. "Miss Swan," he whispered, "go along with me. I need your help . . . badly!"

"What?"

He spun around to face the carriage and slipped his hand in her free one.

Christina stumbled along by his side, her mouth still open. *This is the strongest, most massive hand I've ever held in my life.* She was fighting to regain her breath after the rib-squeezing hug.

"Well, here she is, Lucy — my Christina, the sweetest woman on the face of the earth," he boomed in a voice too loud to be believed.

Kern Yager, you are a big liar. He squeezed her hand, and she smiled at the woman in the white lace dress with rings on every finger. Lucy's nose was petite, turned slightly upward, her eyelashes as thick and dark as her coal-black hair. Her lips were full, her mouth too big for her face. Christina's fingers were beginning to throb.

"You keep her well hidden, Kern," the woman smirked.

"Christina darlin', this is Lucy Atwood. She lives with her daddy over on the Kaweah River. Mr. Atwood has this crazy idea that he can grow orange trees in this county, so I rode over to take a peek. Who should I meet on the road out but Lucy? And she just insisted on coming over and seeing my place . . . I mean, our place."

He squeezed her hand so hard this time she

thought her fingers would fall off.

"Oh," she finally blurted out, "where's my manners, darlin'?" She looked up at the startled woman in the carriage. "Miss Atwood, get down and sit awhile. You kin have the rocker. Kern can sit on the stump, and if I get tired, I'll sit on his lap." She lowered her chin, batted her eyes, and clutched his arm, which reminded her of the trunk of a ponderosa pine.

"I probably ought to go on home. Daddy will be worried," Lucy demurred.

"No, I insist!" Christina added.

Kern's elbow jabbed her side in a way she knew would leave a bruise.

"Well," Lucy hesitated. "Perhaps just for a moment."

"That's good. I ain't got nothin' for us to eat until supper," Christina gushed, "exceptin' that half a tortilla over on the rocker. Miss Atwood's welcome to eat that, ain't she, Kern?"

"That's my girl." He squeezed her around the waist. "Generous to a fault."

His hug took the breath out of her. Christina had to gasp for air.

"Are you all right?" Lucy asked, still sitting in the carriage.

"Oh, yes, indeed. It's just that Kern is so affectionate it makes my heart paulpatater and takes my breath away. Do you know what I mean?"

"Paulpatater?" Miss Atwood snickered. "Perhaps I'll merely have a drink of water and be on my way."

He started to hug her again, and Christina squirmed away.

"Now don't be gettin' all lovey-dovey in front of the company, darlin'. It ain't polite." She turned to the woman in the covered carriage, who didn't seem to have one drop of sweat on her. "You know how men can be sometimes. They jist cain't control themselves."

Christina pulled off her wide-brimmed hat, scratched her head, and pretended to pluck something out of her dirty auburn hair. She pinched it and dropped it to the ground. "Kern, you fetch her some water. Try to find some that looks clear and clean. One of them skunks from that old cabin wandered over here this mornin' and fell in the well and drowned." She put her hat back on and looked up at the woman in the carriage. "I mean to tell you, we are goin' to have one fine stew tonight. You want to stay for supper, Miss Atwood?"

The woman took an embroidered linen hankie from her sleeve and gently patted her cheeks. "No, I think I'll . . . I'll just drive on home. I have a long trip ahead of me."

"Well, that's too bad," Kern piped up. "Tell your father I'll be over next week to check on those lemon seedlings."

"Next week?" Miss Atwood echoed. "But I'll be in San Bernardino next week."

"What a shame," he mumbled.

Christina waved even before the carriage started to roll. "Do stop by and see us again."

This time when he squeezed her hand, Christina jammed her elbow into his side. It felt as if she had bumped into a brick wall.

Lucy Atwood turned the carriage around in the yard.

"Just leave the gate open," Yager called out. "I'll have Christina close it later when she's doin' chores!"

"Tell me, Kern," Lucy asked as she stopped the carriage near them, "why does she carry a shotgun with her?"

"When her man's gone," Christina drawled, "a woman's got to protect her honor."

"Honey, if ever I met someone who didn't need protecting, it's you."

"Thank ya." Christina smiled.

The woman in the carriage shook her head. "Kern, I don't know what to say. I never figured you for the type. Where in the world did you find her?"

"At an auction," he grinned.

"What? You bought her?" Lucy gasped.

"No, of course not. She had a pig to sell, and I bought it. She was quite fond of the pig and followed me home to see that it was taken care of . . . and never left."

"That there was the tastiest pig I ever raised," Christina added. "I called him Jedediah. That is, I called him that until we ground him up for sausage. After that, I jist called him breakfast."

The woman in the carriage stared down her nose at Kern Yager. "Well, you should buy her a skirt that isn't ripped and a new shirt that isn't worn out and too tight." She slapped the lead line on the horse's rump and rolled out the driveway.

For the first time since she woke up, Christina remembered what she was wearing. She broke free from Kern Yager and trotted alongside the carriage. "He bought me these here boots at the secondhand store . . . and it ain't even winter! Kern is good to me, Miss Atwood."

"I don't know which of you two I pity more," she called back. "Perhaps you deserve each other."

Christina stood by the driveway as the carriage rolled off. Then she turned and walked back up to where Yager stood grinning.

"What in the world was that all about?" Christina asked. "And why are you grinning?"

"I was hoping you'd support me with a line or two, and you put on a whole performance."

"Was I good?" she asked.

"No one but Lucy Atwood would have believed you. Fortunately, she has no discernment at all. You are an educated lady with class and style. You can't cover it up with that costume and a drawl."

Christina stood up straighter and pulled off her hat. "Mr. Yager, thank you for the nice compliment, but you owe me an explanation."

"Do you owe me one?" he countered.

"About being over here? I came to check on your place for Joshua, and your rocker was so tempting I ate my lunch here and must have fallen asleep. I took my siesta in your arcade."

"That's fair enough. I'm certainly glad you were here." They strolled back up to the shade under the shed roof. "Lucy's father is an expert horticulturist," he explained. "He is perhaps the top citrus man in the state, if not the whole country. Whenever I can, I like to go over and talk to him. But Lucy has it in her mind that I'm really coming to see her. She's so pushy, it's embarrassing."

"Embarrassing?"

"She has a habit of forgetting to fasten all her garments when I'm alone with her. Anyway, it got to the point that I wait until I know she's gone before I go over there. Well, this time she captured me in the drive as I was leaving and insisted on coming to see my ranch."

Christina pulled off her hat and tried to untangle her hair with her fingers. "And you told her you had a little woman waiting for you?"

"Something like that. I presumed she'd get the picture and turn around. Well, the longer she followed along, the wilder my story got. Anyway, please forgive me for pulling you into this. It's not my nature or my faith to lie like that." He was standing close enough that she could have reached out and touched him, but she didn't.

"Nor is it mine, Mr. Yager."

"I'll pray for forgiveness for both of us," he said. "I just don't know how to get rid of that woman. I've told her I'm not interested in her.

131

She is exactly the kind of woman who repels me."

"What kind is that, Mr. Yager?"

"Domineering, pushy, selfish, and totally lacking in common sense."

Christina glanced up at the thick brown eyebrows above his sky-blue eyes. *And you, Mr. Yager, are perfect, no doubt.*

He was obviously uncomfortable with her stare. "Anyway, I don't think I'll get rid of her until I'm married and have children bouncing on my knee."

"Be gentle with them, Mr. Yager."

He leaned closer. "What? With women like Lucy?"

She very much wanted to lean closer herself. But she didn't.

"No, be careful with those children you plan to bounce on your knee. You are very strong. Be gentle with your children."

He stepped back. "Oh . . . did I hurt you with that little squeeze?"

Little squeeze? No woman on earth could live through one of your big squeezes! "I'm still a little sore from fixing fence the other day."

He pulled off his hat. "Miss Swan, I want you to know —"

You need a haircut, Mr. Yager. "Could you call me Christina? I don't have a relative or a friend within 100 miles, and I'd like someone to call me Christina. Joshua insists on calling me La Dueña."

"Christina, I owe you a great favor."

I could cut it for you if you ask. I always cut Uncle Joey's hair. "Your kindness the other day when I fainted is sufficient."

"That doesn't count. I was not in a very good mood when I did it. Virtuous behavior with an unvirtuous attitude hardly counts as an act of grace."

"Are you in a good mood today?"

A smile broke across his face. There was a dimple on the right side of his cheek. "Yes, I am. And I mean it. I'm sure someone as attractive as you has had a few admirers that you've had difficulty getting rid of. If you've found a way to politely dismiss them, please tell me your secret. And if you ever need a temporary beau to scare them off, I'll volunteer."

"Why, thank you, Mr. Yager. I just might —"

"Just call me Kern. I don't have a relative or a friend for 1,000 miles, and I'd like to have someone call me by my name. All Busca ever calls me is 'Bark!' "

Christina started laughing and found that she couldn't stop. Finally she caught her breath. "Kern, I haven't had this much fun since high school."

"Summers in the southern San Joaquin Valley don't leave us much to laugh about, do they?"

"Not so far," she concurred. "I just had the strangest dream while sitting in your rocker. Then I woke up to the wildest charade I've ever been a part of."

"At least it won't be boring to write in my journal tonight. For the past month mine has contained little more than the weather and soil conditions, except for an entry about a neighbor lady and a heat stroke."

"I'm glad I can perk up your journal. And you certainly added to mine this afternoon."

"I was serious about helping you out like that sometime," he repeated.

"If I need a temporary beau — and I very well might on more than one occasion — you get the job."

"Thank you. Do you prefer the big, dumb-ox boyfriend? The professional boxer boyfriend? Or the *summa cum laude* college graduate boyfriend?"

Summa cum laude? In what field? "I'll probably need all three sooner or later," she replied. "I do need to get back to my place." She jammed on her hat, clutched her saddlebags and shotgun, and started down the drive toward the road.

"Aren't you going to cut across that field?"

She glanced back up the hill at him. He looked even taller than usual. "If I have to crawl through the wires one more time, this dress will be in shreds."

His voice was quiet, almost bashful. "Would you like me to walk you home?"

"Good heavens, no," she called back. "I need to check the fence line along the road."

They were now nearly 100 feet apart. "Listen," he hollered to her, "I hope I didn't squeeze you too hard. I was distracted, you know, with Lucy. It was nothing personal — you know what I mean?"

"I understand perfectly, Kern," she called back. "Don't give it another thought."

Each step toward the gate seemed to be lighter than the one before. The air was not nearly as hot as on the previous day. The stiffness in her joints had finally cleared, and she felt as if she could hike for hours.

I know exactly what you mean, Mr. Kern Yager. What you mean is that deep in your heart you know that it was very, very personal!

Christina found that Joshua had repaired the fence all along the front road, and it took little time for the inspection. Starting with "Beautiful Dreamer," she sang every Stephen Foster song she could remember. By the time she reached the home gate back up by the barn, she was humming a special adaptation of "Christina with the deep auburn hair . . ."

She hiked within 200 feet of the unpainted clapboard-sided remains of a cabin.

"Lord, I have a skunk problem here. I know You created them just the way they are. For what reason, I cannot fathom. It's not that I want them dead. I just want them on someone else's ranch. Not Kern's, but someplace. How about on top of Stokes Mountain? Couldn't You just give them a signal tonight and lead them to the top of the mountain — the way you led Moses and the chosen people to the promised land?"

Halfway up the hill she ran out of Stephen Foster songs. She was tired.

And hot.

And extremely sweaty.

When she reached the metal stock tank, she rolled the sleeves of her flannel shirt up to her elbows and dipped her forearms into the clear, cool running water.

Joshua's right — this is wonderful! I should soak my hands until they shrivel like a raisin. It even makes the blisters feel good!

Even though the tank was now in the sunlight, she pulled off her hat and hung it on a corral post. Then she took the combs out of her hair and let it fall down to her shoulders. She returned to the tank and bent over, splashing water all over her face.

"Oh, my!" *I didn't know our spring was that cool. Or maybe it's because my face is flushed.* "Oh, Christina, oh, don't you cry for me. I'm goin' to Californy with a banjo on my knee." . . . *Whoa, that feels wonderful. . . . I should have brought a towel to dry my face off.*

She stared at her wavy reflection in the water.

No wonder dear Miss Atwood found me incredulous. I look like something between a beet and a sweet potato . . . with dirty red hair. Well, it will give her something to giggle about at the church social.

She held her nose and stuck her entire head under the water, then quickly jerked it out again.

"Oh . . . Oh! . . . Oh, that's cold. Really cold."

The water poured off her hair onto her flannel shirt. *My, it does feel good. Maybe I should do this at the end of every day, provided Joshua looks the other way. I don't care how old he is, he's not going to see me with wet hair.*

Christina splashed her arms in the water until they were used to the temperature.

I wonder what it would feel like to . . . I mean, I'm supposed to live life to the fullest . . .

She walked over to the corral and unlaced her boots, slowly tugged them off, and yanked off her stockings. Gingerly, she crept barefoot across the hot, dry, rocky dirt to the tank.

Lord, may I not freeze to death in this tank and have someone find my body bobbing like an apple. Now . . . do I want to face the driveway? Or the sunset? Definitely the sunset.

"Lord, I know it looks very strange to climb into an open stock tank fully clothed, but it's as much adventure as I have the nerve to squeeze out of today."

It took over fifteen minutes and four Stephen Foster songs for her to ease herself completely into the tank. She found she could sit on the bottom and lean her head against the rail, with everything below her neck covered by water.

Clean.

Cold.

Water.

This, Lord, is one of the greatest moments in my life. It's just like Your promise: "I will make the wilderness a pool of water, and the dry land springs of

137

water." Here I am . . . in the promised land.

I love it.

I love it.

I love it.

I love him.

I didn't mean that, Lord. What I meant was, I didn't mean to think that. At least, not for a while.

The sun was a bright sinking ball, filtered orange by the dust clouds from dry alkali lake beds far to the west. The air was still, stagnant, warm, but Christina was cool, and her heart kept singing.

I knew the minute I put my hand in his that he was the one. You know it, too, don't You, Lord? This is my place; he is my man; this is my life, and I'm going to live it to the fullest.

There's just one thing I'm wondering. Are You going to tell him that he's the one, or do I have to? I think it would be more socially acceptable if You do it. Maybe You could speak to him in a dream or something like that. I don't mean like Joseph and Mary. I just meant that You could kind of whisper in his ear, "Hey, Kern, she's the one!" But You might have to shout.

"You are a beautiful dreamer, Christina!" she muttered. "I'm also a beautiful schemer, and that bothers me. Lord, not my will but Yours be done."

She was still in the tank, splashing water on her face and singing, "Doo-dah, doo-dah," when she thought she heard something. She turned around. Kern Yager and Busca were no

138

more than thirty feet away, coming down the slope of the hill.

"Go away!" she shouted and immediately plunged her head under the water. *This is not fun, Lord. Send him away.*

Finally she raised her head up out of the tank, dripping wet and gasping for breath.

Busca barked.

Kern grinned.

She scowled. "Are you still here? I told you to leave."

"We were waiting to see if you were going to drown."

"Well, I'm not. . . . What are you staring at?"

Yager looked away at the sunset. "Tell me, did you accidentally fall into the stock tank, or do you always take your bath fully dressed?"

"How and when I bathe is no concern of yours, Kern Yager!"

"No, ma'am. You're right about that. Forgive me for the intrusion. I didn't come over here to see you wet."

"That's nice to know! Why did you come over?"

"Did you want me to fetch you a towel or something?"

"Why would I want that? I have no intention of getting out of this water until you leave."

"But you have all your clothes on."

"Indeed," she snapped, "but wet clothes do not fit me as comfortably as dry ones. Now what did you want?"

"First off, I wanted to let you know that I hung a gate on the east fence over near my plowed ground. If you are ever checking on my place when I am gone again, I wouldn't want you to rip your dress."

"Thank you, Mr. Yager. If that situation ever presents itself again, I will appreciate it. Is there more?"

"Ol' man Lawrence came by on his way up to the King's River and gave me a message from Joshua."

She sat up until her shoulders were above the water. "My hired man sent you a message?"

"Yep. He said that the verdict in the 76 Land and Water Company suit with the railroad will be handed down tomorrow at 10:00 A.M., and he wants to hang around and find out what they decided."

"What they decided? You mean the jury is through with it?"

"I think they settled out of court."

She flopped her wet hair back out of her eyes. "My goodness, that could be interesting."

He pulled off his hat and held it in his hand, letting the sunlight fall on his clean-shaven face. "Since you and I are holding lieu land, it could be critical."

Christina stared off to the south. "Well, I'm glad Joshua stayed in Visalia. But I still don't understand why Mr. Lawrence couldn't have brought me the message directly."

"I reckon he doesn't like the skunks. Anyway,

Joshua asked me to look after you until he got back."

"Look after me?" She threw her shoulders back and reared out of the water. "Just exactly what does that mean to you, Mr. Kern Yager?"

"Me and Busca can sleep out here in the yard, like Slashpipe, just so you'll feel more comfortable."

"Look at me, Mr. Yager. I'm not a little girl who needs a protector."

He stared at her.

She slipped down until only her head was above water. *I didn't mean look at me like that.*

"No man on the face of the earth would mistake you for a little girl," Yager commented. "Some gals appreciate extra security. Busca could take care of things fine for you, but he misses me. So I'll just hang around so he has someone to talk to."

The dog barked twice.

"Thank you, both. That is a very generous offer, Kern and Busca. But, seriously, this is my ranch, as primitive as it is at the moment, and I feel very safe and secure here. I do have a shotgun, as you know, and I seldom miss anything I'm aiming at. The one advantage of those skunks down there is that they slow down traffic up to the barn."

"Look, Christina, I can go back to my place now and just come over after dark. I'll stay out of sight."

"Kern, I'm serious. I really need to know that I

can take care of myself. Thank you anyway."

"Okay, but promise me — if you wake up worried about anything, fire the shotgun, and I'll come check on you," he said.

"Yes. I will do that." She reached back and tried wringing some of the water out of her hair. "And if you wake up worried about anything, fire your shotgun, and I'll come check on you."

A wide grin broke across his face. "You would, wouldn't you?"

"Yes, I would. Now if you two don't go home, I'm going to be permanently blue and wrinkled."

He was slow to start down the slope of the hill. "Eh, I . . ."

"Was there something else?" she called out.

"I surely hope things turn out to our advantage with that lawsuit," he muttered.

"As do I, Kern."

He went down the hill a few more steps, then turned back. "By the way," he hollered. He pulled off his hat. "Miss Christina Swan, you really do look mighty handsome — even wet."

"Thank you, Mr. Yager," she yelled back. "Perhaps I'll always entertain gentlemen from inside the stock tank."

"What?" he called out.

"I was teasing, Kern," she shouted.

For a moment it seemed as if they were the only two people on the face of the earth. "Shall I check on you in the morning, or would that be insulting, too?" he asked.

"That would be fine. Good-bye, Kern."

"Evenin', Christina." He waved a quick hand at the dog. "Come on, Busca, let's go home."

The dog barked twice.

She watched man and dog hike down the one-mile path to the eastern side of the ranch. Then, with her clothes feeling as if they weighed a ton, she pulled herself out of the tank.

He knows, too, doesn't he, Lord?

I know that he knows.

And he knows that I know that he knows.

Dragging her wet skirt in the dirt, she plodded barefoot up to the barn singing, "Oh, doo-dah-day," at the top of her lungs.

Five

The fire in the beehive-shaped adobe oven had gone out long ago, so Christina had a supper of one apple and two cold tortillas. If she had thought about it, she would have realized that the food was nearly tasteless and not at all the healthy meal her mother always demanded she eat.

But she didn't think about it.

She sat on her padded stool and watched the June summer sun drop behind the low coastal range of mountains eighty miles to the west. Their rounded silhouettes stretched out in direct contrast to the jagged, towering peaks of the Sierra Nevadas in the sunrise.

Her legs stretched out in front of her, she sipped a tepid cup of coffee that did have a taste — bitter.

Lord, I don't think I've ever heard anything like this.

Nothing.

No sounds at all.

There are no trees for the birds to nest in.

No dogs to bark.

No chickens to cluck.

The horses are gone.

Joshua is gone.

144

Maybe I should run and throw a rock at Mrs. Manchada in the corral. If she bellowed a bit, at least I could hear something.

"Mrs. Manchada, are you still over there?" she hollered.

You see, Lord, even the cow is quiet.

Christina pushed the cuff of her cotton dress sleeve halfway up her elbow and placed the inner part of her wrist to her ear.

Good. I can hear my heartbeat — that's always a nice sound. I think I should get a dog, a cat, some ducks . . . perhaps some chickens and a peacock. That should do it.

A female dog.

Medium size.

Who likes to work cows, of course.

The backs of her thighs felt stiff as she sauntered to the table and abandoned the half-filled tin coffee cup. Christina pushed her curly, damp auburn bangs back off her thick eyebrows and strolled over to the corral. She laid her arms on the top rail and her chin on her hands as she stared at the cow in the middle of the pen. "Mrs. Manchada, I hate to put pressure on you, but you have to produce a calf, or Joshua says we'll hang you for meat this winter. It's a cruel world. Produce or else."

She stood on the bottom rail and gazed across the three-section ranch.

"Well, Christina, the upper 1,200 acres will always be too shallow and too steep to farm. But by fall we'll have a nice pen of cows and calves.

And down below we'll have 320 acres of wheat, 160 acres of hay, and 160 acres for fruit, vines, nuts, and vegetables."

Maybe only 155 acres of those things. The other five belong to the skunks!

Lord, I'll never have that much in crops without that ditch company bringing water in here. Now I don't want something for nothing; I just want an ample supply of water at a fair price. The ruling is going to be tomorrow, and I would rejoice in You greatly to have a ruling that provides just that.

Is that asking too much?

She stared to the east where the distant fence separated her place from Kern Yager's. She tugged at her small, round abalone earring.

And one other thing, Lord — right over the horizon in a used white army tent is a big, strong man. I want him over here, and I want him over here right now!

Even though it was still fastened, she held the collar of the dress tightly under her chin. *Christina Alena Swan, why in the world did you chase him off tonight?*

Like a condemned prisoner advancing to the gallows, she marched straight to the stock tank and plunged her face, not her entire head, into the cold water.

"That tank's handy for a lot of things," she muttered as she trudged back to the barn, letting the cold water drip on her sleeves which were now tightly hugged around her chest.

She had her loft arranged for the night before

it got completely dark. The lantern hung from a peg on the post beside her bed of freshly fluffed straw. The journal, her Bible, and some stationery were neatly arranged on the floor next to a bottle of India ink and a pen.

The double-barreled shotgun lay parallel to the sleeping area. Two cartridges were lined up beside the receiver. A fresh pan of water perched across the loft on an empty barrel. Near the steps down to the barn floor was a stack of neatly folded filthy clothes.

She sat on the floor, her knees tucked up under her chin as she unlaced her boots. "Lord, I know this is strange for me to keep talking to myself aloud, but I like hearing someone talk, even if it's me. I need to write to Mother and Uncle Joey. Mother said that after two days, I might grow tired of all this. She's wrong this time. I should tell her about Kern Yager, as soon as there's something to tell. She always told me to find someone as solid as Grandpa and Loop."

A smile broke across her face.

"Mama, this man is solid. Solid muscle."

Lord, if I keep this up, I'll need another trip to the stock tank! Perhaps You can help me change the subject.

A faint screeching sound, not much more than a small child's fingernails on a slate board, drifted across the loft.

"A varmint! A least I'm not alone. Well, perhaps You did bring me a visitor. I trust it's a squirrel or a . . . But I don't have any trees." She stood up in her stocking feet. "I don't mind mice. I just hope they aren't rats. I don't want rats, and especially I don't want them in the loft. That's my prayer, Lord, and You know it comes from a sincere heart."

She strolled over to the edge of the loft carrying the kerosene lantern, looked down into the flickering shadows of the barn below, and cleared her throat. "Well, whatever you are, you are welcome as long as you . . ."

A shadow swooped down from the peak of the barn roof and flew straight out into the night. She jumped back.

"Bats? No, no, no, Lord, not bats! I didn't say bring bats. This is not funny. I'm not laughing. I do not like bats. I hate bats worse than I hate rats . . . and You know it."

Two bats swooped into the barn and attached themselves to the peak of the ceiling; then a third came.

Christina paced the loft. "Lord, I don't understand this. I have been here five nights, and there have been no bats. Not one. Now the first time I'm alone, the bats come in. Can You give me one good reason why that has to be? I know You appointed a worm for Jonah, but a bat? I already have skunks — isn't that enough?"

She set the lantern down on the loft floor and marched back to retrieve the shotgun. She hiked it to her right shoulder and pointed it at the pitch-black images of small, winged mammals.

"All right, bats, here's the deal. You can spend

the night, one night, but you get out before day-light, and if you so much as come near the loft tonight, I'll blast you right off to . . . to wherever it is that bats go when they die! Don't mess with me. I mean it."

For the next half hour, she sat cross-legged, her Bible in her lap, shotgun by her side. Once she decided that the invasion of the bats had ceased, Christina stretched out in the straw on her stomach and propped herself up on her elbows. After two half-written letters, re-reading each several times, she screwed the lid down on the ink jar and turned out the lantern.

She rolled over on her back on the blanket-covered straw, barefoot, but fully clothed. She unfastened the top three buttons of her brown cotton dress.

I will wash clothes first thing in the morning and hang them out to dry. I wonder when Kern will be coming over? I certainly don't want him to see my clothes hanging out.

But I hope he's coming over.

If he doesn't, I'm quite confident that I'll humiliate myself in some manner by going to visit him. The trouble with living alone is that I know myself too well, but I never get a break. I'm stuck with me.

She rolled over on her side and tried to see the moon through the cracks in the barn siding. *Perhaps I'll try baking some bread in the adobe oven. Old Piedra showed me how to do it one time up at Rancho Alazan when I was a little girl. Heat the oven, scoop out the coals, stick in the bread, and then wait forever. At least, when I was ten it seemed like forever.*

Then while it's baking, I'll stake off where the new fencing will go to keep the cattle up on the hillside. Yes, I knew I'd think of it. And while I'm over near the east fence, I'll chat with Kern about . . . eh, planting tomatoes. Yes, he had lots of seed and dynamite.

Please, please, Lord, don't let him turn out to be a train robber or an anarchist, because I think I'm going to fall in love with him no matter what he is, and certain occupations will be difficult to justify to You and my mother — not necessarily in that order.

The only sound for the next hour was what she produced crunching the straw as she tossed and turned. No matter which way she moved, there was a twitch or a pain. Try as she might, she couldn't keep her eyelids closed.

About midnight a horse-thief moon lit up the barn. A blanket of dim stars washed across the San Joaquin Valley sky. With the skirt of her brown cotton dress hiked up to her hips, she sat on the edge of the loft, her legs hanging down toward the darkness of the barn floor. Her arms were wrapped around her chest as she rocked back and forth and hummed "Beautiful Dreamer."

Lord, I don't know what's keeping me awake. I didn't drink that much coffee tonight. I didn't take any Female Remedy. I don't know if it's being alone . . . or the bats . . . or because I'm anxious to see what happens next.

I'm not in a hurry, but if that man with arms like an anvil is the one — and I know he is — well, that means something's going to happen to move things along, and I'm looking forward to what that might be.

Should I visit him tomorrow or wait for him to visit me?

Should I tell him I know that he knows, or should I wait for him to tell me that he knows that I know?

Should I write any of this to Mother? She and Loop would come down the next day if I did. No, I should wait until there is something more definite. Maybe something definite will happen tomorrow. Maybe I won't even see him tomorrow. What if I never see him again? What if that dynamite blows up, and there's nothing left of him but big bone fragments? Then I'd never know if he was the one! Maybe I should go wake him up and find out right now once and for all!

She continued to rock back and forth.

Back and forth.

Of course, I know he's the one, so I don't need to wake him up.

She lay back on the floor of the loft, her feet still hanging over the edge.

The noise was so soft, so faint. Only in the dead silence of a deserted ranch could she have heard it.

Somewhere, far down the drive . . .

Clop.

Clop.

Clop.

Clop.

151

A cold chill swept around her neck like a frigid muffler. She quietly scampered back to her straw bed and clutched the shotgun.

Someone's leading a horse very quietly up my driveway. I don't know who it is, and I don't like it!

Maybe Joshua decided to come home after all. But why would he do that in the middle of the night? I don't hear any wagon wheels. Our wagon squeaks. Besides, he has no reason to sneak in.

But who else even knows I'm back here?

Kern?

Kern Yager, if you think you're going to come over here and camp out in spite of what I told you . . . and secretly protect me in the middle of the night . . .

She crept to the edge of the loft but could see nothing but moonlit darkness.

Why would Kern lead a horse over here? He could walk over, and it would be a lot quieter. He might already be here. Maybe he came back and has been listening to everything I said. What did I say? I only hummed out loud . . . didn't I?

She paused. The horse stopped somewhere out in the yard.

Nobody knows I'm back here. It's not someone looking for me. Maybe he thinks no one is here, that it's an abandoned barn. Maybe he thinks he's just going to bunk for the night and . . .

Scooting to the side of the loft, she lay down on her stomach, propped the gun to her shoulder, and pointed it out the opening of the doorless barn below.

I'm a little nervous here, Lord. I've never shot

anyone. I do not want to shoot anyone.

Christina, do not shoot Kern. I can see the news-paper headlines: "Woman Finds Perfect Man . . . and Shoots Him."

And do not shoot Joshua.

Do not shoot anyone.

She heard one boot heel, then another.

A horse snorted.

Then another step.

Sweat beaded on Christina's forehead. She licked her chapped lips.

There was another step.

She chewed on her tongue.

And another step.

The shotgun felt heavy in her hands.

Lord, don't let me shoot him until I know who it is.

There were two more steps.

Then I'll shoot him.

A man's silhouette appeared in the door-way.

Male . . . medium height . . . wide-brimmed hat — that covers most of the men in the state.

Except the one who lives next door. It's definitely not Kern Yager.

"Psst! Christina! It's me — Cole. Put down the shotgun!"

No . . . no . . . no, not Cole. He doesn't know I'm here. He can't see me. I'm having another bad dream.

This time the voice was a little louder. "I can't see you, Christina, but I know you're up there. I can smell your pink rose perfume. And I know you aren't asleep because you mumble when you sleep!"

I most certainly do not. Besides, Cole Travis, how do you know what I do when I sleep? Maybe on that train ride from San Francisco, but that doesn't count.

"Put the shotgun down, darlin'. I need to talk to you."

Does he think I can't handle the likes of him without a shotgun?

She jammed the double-barreled shotgun back under the hay at the side of the loft.

"Christina?"

"Cole, would you please leave now." She tried to make her voice sound demanding, but it had a whiny ring to it.

"Darlin', I knew you were in there. I need to talk to you. Have you got a lantern?"

"I have a lantern, but I'm not going to light it. You are not welcome to stay. Please get on your horse and leave my ranch." She stood and crept over to the ladder.

"I'm not leaving until we talk."

"How do you know I'm alone?"

The shadow in the doorway didn't move. "You ain't got a man up there with you — I know that. A buffalo has a better chance at tap dancin' than a man being in your loft."

You came very close to being wrong, Cole Travis! "I would expect such thoughts from you. I was talking about my hired man."

"I know that the old toothless *vaquero* that

154

works for you is in Visalia."

Lord, all night I wanted to talk to a man, but this is not the man. "How do you know that?"

"I ran across him at a saloon just west of town. How in the world do you think I knew you were out here?"

She placed her palms on her cheeks. Her face felt flushed. "Joshua told you how to find my place?"

"Of course. When I heard him mention Christina Swan, I told him I was your beau."

Lord, this is like the same frightening dream over and over again. "You are not my beau, Cole."

"Are you startin' in on that again?"

"No, I am not. I want you to leave. I want you to leave right now."

"Now, darlin', I can't do that. I need to cross Stokes Mountain and end up at Badger, and I can't do that at night. We aren't leavin' until jist before daylight."

"We?" The word flew out of her mouth like a bullet. It seemed as if every muscle in her body locked up at the exact same moment.

A sulfur match flickered in the doorway below as another man appeared next to Cole Travis. In the dim glimmer of light both men looked unshaven or dirty-faced or both. She could see that the new man held a revolver, had big ears, shaggy hair, scowling eyes, riveting, sweeping eyebrows — and an old Confederate cap pulled tightly on his head.

"This here is Billy!" Cole called out. "He's my pard."

Christina staggered back and propped herself against a post.

It was all she could do to keep her voice from quivering. "What did you say his name is?"

"Billy! Like in Billy the Kid, only Billy the Kid's dead, and this Billy ain't."

Something's going on, Lord, and I don't know what. I can't tell what is a dream and what is real. Something's happening to me that I don't like. I'm losing control.

"Christina?"

"She don't have no shotgun, Cole."

She felt frozen to the post, unable to move. *He's like the one in the other dream, the one who was supposed to be a brother that I don't have. I don't understand . . .*

Someone climbed up into the loft. "Christina, are you all right?"

Another man climbed the ladder. "Where is she, Cole? I cain't see her."

Another match was lit. Cole Travis held it only a few feet away. He marched right past her to the lantern, lit it, and then squeezed out the flames between his fingers.

"She's got on her dress," Billy sneered. "You said she'd be in her nightgown."

Christina spun around, her back to the men, and buttoned the high collar of the cotton dress. She felt dizzy. She couldn't think what to say. *I want to wake up now, Lord. I don't like this dream.*

Please, Lord, I want to wake up.

There was a decided gap between Billy's two front teeth. "You didn't tell me she had purdy red hair, Cole. You aren't plannin' on savin' her all for yerself, are ya?"

Christina ran her tongue across the slight gap in her own teeth.

Cole Travis pulled his revolver out of his holster and jammed it against Billy's head. "You get over on the other side of the loft and stay there," he snarled. "Don't you talk about Christina that way!"

Billy jammed his own pistol back in his holster. "That ain't the way you talked about Juanita last week."

"This isn't Juanita. Christina is different. Get over there, Billy — I mean it!"

Christina felt her chin tremble. She bit her lip and inched away from the two men.

Billy reached inside his half-buttoned, dirty blue shirt and scratched his chest. "Ask her if she's got anything to eat or drink."

"I told you, she's temperance." Cole turned back to Christina. "Billy's hungry."

"There are a few tortillas and pork and hot sauce down in the pantry box out in the yard," she instructed.

"You got any biscuits?" Billy asked.

Christina shook her head.

"I really like biscuits and jelly. Think I'll go take me a look," Billy decided. "Can I take the lantern?"

"No, you may not," she snapped.

His right hand went to the grip of his revolver. "I didn't ask you."

"Leave the lantern," Travis instructed.

When Billy disappeared out of the loft, Cole Travis sat down on some straw near where she had buried the shotgun. He patted a place next to him. "Come on over here, darlin', and sit down. Let me tell you what happened."

She remained on the opposite side of the loft and sat down, cross-legged, facing him. Both of their shadows cast eerie reflections on the slanting barn wall. She could hear Billy curse and bang dishes in the grub box out in the yard.

Christina clutched her hands together in her lap until they almost turned white. "Cole, why are you here, and who is that man?"

He kept his revolver in his right hand, but let it rest on the loft floor. "Billy's just one of the gang."

She could feel her heartbeat throb in her temples. "What gang?"

"My gang."

"What does your gang do? Blow up trains?"

"I'll tell you what we did this time. We were just as bold as sin. It had 'em tremblin' in their boots and beggin' for their lives. Me and Billy held up the land office of the Los Angeles and Pasadena Tulare Improvement Company."

"Where is that?"

"In Waukena. We got $7,000 cash dollars right out there in the saddlebag."

"Where's the justice in that, Cole? Where's the great cause? How have you stood up for the small farmer in that? You going to tell me that's a strike against the railroad's monopoly of the land?"

"You don't understand, Christina. Sometimes we've got to take what we can just to keep going until something more noble comes along."

"There isn't any noble crime. Sin is lawlessness, and you're a lawless man. Cole, at one time you were a principled man. Now you're just an outlaw. And if you keep going like this, soon you'll be a murderer."

He stiffened his shoulders. "I didn't kill that man."

Something in the pit of her stomach became twisted in a knot. "What man?"

"The land agent in Waukena."

Christina leaned forward, put her hands on the loft floor, and took a deep breath. "Someone got killed?"

He pushed his hat back. She could see his shallow eyes more clearly. "He was stupid. We weren't going to shoot him, but he grabbed for his carbine. Billy shot him through the neck. Sometimes it's shoot or be shot."

She struggled to her feet and marched halfway toward him. "Get out of here, Cole. I do not want to ever see you again in my life."

When he stood, she was afraid he would step on the shotgun. "Christina, I ain't leavin' this loft, and I'll tell you why. First, because we can't cross Stokes Mountain until the break of day, and, second, because I can keep Billy out of the loft, and you can't."

"Are you saying if I don't let you stay up here, you'll turn Billy loose on me?"

"That isn't the way I put it, but you get the picture. We leave as soon as dawn breaks."

"And never ever come back this way again?"

A sly grin broke across Cole Travis's face. "I didn't say that. I'm sure we'll need a place to hide out ever' once in a while."

She paced over to where the basin of water waited on the barrel. The air in the loft felt warm, stuffy. "I will get word to the sheriff as soon as you're gone."

She was glad to see him step away from where the shotgun was hidden. "There isn't anyone around for five miles — the old man told me that."

He didn't tell you about Kern? Did Joshua suspect something with Cole? "Yes, but once I get the sheriff, I'll show him your trail."

"By then it won't matter. We'll be in the mountains," he bragged.

She ran her tongue across her chapped lips. "You're in serious trouble, Cole Travis. They'll track you and hang you both."

"They can't track Billy. He's a half-breed, and he grew up in the mountains. He knows 'em like a wolf. Once we make it to Badger, the entire U.S. Cavalry couldn't find us."

"Where's the future in this, Cole? It can only

lead to your death."

"You made it plain your future wasn't with me. So don't go preaching at me. If you had told me somethin' different, I might still be workin' for your Uncle Joey."

"Are you blaming me for how your life turned out?"

"I'm just saying that I don't need your moralizin' anymore." He sauntered closer. She smelled the rank scent of sour whiskey. "Which is it going to be, darlin'? You let us stay until mornin', peaceful like . . . or I go on down and turn Billy loose?"

"I can't believe you're doing this to me. What happened to you? It's like everything that was decent and good in you just dried up and disappeared."

" 'Cause I got tired of bein' good and decent. It don't buy you nothin' more than hard work and a bowl of beans. I want more out of life than that. You ought to know. You were never satisfied with a simple life either. Don't kid yourself. You exiled yourself to school to please your mama, but you hated it. You exiled yourself down here to please your Uncle Joey, but in two weeks you'll hate it, too. You never liked ridin' in the caboose. You always wanted to be up in the engine with your head out in the breeze. Well, there ain't no breeze here, darlin'."

Her mouth dropped open to respond, but no words came to mind.

"You ought to come up into the hills with us.

I'll ditch Billy, and then you and me can head for Denver or St. Louis and have a grand time. At least until the money runs out."

Christina brushed her fingertips across her lips. "I can't believe you'd even ask me that. It's like you have no memory of who I am. You're treating me like some dance hall girl on morphine."

"That's the way it always was. You'd lead me on with your flirtin' and then suddenly become snotty. Well, it isn't too high and mighty living in a broken-down barn with no doors out in the middle of an abandoned ranch. There are a lot of dance hall darlin's sleepin' on silks and not straw."

"This ranch is not abandoned. It belongs to my Uncle Joey, and I'm going to develop it for him. We'll start building a house as soon as the lumber arrives, and by —"

"Oh, yeah, sure, and I'm going to be governor of California someday."

"You're a common crook, Cole Travis."

"So's the governor. I've heard you say so."

"Cole, we used to be friends. Good friends. Would you please honor that friendship by leaving, with Billy, and never coming back?" She clutched her hands together in front of her waist.

"Why should I do that? What advantage would that be to me?"

"Then you would know that no matter what happens to you in the future, I will at least have pleasant past memories of our friendship."

"That ain't a very motivating speech. You'll promise to think about me as a former friend. Isn't that wonderful! What if I don't care whether you remember me as a friend? I'll remember you as a selfish, superior prig."

"It is obvious from the way you talk to me that you hate me. I don't know why you came here."

"It was on the way. I figured you might be impressed."

"Why would you ever think that?"

" 'Cause I know how hard it is to impress you — that's why."

"I'm impressed with honesty, integrity . . . faith. . . . You know that."

"And you're impressed with men who have college degrees, big bank accounts, and social standing."

"That's not true."

"You're talkin' to Cole Travis, Christina Alena — not the women's auxiliary at church. . . . We're stayin' until first light."

"Not in the loft. Why don't you go out there and get something to eat with your great pal, Billy."

"Because you might try to slip out."

"What if I did? It would take all night to reach a neighbor. You said there's no one within five miles, remember?"

"But your shotgun is somewhere in this loft. You always had one at home. You had one in the

163

schoolhouse. And I know you have one out on this ranch."

"Joshua took it to town."

"An ol' *vaquero* toting a shotgun? Nope, that don't ring true. He's a *pistola* man if I ever saw one. I'm going to stay right here."

Billy entered the barn below the loft. "Cole, you want something to eat? There's some salt pork and tortillas," he called up. "This here pork ain't spoiled or nothin'."

"I'll eat later."

"How much later?"

Christina walked to the edge of the loft. "Billy, have we ever met before?" she asked the man with hot sauce on his scraggly, dirty beard.

Even in the shadows she could see him squint and stare at her from head to foot. "Nope, but Cole told me all about you."

"Where did you grow up, Billy?"

"In the Sierra Nevadas. In the Carson Range. You ever been there?"

"No. Did you ever live in Stockton?"

"No, I ain't. Now why are you askin' me all these things?"

"I thought we might have met sometime," she stated.

"I told you we didn't. I'd remember meeting a woman like you."

"And I'd certainly remember meeting you."

The man down in the barn took a few steps toward the loft ladder. "Cole, are you two finished up there?"

"We've got more talking to do," Cole Travis called back down. "Don't we, Christina?"

"Probably," she muttered.

Billy wiped his chin on the sleeve of his shirt. "Well, hurry up. I want to talk to her, too. I think she likes me."

"You stay down there," Travis called down. "I need you to be the lookout."

Billy walked over to the barn door and looked out at the dark yard. "We don't need a lookout. There ain't no one followin' us. Swingin' out east toward Farmersville threw them all off our trail."

"Maybe that old man told someone we were headed this way," Travis cautioned.

"He ain't goin' to wake up till tomorrow, the way you cold-cocked him."

Christina turned toward Cole. "You did what to Joshua?" she demanded.

"He's all right. I did it so Billy wouldn't kill him, just like you did good ol' Harvey up at the schoolhouse."

"How come I got to be the lookout?" Billy hollered.

Cole kept his eyes on Christina as he talked to the man below. "Because you're a better shot than me."

"That's true. Maybe we could trade off after a while."

Lord, You didn't lead me to the right place — and the right man — to have it end like this. Deliver me from my enemies. Now would be a good time to send

165

10,000 angels to help me.

Suddenly Billy looked straight up at the peak of the barn roof. "You got bats in here, lady."

"Yes, I know."

"I don't like bats very much. Once they move in, you can't get rid of them without you shoot the whole passel."

"How good a shot are you, Billy?" she asked.

"You mean, can I shoot them bats for you?"

"I would appreciate it."

"How much would you appreciate it?" he demanded.

"Billy, me and Christina have to talk," Cole called out.

"I ain't talkin' to you. I'm talkin' to Miss Christina. How much would you appreciate it?"

"If you can kill all those bats, I'll come down after a while and cook you both some breakfast with a big basket of biscuits and jelly to take when you leave."

"That ain't what I had in mind," he insinuated. "You can keep your bats."

"I understand if the job's too hard for you. Bats are hard to hit. Sure, you could kill the first one, but then the others would fly around, and you probably wouldn't be able to hit them," she challenged.

"You sayin' I cain't do it?"

"I'm saying that I realize how difficult it is."

"Bring that lantern over here," he called up.

"Don't be wasting bullets," Travis cautioned.

"There's only three of them. I only need three

bullets," Billy bragged.

Christina carried the lantern to the edge of the loft. Billy took aim and fired. The explosion pounded Christina's ears and filled the barn with gun smoke.

One bat dropped to the barn floor. The other two soared for Cole Travis's side of the loft. He dove back into the straw and came up carrying her shotgun.

"Well, here's what I was lookin' for."

"I'm coming up," Billy called out.

"You only shot one," Christina insisted. "I could have done that well myself."

"The others are up there. How can I shoot 'em if I cain't see 'em?" Billy complained.

"Here they come back," she roared.

There was another explosion. Another bat dropped to the barn floor.

"The other one flew out the door," Billy reported. "I cleaned them out."

"But you didn't shoot all three," she challenged.

"I cain't shoot them if they fly off in the night. They ain't in your barn no more. Now send Cole down. It's my turn to come up and visit."

"That third bat will come back. You told me that yourself. You know how they like to roost in the same place," she argued. "Just wait a few minutes. It will return."

"And then I can come up there, right?"

"We can visit while I cook those biscuits."

"My daddy ran off before I was born, and my

mama died when I was twelve. I grew up by myself. I ain't too good at talkin'."

"I am."

"Maybe I'll come up there and wait for the last bat."

"There are no bats up here," she insisted. "Look around the eaves of the barn. I'll bet he moved to the outside."

"I can't see out there. Hand me the lantern."

"There's another by the oven out in the yard. Why don't you light it?"

"Maybe I will. Reckon I could find something better to eat."

She watched him disappear into the darkness and then turned around to face Cole Travis, who had holstered his revolver and carried her double-barreled shotgun.

"He'll be back, and he'll want more than talk."

"Look, Cole, you and your Billy go down there and take all the food you need. Even take a lantern if you want. Go on over Stokes Mountain right now. I can't do anything until daylight, and, chances are, Joshua won't be back till noon if he wakes up with a blue lump on his head. That means it's tomorrow night before I can get word to Visalia. You two will be safe by then. Isn't that what you want?"

"I want you to come with us."

"Cole, I have no more desire to be with you than to be with good old Billy. And there is something extremely eerie about him. You are a former boyfriend, but at this point I don't think of you as a friend at all. And I don't want you ever to come by this ranch again."

"You know I could kidnap you and take you to the mountains anyway," he threatened.

"No, you couldn't. Billy could. He's got the moral restraint of a slug. But I'll tell you why you'll make a lousy outlaw and probably die young. You can't kidnap, you can't rape, and you can't kill. No matter how tough you try to be, you can't do it."

"Don't preach at me," he fumed.

"I'm not preaching, Cole. It's your grand-mother's prayers that are preaching. You forget that I knew your grandmother for over a year before she died. And she prayed for you, Cole Travis. My, how that woman could pray!"

"I'm not listenin' to this anymore." Travis headed for the ladder.

"Leave me my shotgun, Cole."

"I'm not having you shoot me in the back."

"You know for a fact I couldn't shoot anyone unless I thought my life was threatened."

"I'm not leaving you the shotgun. If prayers are so powerful, yours can save you," he snarled.

"Cole!"

"You always pretended to be too good for me, Christina Swan. Now we'll see if you're too good for Billy."

He was still at the top of the ladder with the shotgun when Billy trotted into the barn. "Hey, I didn't know she had a dog," he called out.

A medium-sized black-and-white dog trotted

into the barn, looked up at her, and barked.

I called to the Lord, and He delivered me. "Busca!" she shouted out.

"How come that dog didn't show up sooner?" Travis remained perched on the top step of the loft ladder.

"He was probably out visitin'," Billy suggested. "I had a dog like that who chased the lady dogs ever' night."

"There's not supposed to be any neighbors to visit around here. Check out in the yard, Billy," Travis ordered.

Billy had just spun around in the open doorway of the barn and drawn his revolver when a massive fist connected with his jaw, making a sound like a picket fence being hit with a sledge hammer. Billy fell to the barn floor unconscious. Cole scrambled back up to the loft and grabbed Christina as a shield.

A tall man stepped inside the barn, a carbine at his shoulder. "I'll get you out of this, darlin'," Kern drawled. "Turn loose of her, mister, and come on down here."

"I'm not going down there," Cole growled to Christina. "That guy's crazy. He killed Billy with one punch."

She tried to relax so that her twisted arm would not hurt as bad, but Cole took her yielding as an excuse to twist harder.

"He isn't dead, but for a few days he'll wish he was." Kern continued to hold the gun pointed at the outlaw.

Cole backed them away from the edge of the loft. "Who is that guy down there?"

"He's my — my future husband," Christina blurted out.

"Your what?" Cole shouted.

"Kern and I are going to get married . . . soon," she added.

Travis shook his head so decisively that it shook Christina as well. "I can't believe you're going to marry," he declared. "What happened to that other guy in the schoolhouse?"

"You better believe it, mister," Kern hollered. "Now turn loose of my precious honey-girl before I put a 200-grain bullet in your head."

Christina tugged at her wrist. *Precious honey-girl? You're not very good at this, Mr. Kern Yager.* "You're hurting me, Cole."

He lessened his grip a little. "But you've only been down here a couple weeks. How can you decide to marry someone so quick? You went with me two and a half years and never wanted to marry me."

"We went together six months. I've been trying to get rid of you for two years," she corrected.

"Where did you meet him?"

"Put down the shotgun and turn loose of my pumpkin," Kern demanded.

Horrible! You are absolutely the least smooth-talking man I've ever known, Kern Yager. "We had a class together at the University of California."

171

"He went to college?"

Kern looked up at her. "The college graduate one? I thought I was supposed to be the dumb-ox guy."

"What'd he say?" Travis looked confused.

"He said he graduated *summa cum laude*," she replied.

"What did he study — boxing?"

"Marksmanship," she announced.

"You don't want to die, mister," Kern growled. "Put down the shotgun. I'm a jealous man. When someone touches my Christina, I can get mighty angry."

"No one has to die. I just want to get on my horse and ride away," Cole retorted. "Bring my sorrel horse over to the barn, and I'll ride off."

"Turn loose of my Christina."

She studied Yager's eyes. *My Christina . . . now that sounded more authentic.*

"I ain't goin' to turn her loose. I do that and you'll kill me. Bring me my horse," Travis commanded. "I won't hurt her. She knows that. I just want to ride off."

"Do it, Kern," Christina directed. "I don't want anyone killed in my barn."

"What are they doing here?" Kern asked.

"Just passing through," she replied.

When Kern Yager stepped back into the yard out of sight, Cole Travis descended the loft ladder, dragging Christina along behind him.

"What's taking him so long?" Travis pressed.

"I don't know. Why don't you go out there

172

and look?" she suggested.

"You just want him to shoot me," Travis growled.

"Cole, I honestly do not want you shot. I do not want anyone shot."

"You go out and check on what he's doin'," he insisted.

"Turn loose of my arm," she demanded.

"I'm not turning loose of your arm. Now look out there. Where is he?" Keeping out of sight next to the barn wall, Cole shoved her to the open doorway. His hand clutched her wrist so tightly that she felt her fingers turn numb.

In the flicker of the lantern setting over by the oven where Billy had left it, she spied Kern Yager next to the outside of the barn wall a couple of feet away. She did not turn her head to look at him.

"Can you see him?" Cole asked.

"Yes, he's out there."

"Mister, bring me my horse!" Cole screamed. "What's he doing now?"

"He seems to be waiting for something," she reported.

"Tell him to hurry up."

Kern pointed to his head and then put his fist up next to the barn wall.

"Kern, sweetheart," Christina yelled as if he were 100 feet away, "Cole says to hurry up!" *What in the world is he signaling? Head? Fist? Cole's head?* She glanced back into the barn to see Cole leaning his head on the barn wall, trying to hear Yager's response.

"What's he doin'? I didn't hear him!"

She peeked back into the yard and pointed her thumb down. Kern lowered his clenched fist until she nodded slightly. "He seems to be about ready now."

Kern pointed to her, raised three fingers, and pointed to the ground.

This is my last clean dress, Kern Yager. I am not dropping to the dirt on the count of three. Not for any man.

"I don't hear him bringing my horse," Travis complained.

"Listen . . . Don't you hear that?" she replied.

Travis leaned his head against the barn wall.

Christina peered back outside and nodded at Kern.

Yager signaled with his finger — one, two, three, and then brought his clenched fist back about a foot.

Busca barked.

Christina stood still.

Kern slammed his fist through the faded, old one-by-twelve barn board and connected with Cole's head. Cole Travis pulled the trigger of the shotgun as he crumpled to the floor, unconscious.

Yager swung one arm around her waist and hefted her a foot off the ground as he scurried into the barn.

She gasped for breath. "You busted my . . ."

He quickly set her down on her bare feet. ". . . barn wall."

"When you didn't drop, I just knew he was going to shoot you. In my heart I about died when you just stood there."

She stared down at Cole Travis. "I didn't want to ruin my dress."

Kern Yager paced next to her. "You worried about a dress at a time like this?"

"All my other clothes are filthy," she complained.

"I can't believe this. A man holds a shotgun on you, and you worry about what you're going to wear tomorrow?"

"Of course."

Yager pushed his hat to the back of his head and scratched his neck. "That's unreasonable and irrational."

"It makes sense to me."

"He could have easily pulled that trigger."

"He did."

"He pulled the trigger, and the gun misfired. That was the Lord's protection."

"I don't think so." Christina pulled two shotgun shells out of the pocket of her brown dress. "I got so nervous when they first rode up that I forgot to load the gun. But I'll tell you what was the Lord intervening."

"What?"

"The bats."

"What bats?" Yager asked.

"That's what all the shooting was about. I got

175

Billy to shoot at the barn bats as a signal for you."

"Which one is Billy?"

"The one you first laid out. Do you normally end fights with one punch?"

"Normally I don't get in fights."

Yager grabbed up both men by the shirt collars and dragged them out into the yard. "Was this Billy one of your old boyfriends, too?"

"No, but he looks like a man I dreamed about while sitting on your porch yesterday. There's something uncanny about him."

The lantern was starting to weaken. The June stars sparkled. "Have you got some rope?" he asked.

"Yes, in the barn."

"I'll tie them up. Then maybe we can sort out what's real and what's a charade around here."

She returned from the barn with a brand-new fifty-foot coil of five-eighths-inch sisal rope. "What do you think Busca is doing over there by the corral?"

"He's buryin' bats. Now, Christina darlin', what's all this about?"

That's better, Mr. Yager. A couple more times and I'll believe you mean it.

When the sun finally came up above the Sierras, it came up hot. Christina, Kern, and Busca moved to the shade of the open barn.

"Will you be all right with those two in the corral while I go hitch my team and bring a

176

wagon over?" he asked.

"I think they're hurting too much to try anything, but I'll keep the shotgun on them in case."

"Are you going to put a shell in it?" he asked.

She raised her eyebrows. "Perhaps."

"Christina, I enjoyed sitting here and talking with you most of the night. I've learned more about you than any other gal I've known. But I have one question I need an answer for."

"All right, you may ask just one question," she said.

"Have I been visiting with the real Christina Alena Swan or just a gal who spins a real good yarn?"

"I'm afraid this is the real me," she admitted. "Did I ramble on too much?"

"Not any more than I did."

"Busca slept through it all."

"He is very happy to have you around. Now he doesn't have to put up with my discussions."

"Now I have one question for you, Kern."

"All right, you get one question," he grinned.

"What drives you, Kern Yager?"

"Drives me?"

"Why do you do what you do?"

"I've never been asked that before."

"I've never thought about it until just now. I think that for a lot of my life, family tradition and pride have driven me," she said. "That's not all bad, mind you, but down here on this ranch . . . I need a drive that will last when I'm the only family member around, and no one cares whether I'm a university graduate or not. So what drives you?"

He rubbed his chin. "Like most ever'one, I try to escape the past by pushin' into the future. So I think it's the parable of the soils that motivates me."

"From the Bible?"

"Yeah. I want to plant seed, tend it, water it, and have it produce a hundredfold to the glory of God."

"Are you talking about farming?"

"Farming . . . ranching . . . friendships . . . faith . . . family — I'm driven to produce a good crop."

"And children?" she challenged.

"A hundredfold."

Her mouth dropped open. "What?"

A wide grin broke across his face. "You're easy to tease, Christina Swan."

"That's what people keep telling me. I'll be even easier to tease later today."

"We'll both be tired, won't we?"

"I'm sure I will. I don't do well without sleep."

"You get some rest while I'm taking these two to Visalia."

"I'm coming with you," she announced.

"Why?"

"After all we've gone through and said, I think that's obvious," she ventured.

"I think perhaps I missed something. I got confused in the middle of the night when I came over, and we bantered back and forth about marriage and all that. You sounded awfully convincing."

"Me?" She thought about poking a finger in his ribs, but hesitated when she thought about the pain it would cause her. "How about you?"

"It didn't feel as much like a charade as it did with Lucy Atwood," he admitted.

"Didn't it?"

"We were still just playing a game tonight with all that talk, right?" he pressed.

"Was it?"

He scratched above his ear as if in frustration. "Well, you were just playacting, right?"

"Were you?"

"Were you?" he quickly replied.

"I asked you first," she countered.

"No, you didn't."

"What are you saying, Kern?"

"Christina, what I'm saying is, you're a captivating woman. If we play this game a few more times, I sincerely think I'm going to believe it."

She bit her lip. *Keep quiet, Christina. Don't say it.* "Then let's keep playing the game and see what happens," she blurted out. *I told you not to say that, Christina. You don't even know this man. Of course, you can't stand the men you do know.*

"Are you leading me on, Christina Swan?" He stared out at the yard and refused to look in her eyes. "I aim to lose my heart only once in my lifetime."

Compose yourself, Christina. Be wise. Honest. Subtle. "I'm scared to death I lost my heart yesterday afternoon," she blurted out. *That was about as dainty and subtle as a bull, darlin'.*

He looked in her eyes. "When you held my hand?"

"No," she corrected, "when *you* held *my* hand."

"Same thing."

"Oh, no, Kern Yager. . . . I've held other men's hands."

He slipped his hands in the back pockets of his jeans. "Yours was the first for me . . . I mean, to hold that way."

"What way?"

"Like I meant it. What are we going to do?" he quizzed.

"Well, it's not exactly a deadly disease."

"I don't know," he sighed. "I hear there's no cure for it once you get it."

"Maybe we only have a mild case."

He tugged his left hand out of his pocket and slipped his fingers into hers. "I've been wanting to do that all night long."

"Okay, so it's not a mild case."

"I reckon we'll just see how this all develops over the summer."

Summer? How about today? Tonight? This week? What are you doing next Saturday? I need to buy a white dress. I need to write to Mother. You need a haircut. Do you own a suit and tie? I'll have Loop give me away. Francine can be my matron of honor.
"Yes. . . . It should be interesting to see what the summer brings," she murmured.

"Well, I do have to tell you one thing my daddy always told me," he explained. "He said, 'Kern, you have no right to marry any woman until she's seen one of your bad days.' "

"Have I seen one of your bad days?"

"Once you see one, you don't have to ask."

"I thank your father for that wisdom. Do your parents still live up at the mother lode?"

"Nope. Mama died when I was young. After a while Daddy remarried and is the marshal of Lordsburg, New Mexico."

"Have you had any of your . . . bad days . . . since you began developing the land? How about last week when my cow ran over your tent?"

"That day wasn't even a blink in comparison to a real bad day. But I don't want to talk about it. How about you, Christina Swan? What advice did your mama give you about who to marry?"

"You mean, besides the usual — that he must be a Christian man, a non-boozer, not pronc to violence, honest, hardworking, loving, loyal, and he must make my throat tickle when he talks and my heart leap when he touches my hand — you mean, besides all that?"

Kern laughed. "I'm going to have to make myself a list. How can I ever reach that goal? But, yeah. What else did your mama tell you?"

"She said absolutely never marry a man until he has a house built for me to move into."

"You're teasing me. Your mother actually said that?"

"Yes, she did. Daddy promised to build her a house, but they had to live in a big, old room above the store, and she never got that house. Until after Daddy died."

"When did that happen?"

"When I was one. Some outlaws burned down the store and shot Daddy while he was saving me and my mother."

Yager stared across the mountain.

"Kern?"

He turned to her with sorrow in his eyes. "That's tragic. But it was good that he was there."

"I always lived with it. After twenty-four years, I've decided there are worse things that can happen to a girl than to have a heroic father."

His fingers brushed his face. "You're right about that. We don't know much about each other yet." He turned loose of her hand and started to slip his own around her waist, then pulled back.

"More than we did yesterday. I know that I have to wait and see one of your bad days." She tugged his arm around her waist.

"And I know I have to build you a house." He gave her a squeeze.

She discovered that if she relaxed, she could actually breathe.

Six

The old conical Californio parasol kept the direct sunlight off Christina's face as the wagon crossed the Antelope Valley road and rumbled south toward Visalia. But it did nothing about the sweat around the collar of her brown cotton dress or the moisture between her toes. And they were still in sight of the ranch.

Joshua's right. The sweaty flannel shirt is cooler, once it gets wet. But not very glamorous. Of course, a plain brown dress covered with road dust isn't the latest style from Paris either. Not that I need to be glamorous. But this man beside me has never seen me dressed out. He's seen me dirty, sloppy, wet. I've never seen him dressed up either. Nor have I seen him wet.

She stared across a thousand acres of undeveloped hog wallows and hardpan, the last notion lingering in her mind.

His words erupted like a wagon wheel rolling over a pumpkin. "What are you thinking about, Christina?"

Startled, she sat back, straightened her shoulders, and brushed down the skirt of her dress. "I was thinking about this land. What would it be like if we could actually get the ditch company to bring water in?" *I know it's a lie, Lord, but this man doesn't know me well enough to hear what's really on my mind.*

He pushed his hat back and waved his hand across the empty valley. "I've spent a lot of evenings in that rockin' chair lookin' south and wonderin' if the day will come when there is nothin' but farms, dairies, and ranches between our place and Visalia. Wouldn't that be somethin'? There would be homes and barns and packing sheds, drying yards, cows and chickens, stores and churches and children playing in yards and old folks waving at us from porch swings. Won't that be swell?"

She glanced at him out of the corners of her green eyes. "You mean . . . our places?" she quizzed.

He looked straight down the flat dirt road. "What did I say?"

Even that tanned face of yours can't hide the blush, Mr. Yager. "You said, 'our place,' as if you assumed some future merger."

He gave her a little-boy-caught-with-hand-in-the-cookie-jar grimace. "Okay, Christina Swan, you shamed me."

"How did I do that?"

"You were sittin' there thinking about ditch companies and developing land. I've spent a lot of time ponderin' this land, but that wasn't my thinking just now. I was thinkin' about you and me. Mostly you. But you snapped me out of it, and I thank you for that."

He abandoned the wagon lead lines in his left

184

hand and reached across the wagon seat with his right. Christina bit her tongue and held her breath. Then she watched him pat the black-and-white dog on the head.

Nice work, Christina. You successfully changed the subject. Mr. Yager, if you'd like to continue to think about you and me . . . mostly me . . . it's quite all right.

Kern pointed a thumb toward the back of the wagon. "Busca, go watch the men."

The dog let out one bark and leaped to the back of the wagon where two bound-and-gagged men sat with hats jammed low on their heads in the June sun.

Christina glanced back. "What will he do?"

"He'll bite them in the heels if they try to run away."

She laughed. "I don't think they'll run away — the way you tied them."

He rubbed his freshly shaved square jaw. "I did yank it tight."

You yank everything tight, Kern Yager. My first goal is to teach you gentleness. And quickly. "They're still breathing. I suppose it's all right."

"That's not really why I sent him back there."

"Oh?"

He looked down as if inspecting the top of his jeans. "I was thinkin' . . . we might want to talk about some things . . . and, eh . . ."

She tilted her head and raised one of her thick auburn eyebrows. "And you didn't want Busca listening in?"

"Christina." His voice contained a scolding lilt at the end of her name.

So, Mr. Yager, I believe that's the first time I've heard that particular "Christina." But not the last time, I hope.

"You surely do make me act in ways I'm not used to actin'."

"What did I do?"

"I sent the dog to the back of the wagon so that you would scoot over on the bench next to me."

"Oh!" She started gently to rock back and forth but remained on the far side of the wagon seat.

His focus now turned to the rump of the lead horse. "Do I have to beg you?"

"I'm not sure. Are you very good at begging?" she baited.

With no more effort than it takes to glide a candle across a nightstand, he reached over with a massive hand and slid her over until their hips touched.

"Okay, so you're not very good at begging," she giggled. "I can accept that. Now what did you want to talk about?"

He was silent for a moment. She studied his face. The light brown hair curled out from under his hat and framed his suntanned face and steel-gray eyes. His nose was wide, crooked when she looked straight at him. His lips were thin, drawn, permanently serious.

I wonder if he wants to talk about marriage plans? Perhaps about whether to build one house or two. I wonder if he kisses with as much enthusiasm as he does everything else? There's only one way to find out, of course. On the other hand, I hope he doesn't ask something too awkward.

He shook his head and then looked down at her. "This settlement between the 76 Land and Water and the railroad torments me day and night, Christina."

"I've been worried about it, too."

"When I bought this place, I was told that whatever happened, the land was mine. They said there would be money, stock shares, property passed between the ditch company and the railroad, but privately owned land would not be appropriated. But after three years of arguin', they agree on an out-of-court settlement. The whole idea of a settlement sits wrong with me."

You sent the dog to the back of the wagon so that we can talk about this? "Why is that?"

"In a settlement both sides get something. That is, they figure out what they can live with. Everyone is satisfied with the deal, but someone has to pay. So if it's not the railroad or the ditch company, who's making the sacrifice?"

"I guess that's one of the things we'll learn this morning. I don't think they'll take back land that they sold. This isn't speculation land like Mussel Slough. We have patent deeds."

He brushed the sweat off his forehead and wiped it on his jeans. "You're right. I should relax. I probably worry about it too much. But our deeds have a lieu land attachment."

Lord, I want to be real honest with You. I like sitting up close to this man. I like touching. I really, really like it. She licked her chapped lips. "Do you ever relax . . . and trust the Lord?"

"I know, I'm too serious. Everyone tells me that. Lots of times I worry about things that I'm helpless to do anything about. I'm not good at being helpless. I have a hard time relaxing. There are just so many things to get done in a day. I usually finish a day with regrets for the things left undone. How about you, Christina? Do you finish a day disappointed with yourself?"

The rumble and bounce of the wagon kept them gently rocking in unison. "Most of the time, I'm content with the day. I write lists. It's the schoolteacher in me. Sort of a lesson plan of what I want to accomplish each day."

She couldn't tell if it was the wagon jarring them, or if he was actually leaning against her a little more. "Yeah, I know what you mean. I do the same thing — only I keep lists in my head."

"That's not the same."

"It is to me. I don't forget things."

"Nothing?"

"Very little. It's a curse. There are some things in my life I dearly wish to forget, but I reckon we're all that way." He reached over as if to pat her knee, but pulled his hand back to his own knee. "Do you remember the first words you ever spoke to me, Christina?"

She twirled the parasol. *Let's see, the cow had run over his tent. He ran outside wearing no shirt, no*

188

hat, no shoes . . . no shirt. "I believe you had just called me 'woman,' and I scolded you and said my name was Christina Swan."

"Nope. The first thing you ever said was, 'Please show some common courtesy and remove your hat.' "

Her mouth dropped open. She threw her shoulders back. "When did I say that, Kern Yager?"

"Five years ago, September 16, 8:05 A.M. It was the first day of calculus at the university. I was sitting in the back row next to Tom Roy Hunt when you breezed down the aisle with some well-endowed grinning blonde friend of yours, and without even looking at my face, you said, 'Young man, please show some common courtesy and remove your hat in class.' "

"I did?" she gasped. "I don't remember that."

"Trust me — you did."

"Well, it sounds so haughty and arrogant this many years later. Please forgive me."

"I forgave you years ago. Forgivin' is mostly easy. It's forgettin' that's tough on me. That's why I worry too much."

"Well, Mr. Kern Yager, I hope you have a good day today and accomplish all the plans on that list up in your mind."

"I already feel whipped, and the day's just beginnin'."

"Okay, here's my schoolteacher lecture. You need to make a shorter list. Think it through. Are there any things you can cross off and take care of at another time? Perhaps there are some things I can do for you. Delegation is an important managerial concept, as Moses learned from his father-in-law."

"I've tried to delegate to Busca on numerous occasions, but he balks at accepting a management position."

"You can laugh and tease, but you need to do something, or you'll just end up the day with things undone again."

They crested the bank of Cottonwood Creek. Yager stopped the wagon so abruptly that Busca barked and leaped up to the seat beside Christina.

She stared down at the dry creekbed. "What's the matter?"

"There's a wagon coming this way. We'll let them cross first. If we don't stay in the crossing, we'll get stuck in that sand."

She spotted a wagon rolling through the brush on the other side of the mostly dry creek. "I thought you remembered something on your list."

"I did." He slipped a wide, callused hand behind her head. She turned toward him and pointed the parasol like a shield toward the approaching wagon.

Christina took a deep breath. He pulled her face close to his. *I hope he doesn't bust my lips or crack any of my teeth!*

His narrow lips brushed across her chapped ones. The kiss was so soft it tickled her lips as much as it raced her heart.

Then he sat straight up.

She kept the parasol facing the other wagon.

"There, that takes care of one thing on my list," he announced.

"One little kiss? What kind of list is that?" she blurted out. Then she put her hand over her mouth. "I didn't mean to say that!" she gasped.

He chuckled. "One thing you'll have to put up with — I'm not very good at this spoonin' thing. You can count the number of girls I've kissed on one hand, and most of them were relatives that made me kiss 'em."

"You do fine. It was very sweet. We might want to practice some more, but . . ."

"Hey, what's goin' on over there?" someone yelled from the approaching wagon. "Mister, don't you accost my Christina!"

She dropped the parasol. "Harvey?"

Harvey Jackson stood up in the wagon driven by a toothless but grinning Joshua Slashpipe.

"Who is this guy?" Kern asked.

Joshua reined up the team quickly at the top of the incline of the creek bank. Harvey Jackson tumbled into the wagon bed.

Christina peered at the man sprawled in the back of the wagon. "He's a neighbor boy from Stockton."

Kern sized up the man in the crumpled dark brown suit and tie. "He isn't a boy."

"I think I broke my back," Harvey groaned.

Joshua Slashpipe reached out a hand to assist

the downed man. "He said he was your beau and hitched a ride." Joshua pushed his sombrero back. "The last man who claimed to be your beau left me with this lump on my head. So I thought I'd just save wear and tear and bring this one along. I figured you were having a convention of boyfriends." He studied the bound men in the wagon. "It looks like you got 'em stacked in the wagon like cordwood."

"Kern captured Cole Travis and his partner," Christina explained. "He knocked them out with just one punch."

"Two men with one punch?" Joshua flashed his toothless grin.

Christina shook her head, and sweaty bangs flopped on her forehead. "No, two punches."

"Oh, well, yes . . . that is possible." Joshua shrugged. "A *vaquero* named Big Manuel who rode with me over at La Laguna de Chico Lopez used to knock out a horse with one punch."

Harvey pulled himself to his feet and tried to brush off his suit. "Why would he do that?"

Joshua shrugged his narrow, bony, flannel-shirt-covered shoulders. "Just to impress the ladies, I suppose." He pointed to the men in the wagon. "Who are they?"

"They said they held up the land office at Waukena," Christina reported.

"I heard a man was killed," Joshua commented.

"You should have let me shoot Cole Travis in

the back of the head in the schoolhouse," Harvey insisted.

"Then *you* could have been the one in jail for murder," Christina said.

"I'm getting as confused as Joshua," Kern put in. "These two had a run-in years ago?"

"Just a few weeks ago. I'll explain it later."

"I hope you will." Kern glanced back over at Slashpipe. "We're goin' to take these two prisoners to the sheriff's office. We will be back late tonight."

"What about me?" Harvey complained.

"Are you wanted for any crime?" Kern asked.

"No, I'm not. I'm not like that Cole Travis," Harvey proclaimed.

"Good. Then we won't take you to the sheriff's."

"I could just ride along and visit."

"No, you can't, Harvey Jackson," Christina insisted. "Why did you come down here anyway?"

Harvey loosened his tie. "To visit my darlin', of course."

"I am not now nor have I ever in my life been your darlin'."

Harvey nervously glanced at Kern Yager. "She's quite a tease, isn't she? She's always been that way. Why, I've known her ever since she was flatter than a two-by-six."

"Harvey, I would like you to leave," Christina said.

"I don't have a horse."

"Do you want us to take him back to Visalia?" Kern asked.

"Yes . . . no! He's not going to disrupt our plans. It's not on my list. We've got things to do in Visalia."

"At the rate you are travelin' behind that parasol," Joshua said with a grin, "you won't get there until fall."

"What am I supposed to do?" Harvey repeated.

"Put him to work, Joshua," she suggested.

"Perhaps he's the one to persuade Mrs. Mofeta to leave the cabin?" the white-haired man suggested.

"Oh, Harvey," she laughed, "if you would do that, I would be very grateful."

"How grateful?"

"Let's wait and see how successful you are."

"Is he spending the night with us?" Joshua asked.

"We don't even have a house yet. Harvey really can't stay."

"How about him?" Harvey pointed to Kern. "Where does *he* stay?"

"At his own ranch, of course," Christina snapped. "He's my neighbor."

"Maybe I can stay at that cabin after I get the Mofeta woman to leave. But, from what I hear, neither of you will have them places for long."

Kern Yager spun around so quickly that Busca barked, and Christina nearly slipped off the wagon seat. "What about the settlement,

Joshua? What did they decide?"

"It's posted at the courthouse. Too big a crowd — I couldn't read it all. I do know the railroad gets compensated with undeveloped lieu lands, and 76 Land and Water retains the ditch company."

"How about developed lieu lands?" Yager asked.

"Rumor at the courthouse is that if any land has been developed, they won't touch it."

"What do they consider developed land?" Christina asked.

Joshua pushed back his sombrero revealing a large purple bruise above his right eye. "La Dueña, there was something about crops and trees. There was a lot of loud talk, but I had a headache. I'm glad you are going to town. They have a list of townships and sections that are affected, but I didn't know which was yours. I'm sorry, but I'm just an old man with a sore skull this morning."

"There are several matters about this that I am uncertain of," Christina admitted.

Joshua Slashpipe slapped the lead lines on the rump of General Grant and started the wagon north.

"Are you sure you don't want me to come with you?" Harvey hollered back.

"That's one thing I'm quite certain of," she replied.

Though most of the county offices were closed

on Saturday, several dozen men loitered in the foyer of the courthouse around a lengthy notice on a bulletin board. Kern Yager let Christina off at the courthouse and proceeded across the street to the jail with the two bound outlaws.

Scanning paragraphs of legal jargon, Christina learned that the railroad agreed to settle their accounts by purchasing unclaimed Lieu Lands for three dollars an acre and undeveloped lieu land for the purchase price paid by the current owners. A commission composed of a railroad representative, a county land agent, and a member of 76 Land and Water was appointed to report by September 1 which exact pieces of property would be purchased in northern Tulare County.

Christina carefully copied each word in her journal. "Priority will be given to land still held in public domain; however, privately owned land could be affected. Let it be known that all effort will be made to avoid disruption of established land usage. Developed land with patent deeds will not be attached."

Mulling all of this over, she wandered outside to a bench in the shade of a sycamore. In the still air, heat seemed to rise off the dirt like a steam boiler. A tandem empty of freight rolled out of China Town, going west on Center Street. Two men with silver badges on their leather vests galloped south on Court Street. The dust they stirred up hung in the air.

Christina's dress was soaked with perspiration

two or three inches below her collar. *Lord, this is not the way I planned things. Life was to be quiet . . . peaceful . . . organized. Now everything's confused again. You're going to make my "wilderness a pool of water," remember? So I can't lose the land, can I?*

She stared down at the journal. *In this land it's difficult to look nice and neat and crisp. But this is the kind of weather that makes crops grow quickly. Did You create this valley to grow wheat? And hay? And orange trees? And tomatoes?*

She looked up as a familiar wagon pulled up at the edge of the dirt street. The glance from the broad-shouldered man driving the rig caused her heart and her feet to jump. *Did You create this valley to grow children, Lord? Not a hundredfold, but perhaps five or six?*

Kern hopped down from the farm wagon and greeted her. "What did you find out? Was Joshua right?"

"Yes, but no one will know until September which parcels will be affected." His two hands almost circled her waist as he lifted her up to the seat of the wagon. *Lord, I feel like a rag doll around this man. Please, please, Lord, don't let him be violent on his bad days.*

He swung up beside her. With a flick of his hand, he scooted her over until they touched at the hips. "I have to know a lot sooner than September. They can't stall like that."

"Maybe it won't affect us," she offered. "It was mainly property held in public domain and undeveloped land."

"Were our sections listed as possible lieu lands?"

She put her palms together and held her fingertips to her mouth. "Yes, they were."

He beat his fist on his knee as they rolled south on Court Street. "I knew it! They're going to take it away from us, and I can't do one solitary thing about it! But I've got ground plowed. What does 'developed land' mean?"

Christina felt as if she were reading a sad telegram to a grieving mother. "They spelled it out in detail. Row crops have to be in head or bloom by July 1. Trees and vines have to be two years old. Cattle ranges are not considered developed."

He stared down at his huge, callused hands. "No . . . no . . . I won't let them do that," he murmured barely above a whisper.

"Just because certain land is available doesn't mean they will take it," she offered.

"I've got to do something."

"Kern, we'll figure this out. We've got two college graduates here. We can take on the railroad and the state of California. We'll make a good team."

His reply was too soft to hear.

"What did you say?" she pressed.

"I have to build you a house." His voice had a weary, defeated sound.

"It's all right. I don't need a house at first. That was my mother's idea. It's not that important to me. Look at me now — I'm living in a barn loft and couldn't be happier. That's one thing you don't have to worry about." *Why did I ever tell him about needing a house?*

"You don't understand," he snapped at her. "I've got to do something. God help me, I've got to do something."

His whole body stiffened as if bracing for a fall. For several minutes they drove south without talking. At the edge of town he turned the rig on a meandering road to the northeast.

Christina stared at a tiny white farmhouse set back in a cornfield. "Where are we going, Kern? This isn't the road to Stokes Mountain, is it?"

With his jaw seemingly locked in position, he stared out over the horses' ears.

She placed a hand on his cotton-shirt-clad arm. "Kern, I have a few things I need to do in town before we head back. I need to stop at a clothing store, and . . ."

His eyes seemed to gaze all the way to Colorado.

He's not hearing a word I say. This is very rude, Mr. Kern Yager. The only sound was the rumble of the wagon and squeak of the wheel hubs.

"Honey, we'll figure something out. The Lord will take care of us. We just have to trust Him," she encouraged him. *I don't know why I called him that. I've never called any man "honey" in my entire life. Speak to me, Kern Yager, before I say something else dumb.*

"Do you need to talk about this?" she prodded.

As if frozen in a Sierra winter stream, he clutched the reins and stared ahead without as much as an eye blink. Christina closed her eyes and dropped her chin to her chest. When they reached the St. John's River, he turned east and drove along its southern bank.

"Kern, just talk to me, please. This is bothering me. It's like you're mad at me, but I honestly don't know what I did."

His eyes squinted in the bright June daylight. The creases at the corners seemed permanently etched in his bronzed face. He did not seem to hear her.

Lord, I don't like this. What is going on? It's like he's not even here. I don't have to put up with this.

"Kern Yager, this might be the way you handle problems, but it's not working for me. Stop the rig. Let's talk this through. You're not by yourself out in a tent now. You owe me an explanation."

The continual squeak of the wagon wheels nagged at her temples. She wiped her forehead and retied her hat. When they reached some shade trees, she placed her parasol in the back of the wagon and lifted the lead lines from his fingertips. He didn't seem to notice.

She pulled back on the lines. "Whoa, boys . . . whoa!" she shouted. The horses immediately halted. Reaching across his lap, she tied the leather leads to the wooden hand brake. "Mr. Yager, we seem to have a little problem. Are you worried about losing the land? Well, so am I. We

200

will figure something out together. The Lord does not abandon His children. Are you worried about our future?"

He turned away from her, jumped to the ground, and walked away from the wagon.

"I'll take that for an affirmation," she called out as she climbed down after him.

Yager marched to a big sycamore, sat down in its shade, and faced a river that was no more than thirty feet wide and a foot deep. He pulled his knees up in front of him and rested his arms on his knees.

Christina walked straight up behind him and clutched her hands together. "Kern, I'm scared. I'm so scared I'm about to cry. I don't know what's happened to you. I don't know what I did. You just switched off like a train on a siding. I'm sorry you feel bad. I know it's crushing to think about losing the ranch, but we can work something out. If not here, someplace. . . . Maybe the Lord has something better. Maybe we were supposed to come here just to meet each other. That makes it all worthwhile, doesn't it? Isn't our relationship more important than the property? My heart is dying, Kern — talk to me. You left and didn't tell me where you were going. How can I get close to you if you hide?"

He leaned forward, his head on his arms, his eyes shut.

"Kern, don't shut me out," she hollered. "You are going to ruin everything. Yell, scream, argue, get mad at the railroad, get mad at the ditch company, get mad at me, hit me — anything . . . but don't shut me out. I can't do anything for you."

The tears streamed down her face as she paced behind him. "I can't handle this, Lord. This is ugly. This is bad. Something's drastically wrong. It's a bad day — a very, very bad day." She spun around until she was standing only a couple of feet behind his back. His head, still on his arms, remained even with her waist.

This is his bad day? This is his daddy's bad day, isn't it? He can't help it. It's just the opposite that I was so worried about. He doesn't get violent. He just becomes catatonic!

She stepped up close to his back and reached out her hands. *Lord, I don't know if I'm doing the right thing.* She took a deep breath and placed her hands on his shoulders. She left them there for a moment. Then she began to rub his neck and shoulders. *This is like massaging a cast-iron stove.* She pushed her thumbs into his shoulders and neck the best she could.

"Honey, it's okay. I understand now. I mean, I don't understand what causes this. But I know you can't help it. It's okay, honey, it's okay. I'll sit here for two hours or for two days, whatever it takes." She pulled off his wide-brimmed hat and placed it beside him. Then she pulled off her own hat. With her curly red hair lying hot against her sweaty neck, she rubbed his shoulders again, this time running her fingers through his coarse, light brown hair.

"It's all right, darling. You sit there. I'll take care of you." She pulled his head against her stomach and began to rock back and forth, cradling him in her arms. As she stared across the little river, she stroked his cheeks and then lifted her fingers to see them covered with tears.

She started to sob.

She took a deep breath, wiped her eyes on her dress sleeve, and tried to stop sniffling. "What happened, baby? It's okay. Really . . . I'm here with you, honey."

She bent over and kissed the tears on his leather-tough cheeks. "It's all right. . . . We'll just wait it out together." She kissed both cheeks several times and then his forehead, but she avoided his lips. She stood back up and rested her hands on his substantial shoulders.

Suddenly he reached back, took her hand, and pulled it close to his cheek. She began to rock his head back and forth and rub his cheeks. "Sure, honey . . . I'm here. You feelin' better?"

He let out a long sigh like a deep well that's run dry. She continued to rub his shoulders.

The unexpected deepness of his voice made her jump. "I can't do anything, and I can't get them to stop it. Never again. Not this time. This time I win. If they're going to take my land, they are going to take developed land," he announced. He lay over on his side in the dirt. "I need to sleep," he mumbled.

Then he slept.

That's it? He lays down and goes to sleep? Lord,

what has this man gone through that so affects him?
He's too young to have been in the war. Oh, Lord,
give peace to his troubled heart. Please, Lord. I've
never hurt for someone else so bad in my life.

For the next half an hour, Christina sat by his side, shooing off flies and mosquitoes. Her head was nodding, and she was just about to fall asleep when her fanning hand brushed against his nose. He grabbed her wrist and pressed her fingers to his lips. They felt dry, yet soft.

Her eyes blinked open, and she sat straight up. "Are you doing better, honey?" she asked.

For the first time in two hours he looked straight into her eyes and nodded.

She stroked his cheeks. "You had me worried."

His voice was very quiet. "I'm sorry."

"It was one of your bad days, wasn't it?"

Again he nodded. Then he looked away. "I'm ashamed to put you through it. I can usually sleep it off."

"It's okay. I know it's something you can't help."

He glanced back at her. "I don't want to be this way."

Lord, I don't think I've ever known so strong a man look so weak and helpless. "I know . . . honey . . . I know."

"Sometimes when I'm by myself, it lasts for days. I just stay in bed and don't get up."

"You aren't going to be by yourself anymore. I'll help you through," she soothed him.

"I can't ask you to put up with this, Christina. No one should have to put up with my melancholy spells."

Melancholy? Melancholy would be a party compared to this. "Kern Yager, you aren't chasin' me off this easy."

Again he looked straight into her eyes. "I love you, Christina Swan."

She cradled his head in her lap. "I know, honey. I know you do."

He closed his eyes. "I've never told any woman that before."

"Well, I've been foolish enough to say those words to other men, but I didn't feel it in my bones, like I do with you. I love you too, Kern Yager. And we're going to whip this."

"The melancholy spells?"

"And the railroad, the ditch company, the heat, and the hardpan."

"How about the skunks?" he probed, without opening his eyes.

She swung her head back until she was staring up at the sycamore leaves far above her and began to laugh. Tight, taut muscles all over her body began to relax. "Yes, Kern Yager, we will whip the skunks. They haven't a chance in the world against you and me!"

He sat up, brushed off his shirt sleeve, and then stood and offered her a hand. He plucked her off the ground like a child snatching up a favorite toy. He pulled her toward his chest, and she held her breath, then relaxed as he tenderly encircled her shoulders with arms as thick as most men's thighs.

"What are you going to do about me, Miss Swan?" he whispered in her ear.

"My first thought was to shoot you," she replied.

"Smart girl. What was your second thought?"

"I was wishing the Lord would bring a minister along right now, and I'd marry you right here on this riverbank."

"You couldn't do that," he protested.

"I most certainly could."

He continued to hold her close. "But I haven't built you that house yet."

"You're right. We are not getting married today."

"That takes care of one problem."

"That's what I am — a problem?"

"Yes, you are. You are the most delightful and beautiful problem I've ever encountered. And I have plenty of problems, as you can tell."

He stepped back away from her.

"Kern, you don't have to tell me if you don't want to, but . . ."

"I can't talk about it, Christina — not yet."

"It's okay. Really."

"Someday . . . someday before we get married, I'll try to explain."

"It's all right if I never know."

"No, I have to tell you. But not now."

She slipped her fingers into his hand. "Then tell me the day my big house is built."

They strolled along the riverbank. "Big house? You didn't tell me it had to be a big house."

"Didn't I mention the two stories, Victorian wraparound porch, and separate living quarters for the maids?"

"Maids?" He gave her a tight squeeze. "That might be nice."

She struggled to catch her breath. "Elderly . . . fat . . . maids."

"It doesn't matter. It's too late to put in your order. What I have in mind is a little bungalow with living room, kitchen, and bedroom. I can build it before September."

"There must be two bedrooms," she corrected.

"Two?"

"I'm not having a hundredfold children in our bedroom, Mr. Yager."

He began to laugh.

"Did I really say that? Did I really talk about sharing a bedroom with a man I've not even known two weeks?"

"Yes, you did. And your face is two shades darker than your beautiful auburn hair."

"That settles it. I have to marry you now," she announced.

"Why's that?"

"Once you talk about sharing a bedroom with a man, you have to marry him. It's the only honorable thing. Didn't your mama teach you that?"

He gazed across the river. "No, I didn't learn that one."

"I'm sorry, Kern. I know how it hurts to lose a parent. Believe me, I know. Can we change the subject before I say something worse?"

"I'm not going to sit by this summer waiting to see if they confiscate our lands."

"What did you decide to do?"

"We're going to plant orange trees."

"Really? I thought citrus needed a more sheltered location."

"They don't have to live through the winter — just through September."

"Seedlings won't count. They have to be two years old."

"I'll buy 100 two-year-old trees from Mr. Atwood. I'll dig them, wrap them, and transplant them. By September 1 we'll have two-year-old trees on our places."

"Isn't that deceitful?"

"I'm not going to lie. They said they wanted two-year-old trees — well, that's what we'll have." They strolled toward the wagon. "Not only that, but I'm going to build you that house."

"Even before settlement?"

"That's right. Any greedy commission can kick a man out of a tent, but it takes a real rogue to kick a family out of a house."

"A family? We're not going to have a family this summer, unless you plan on buying two-year-old kids to go along with your two-year-old trees."

"I know that. I'm pretty dumb about women,

but I do know that. We've got to get back and make some plans. We'll need more help. Do you think I should hire good old Harvey for a couple weeks?"

"If you'll keep him at your place. I can't tolerate him around me for long."

"At least Cole Travis and that other fella won't be pestering you."

"Oh! I forgot to ask," Christina said. "What happened when you turned them in? Was the sheriff pleased?"

"He was angry."

"Why?"

"He wanted them captured in someone else's jurisdiction."

"Why on earth?"

"The land agent down at Waukena was very popular. There were rumors about lynching those two even before I brought them in."

"But they won't lynch Cole. He didn't shoot the man."

"I don't think that will hold much weight. If they don't lynch them together, they'll certainly hang them together."

"But Cole isn't a killer. I do know that much about him. It was this Billy character. He's really creepy."

"It wasn't the first time Billy was arrested. Sheriff said he cut up a dance hall girl on New Year's Eve. He spent two months in the county jail."

"Did you find out his last name?" she asked.

"Billy Hays," Kern replied.

Christina's response exploded from somewhere deep in her chest. "Billy Hays!"

"What's the matter? Do you know him?"

Christina felt as if she had just done a belly flop from a high river bank. She struggled to catch her breath. "I — I . . . I never met him before last night, but — but that was my father's name."

He slipped his hand around hers and led her toward the wagon. "I thought your father was named Swan."

"Yes, it was William Hays Swan, Jr. Mama called him Billy because his father went by William."

Yager leaned on the side of the wagon. "That *is* a coincidence."

"But don't you see, Kern — the other day I dreamt about a man who looked similar to this Billy. In the dream he was my brother."

"But you don't have a brother."

"That's what makes this so strange." She could feel her hand quiver in his. "Very, very strange."

"Billy Hays is not an uncommon name. Chances are, you'll run into another man with the name sometime."

"Not one that I dreamt was my brother. Come on," she urged, "we've got to go back to Visalia right now."

"Are you going to talk to this Billy?"

"If I can muster the nerve. Then I'll send a

letter to my mother."

"They won't ship out the mail until Monday morning."

"There's a train that goes from Goshen Junction to Stockton and hacks that run to Goshen all the time. That means that with a sweet smile and a dollar, I can get some drummer to hand-deliver a letter to my mother by tomorrow afternoon. And that means she'll be here by Monday. We'll reserve a room for her in Visalia. Know a good boardinghouse?"

"Hudson's on Church Street. You're inviting your mother to come visit on Monday?" he asked.

"I didn't say I was inviting her. I'm just going to write to her. But I know Mother."

"What are you going to tell her? That you dreamt she had another child that she forgot to tell you about, and you met the guy at the ranch, and he turned out to be a thief and a murderer, and that he's in jail about to be lynched?"

She held her arms up while he set her up in the wagon. "Not exactly. I'll be much more subtle. I'll lead off with something positive."

"Like what?"

"I'm going to tell her about you! That's the reason I know she'll be here on Monday."

"Are you sure telling her about me is a positive thing?"

"Well, it could be more positive."

"How's that?"

"You could hold my hand all the way back to town."

A dozen angry men lounged around the steps of the jailhouse as Kern and Christina walked toward the double front doors.

"Hey, are you the two that brought in those outlaws?" a man asked.

"Yep," Yager replied.

"Where'd you capture them?" another man demanded.

"Near Stokes Mountain," Yager replied.

"Should have shot 'em and saved the county money."

"That's for a jury to decide," Christina asserted.

A man with a thick black beard spat a wad of tobacco juice on the steps. "A jury? There ain't a man in the county that won't hang them."

"Then may the Lord have mercy on their souls," Christina offered, as Kern Yager tugged her past the men and into the sheriff's office.

The jail was dark, shadowy, and the heat oppressive. The stench of sweat and filth seemed overpowering as two deputies led Christina back to the cells.

"Missy, you have to stand against the wall. Don't get any closer to them bars. Them men is killers. I'll be standing right down here, and I'll shoot 'em if they try anything."

"Christina?" Cole Travis came to the cell door. "Look what that bull-ox friend of yours did. My nose is broken. Where is he?"

"He's waiting with the sheriff. I needed to talk to you alone. I'm not sorry about your injury, Cole. At the time you had a gun pointed at me and were threatening to kidnap me."

"The gun was empty, and you knew it," he snarled.

"If it hadn't been, would I be alive?"

"No, I reckon you wouldn't." Cole stared down at his shoes. "I wouldn't have shot you on purpose, but I was startled. They're goin' to hang me, Christina. I didn't kill that man. I ain't a killer. You know that. I get mad, and I get drunk, but I ain't a killer. I told Billy not to hurt anyone. He wouldn't listen. And now they're goin' to hang me."

"Cole, you made disastrous choices, and now you reap what you've sown. That isn't some syrupy church platitude. That's cold, hard biblical fact."

"But I didn't pull the trigger on that land agent."

"You were part of the crime. I don't think a jury will care which of you pulled the trigger."

"I'm scared, Christina. They want to lynch us."

"I know. I saw them outside."

"How many was out there?"

"About a dozen — I don't know."

"It won't happen until after dark, and it will take fifty men."

"How do you know?" she asked.

"The deputies told us they don't intend to take a bullet just to save our hides. They said if the crowd reaches fifty, they'll just walk away. Pray for me, Christina. Pray for me."

"You once told me that you didn't need my prayers."

"Well, I need 'em now. And you once told me that you loved me."

She stared down at her hands, clutched so tightly that they turned white. "Yes, I did once."

"What happened to us?" he said.

"I believe you got bored with a schoolteacher who wouldn't run off to the hills and play outlaw's mistress."

"I should have stayed workin' for your Uncle Joey. I mean it — pray for me."

"Right now?"

"I don't got much time."

She put the palms of her hands on her cheeks. "What do you want me to ask the Lord?"

"Ask Him to close the mouths of the lions, just like He did for ol' Daniel, and deliver me from certain death." There was panic, almost terror, in Cole's high-pitched voice.

"I will not pray that, Cole Travis." Christina's voice echoed down the row of mostly empty cells. "Daniel was a righteous man persecuted for his faith. There is no comparison."

"Pray for me, Christina. Even the thief on the cross deserves a prayer."

"You're right." She bowed her head.

"Hold my hand, Christina."

She looked up and shook her head. "I can't, Cole."

"You mean you won't."

"I can't. The deputy said I have to stay over here. And I won't. I'm choosy what hands I hold. But I will pray for you." She bowed her head. "Lord, You said in Your Word that all of us are sinners. Well, Cole's sin has led him into very serious trouble. I pray that You'll keep him safe so that he will stand trial. I pray for Your justice to prevail. And I thank You, Lord, that no matter what happens, if he confesses his sins, You are faithful and just to forgive him his sins and cleanse him from all unrighteousness. In Jesus' name, amen."

"You jist prayed that I'd get a legal hangin' instead of a lynchin'. That ain't exactly what I wanted you to pray."

"You are free to pray anything you like yourself."

"I still can't believe you'd turn me in like this, Christina — you and me being close."

"You are part of a gang that robbed and killed and then threatened me with kidnapping and bodily harm. What did you expect me to do — kiss you? Of course I turned you in."

"My, oh my, Christina, you had the softest kisses of any gal I ever kissed."

"That's quite a few, I imagine?"

"Hundreds probably," he said.

"I need to talk to Billy now."

"He's the one you'd better watch. If he breaks

215

out of here, he'll come cut your throat from ear to ear. I swear he will. Watch out for him."

"I'm going to talk to him."

"Christina, you have to help me!"

She looked at the pitiful, pleading man. "Cole, tell your attorney that at the trial I will testify of your integrity when you were young. That's all I can say."

"How did I get in this fix, Christina?"

"Just like everyone, Cole — one unrepented sin at a time."

There were two empty jail cells between Cole Travis and Billy Hays. The deputy who walked her down again warned her to stay back. "Lady, I don't know why you want to talk to this one. It's like trying to befriend a rabid dog."

"God did not create this man a rabid dog, Deputy. I need to talk to him." She waited for the deputy to mosey down to the other end of the hall. "Billy, I'd like to talk to you."

The dirty-faced man with a black-and-blue jaw sprawled on his back on the wooden bunk without a mattress, eyes closed.

"Billy?"

"I'll kill you both. That's all there is to say about it," he mumbled. "Your boyfriend busted my jaw."

"I'm sorry that you are in pain, but you held a gun on me and threatened my safety. I'm grateful to be delivered from that."

"I ain't got nothin' to say to you."

"I want to talk to you."

"I don't need any sermon. God ain't never done nothin' for me, and I surely don't need Him now."

"Did your mother love you, Billy?"

"My mother died when I was twelve."

"Did she love you?"

"Yeah, she loved me. I was her only kid."

"I was my mother's only child also. So God did do something for you. He gave you a loving mother."

"And a daddy that ran off with another woman before I was ever born."

"Where was this?" Christina quizzed.

"In the Carson Range. Why do you keep pestering me with personal questions?"

"Is that by Virginia City?"

"No, it's by Carson City. Ain't you never been to Nevada?"

Christina fought back the urge to run outside and get a fresh breath of air. "When I was too small to remember. My mother did not like Nevada."

"Why did you come talk to me?"

"I was startled to find out your name is Billy Hays."

"Why? What's wrong with that name?"

"It's a good name. In fact, my father was named William Hays Swan, Jr., but my mother always called him Billy. He lived in Virginia City for a short time trying to establish a store there. I thought perhaps your father and mother were friends of my father's and named you after him."

"I was named after my own daddy. He was Billy Hays. But like I said, he ran off with some Sacramento dance hall girl."

Christina's hands started to quiver.

"It ain't a purdy story." He turned his head toward her and opened his eyes. "What's the matter with you?"

"What else did your mother tell you about your father?"

"Nothin'. How about your father? Is he still alive?"

"He died when I was a year old," Christina explained. "He was shot by outlaws while he defended my mother and me."

"Mine ran away, and yours died savin' you. Neither of us had daddies, did we? But at least you could grow up proud. That's more than I can say. I don't want to talk anymore."

"Billy, what was your mother's name?"

"I ain't talkin' to you."

"Billy, I'd really like to know."

"Any minute they're liable to bust in here and lynch me. I don't need this, lady."

"You may call me Christina."

He sat up, slamming his feet on the concrete floor. Contempt and hatred rushed out of his eyes and his mouth. "I ain't got to call you nothin'! I'll kill you if I get the chance! I swear to Hades, I'll kill ya."

Christina was surprised at the peace that swept across her chest and calmed her voice. "Billy, please . . . what was your mama's

218

name? It's important."

He glared at her until the deputy came to lead her away. She had walked about ten steps when she heard a quiet voice say, "Her name was Carmela, but I always called her Mama."

Seven

The sound was not gunfire. There was no abrasive impact in the air, no sudden jarring of the eardrum. Christina lay on her back and stared at the bat-free peak of the barn roof. For the first time in over a week, the straw felt rough and uncomfortable under the wool blanket.

Boom.

Distant. Deep. Like a muffled cannon.

This time the explosion brought her to her feet. She searched for her stockings and her shoes. *Lord, I'm getting a little tired of sleeping in my clothes every night, but what else can I do? I'm not going to parade around in an open-air barn in a nightgown.*

With shoes laced and tied, Christina tried to comb her hair. Her hand mirror hung upside down from a nail on a twelve-by-twelve-inch beam jutting out of the center of the loft.

You are a lovely thing, Christina. You look like that time you went bear hunting with Uncle Joey for a week and came back so dirty your mother made you bathe in the front yard. I'll bet Harvey was peeking out his window that day.

Boom.

Distant. But not that distant.

Lord, You gave me this place, and now I'm going to fight for it. The children of Israel had their prom-

ised land, but Joshua led them in battle. Well, my Joshua might not lead, but he will fight. And Kern? He's worth any two men. And now we have Harvey — he's worth . . . well, between him and Kern we have two men.

She left the top two buttons of her brown dress unfastened, but pinned a small butterfly brooch at the third button at the base of her neck. With small, round abalone shell earrings in place, she brushed down her dress and started to descend the ladder.

Boom.

It seemed to roll across the base of Stokes Mountain from the southeast.

The bright June sun was perched a thumb's width above the Sierras when she stepped out into the yard. There were no clouds in the pale blue sky. A tiny breeze drifted from the south straight up the slope of the mountain. It felt morning cool, but temporary.

Joshua Slashpipe was busy at the makeshift table stuffing and rolling tortillas.

"What's going on? It sounds like an attack on Fort Sumter."

"*¿Dónde?*" he smiled, his mouth full of straight white teeth.

She peered over his shoulder at the big, flat tortillas. "Is Kern Yager making that noise?"

Joshua dipped another spoonful of fried ground pork out of the black cast-iron frying pan. "Ah, yes, La Dueña, he is a very determined man."

She meandered to the coffeepot and filled her cup. "What is he doing?"

"Digging holes to plant orange trees."

"No, I meant the explosions. What is that?"

"Like I said, he's digging holes." Slashpipe licked his thin, brown fingers and wiped them on his ducking trousers. "He uses one-half stick of dynamite per hole. He and Harvey have been at it since sunrise."

"I've never heard of ground so hard you must blast a hole in it to let the water drain."

"Mr. Yager is a very determined man. To stand in his way is to throw yourself in front of a train, no?"

Even to snuggle up to him is to throw yourself in front of a train! A slow-moving, tender-hearted, powerful train. She walked back to the table sipping her coffee. "What are we having for breakfast?"

He shoved one of the stuffed tortillas at her. "*Huevos de* Slashpipe."

She inspected the filling. "What's in here?"

"Eggs, sausage, green peppers, cheese, and —"

"No garlic, please. You did not put garlic in them, did you?"

"It breaks my heart, but, no, I did not put in garlic, La Dueña. Just my famous hot sauce and a little chocolate."

"Chocolate? You put chocolate in a tortilla?"

"I couldn't resist. It's an old Scottish recipe," he grinned. "You try it. It's very tasty. In the old

222

days everyone in California cooked with chocolate."

With white, slender fingers extended, she counted the tortillas. "It looks like you made enough for a whole bunkhouse full of *vaqueros*."

"Two bunkhouses. Both the Proud Quail Ranch and the Yager Farms. I told Señor Yager I would cook for them, too."

"Yes, but that is only four people, total."

"And the dog, Buscadero. He eats like a wolf. It's shameful." He began stuffing the tortillas in an empty flour sack. "Perhaps you can take the food to them. I want to stay up here and finish the fencing. We want to keep the cows high on the mountain so we can plant orange trees down below."

She gazed down toward the distant road. "Opposing the land commission, the railroad, and the ditch company sounds crazy, doesn't it?"

"I haven't walked away from many fights," Joshua grinned. "I don't think I will walk away from this one either. I like this place. I won't let some Yerba Buena attorney steal it away."

"Yerba Buena? It's been called San Francisco since '47."

Slashpipe's customary smile faded. "Not by me it hasn't."

Wearing her flop hat and work gloves, Christina trudged through the short brown grass on the sloping hillside to reach the gate near Kern

Yager's plowed field. She watched Kern and Harvey work across the front of Kern's farm, parallel to the Antelope Valley road.

Harvey dug the eight to twelve inches of top-soil off the proposed site of a planting. Kern then took an iron bar and with the strength of his back drilled a hole in the petrified dirt. Next he set the primer and the fuse and crammed the half stick of dynamite in the hole. Then they covered the one-foot-diameter hole with an old piece of heavy, flowered carpet and lit the fuse. He and Harvey jumped back.

Boom.

Dust flew.

Busca barked.

Kern pulled off the carpet, and both men toted huge slabs of rock and dirt to the farm wagon. Then they hiked twenty-two feet west and began the process all over again.

As Christina strolled past Kern's shed and tent, she noticed his flap untied. She tried to peek in as she hiked by but saw only a white shirt hanging on a wooden hanger. Busca met her with a single bark and led her down to the men.

"Are you ready for Joshua's pork sausage and egg tortillas?" she called out as she carried the sack to Kern's wagon.

Harvey looked up. "Now there's a sight for sore eyes."

"Me or the food?" she retorted.

"Why, you, Christina. You're a true vision of feminine loveliness," Harvey insisted.

"Well, don't look too close." She brushed bangs out of her eyes with the back of her hand. "Because this vision could use a hot bath."

Kern's shirt sleeves were rolled up to his elbows. His arms were thick with hair, but it was such a light brown color, it was hardly visible.

"Come on, Harvey James Jackson," she said, "it's time to eat."

"I'm surely glad to see you, Christina darlin'," Harvey blurted out. "This Kern Yager is one of the hardest-workin' men I ever met in my life. And I know for a fact he's the strongest."

She set the flour sack down at the back of the wagon as the men gathered around. Kern slipped his hand around hers. She pushed herself up on her toes to kiss his cheek. He kissed her forehead.

"You goin' to kiss me, too?" Harvey begged.

Kern turned to him and shrugged. "Nope. I don't believe I will."

"I wasn't talkin' to you!" Harvey complained.

Christina ignored the smaller man. "You two have been busy."

Kern pulled the cork out of the canteen with his teeth. "Did we wake you up?"

She curled her nose. "Actually, yes, you did, but it was time to get up anyway."

The wagon was heaped with jagged slabs of yellow, orange, and mostly brown rock. Kern pulled down one of the smaller, flatter ones and tossed it in the dirt by his feet. Then he put the first stuffed tortilla on it for an appreciative

Busca. The second one he offered to Christina.

"Busca likes stuffed tortilla?"

"Yep. But Chinese food is his favorite." Yager plucked up a tortilla for himself. "These don't have garlic, do they?"

She nibbled at the edge of a rather chewy tortilla. "Joshua assured me that these are plain, except for the chocolate."

"I knew an ol' Californio that poured chocolate gravy over fried chicken and mashed potatoes," Harvey reported between massive bites.

"Chocolate is all right," Kern reported, "but Busca doesn't like garlic."

"I wish I had me some garlic," Harvey added. Slashpipe's hot sauce dribbled down his wispy, unshaven chin.

"You like garlic?" Kern asked him.

"Shoot, no. But I bet I could get rid of them skunks if I had some garlic."

Christina wiped her mouth with her small linen handkerchief. "How do you talk the skunks into eating the garlic?"

"Sweet potatoes. Yep, I read about it in the back of *Frank Leslie's Illustrated*. There was an article about gettin' rid of noxious animals. I reckon a passel of skunks is noxious, don't you?"

"I believe you're right about that," Kern said.

"Well, the article said if you take boiled sweet potatoes, mash them up with some cod liver oil until it's kind of like a paste, you could smear it on tree trunks, and it would keep noxious animals away."

"Now that's a handy thing to know," Kern laughed.

Christina rolled her green eyes. "It sounds horrid."

"Well, I was thinkin', what if you did that but added mashed whole garlic and some of Joshua's hot sauce. Don't you think that would dissuade the skunks from hangin' around the ranch?"

"If you could get them to eat it, it would more than dissuade," Kern laughed.

"Maybe I'll jist give it a try. If it works, they'll put me in *Frank Leslie's Illustrated* alongside one of them stories about ol' Stuart Brannon," Harvey said.

"My father's a lawman down in New Mexico," Kern told him. "He knows the real Stuart Brannon."

"He does? Well, I'll be. He's been my hero ever' since I was a pup. I've tried to live my life just like him," Harvey proclaimed.

Kern exchanged glances with Christina.

"Who do you pattern your life after, Kern Yager?" she asked.

"I was hopin' to design a new pattern. But there's a lot of Daddy's influence in me."

"In what way?"

"In working hard. That I learned from my father. So thanks to him, we better get back on the job. Is Joshua coming down to help us?"

"He's got to finish that fence to keep the cows and calves from drifting down on the farm ground. What can I do to help you?" She took the canteen, pulled the cork stopper out with her teeth, and took a big swig.

"This isn't woman's work, Christina," Harvey objected.

Kern laughed and slapped Jackson on the back. Harvey swallowed half of his stuffed tortilla whole and staggered across the field gasping for breath. "Here's some advice for getting along with women. I don't know much, but I've learned never to call one 'woman' and never, ever to tell them what they can and cannot do."

Harvey tottered around the wagon, nodding his head and waving, his face beet-red.

"Are you all right, Harvey?" Christina asked.

"Hah . . . hah . . . hah," he gasped. "That man doesn't know how strong he is."

"Yes, but he can be quite tender when he wants to."

"Christina!" Kern's voice had a high lilt on the last syllable that was meant to end discussion.

She grinned and wrinkled her small, round nose. "But he blushes easily."

"I jist want to know one thing," Harvey demanded as he came back over to the wagon and grabbed up the canteen. "Do you love him?"

"Harvey, that's getting personal," she protested.

Harvey's brown hair curled out from under his hat; his small, round eyes narrowed. "Well, do you, or do you not?"

She looked straight at Harvey. "Yes, I do."

Harvey looped his thumbs in his suspenders

and rocked back on his heels. "How about you, Kern? Do you love her?"

"Yep, I really do love her."

"Okay . . ." Harvey stared off toward the skunk cabin to the west of them. "If that's the way it's got to be, then you two have my blessing."

"Really?" Christina put her hand on Harvey's dirty white shirt sleeve.

"Yep. I like him, Christina."

"Well, so do I."

"I mean, he works hard, he's a college man, he's stronger than a donkey engine, he's got good teeth, he loves you, and he's a man of faith. We spent two hours last night jist talkin' about the Lord. He's a good man, Christina. Now he isn't as handsome as me, mind ya, but you just can't have everything."

"I'm glad you see it that way, Harvey." She hugged his shoulders. "I'm amazed."

"Well, I just couldn't let you up and chase around with the likes of Cole Travis. He's a horse thief and murderer. I always figured you'd be better off with me than with him. But now that Kern's come along, I've sort of got you taken care of, and I can go off and find someone who appreciates my unique charms."

Kern shoved his wide-brimmed hat to the back of his head. "Christina, I like Harvey. He shows a lot of wisdom."

"I'm speechless."

"Me and Christina, growin' up next door, we

was just too much like brother and sister to get too close." He put his arm around her shoulder. "You know what I mean? I remember a time she came home from a bear-huntin' trip with the uncle and had to —"

Christina pulled away. "Harvey! Don't you say another word!" she thundered.

Harvey's grin showed sausage stuck between his upper front teeth. "See what I mean? We fight just like a brother and sister. Besides, Kern has a woman that he wants me to meet. Says she's mighty lonely and will be happy to visit and all that."

"Oh?" She watched Kern toss Busca another stuffed tortilla.

"What did you say her name was?" Harvey pressed.

Kern kept focused on the black-and-white dog. "Lucy Atwood."

"Harvey and Lucy?" Christina gasped. "Never in my life have I known two more dissimilar people. Don't you think there might be a slight, er, cultural gap between them?"

"He already told me about that," Harvey blurted out. "And I promised him I would be kind and not lord it over her just 'cause I come from the city and she's a country girl."

"It will certainly be interesting to see what happens." Christina resacked the leftover tortillas. "And just when do you think we will be going to visit the Atwoods?"

Kern stood up and tried to brush some of the

dirt off his ducking trousers. "Thursday, depending on how many holes we get blasted by then. There's no reason for you to go, especially if your mother comes down."

"You are not going to the Atwood ranch without me, Kern Yager. Not this week, not any week — ever."

"Yes, ma'am."

"Now . . . what can I do to help? You want me to dig holes or carry rock?"

"You drive the team along and help Harvey load the wagon," Kern instructed. "But aren't you going to go to town and see if your mother shows up?"

"Not until this afternoon. She won't be coming down before then. I thought I'd clean up after lunch and have Joshua drive me to town." Christina climbed up in the driver's seat of the wagon and untied the lead lines. "Are you two ready to get back to work? We can't loaf around all morning."

"She's a tough boss," Harvey grinned.

It was not nearly as unpleasant a grin as Christina remembered. She stared at the hardpan in the back of the wagon. "What are we going to do with this rock?"

"How about dumping it along the property line between our places?" Kern suggested. "We'll stack it up to be a little holding corral right next to the road."

"Won't that be somethin'?" Harvey said. "We'll build a stone corral."

The sun was almost straight above, but a thin, high layer of clouds had floated into the valley, diffusing the bright light and making an already hot day sultry. Christina wiped her forehead on the sleeve of her wet flannel shirt. Her petticoats were soaked and sagged under her skirt, which was now the same color as the hardpan in the wagon. Her face was dusted red from the fine powder of exploding dirt that hung in the air after every blast. When she climbed off the wagon and walked over to the men, her shoes squeaked from the sweat in her boots.

Her only consolation was that Kern and Harvey looked exactly the same.

"I think it's time for lunch and a siesta," Kern offered. "This iron bar is getting too hot to hold." He tossed it and the shovel into the wagon. "Let's empty this load and wait for it to cool down."

"Now those are about the purdiest words I ever heard," Harvey agreed as he struggled to carry a heavy slab of rock to the wagon. "I doubt if I will be able to straighten my back up before Christmas."

"You want me to pop your back for you?" Kern offered.

"Pop my back? You'd break me in two like a matchstick. I'd rather be humpbacked than to wake up dead."

Kern plucked up Christina and plopped her in the wagon seat and crawled up beside her.

Harvey and Busca sat on top of the rock pile in back.

"Looks like a drummer's wagon coming to visit." Kern pointed at the front gate to the Proud Quail Ranch a mile away.

"Can you read what it says on the side?" she asked.

"Nope."

"Doesn't matter. I wouldn't mind picking up a few things, but I'm not about to have anyone see me like this."

"I think you look fine," he murmured.

"Yes, dirt is a rather nice color on me, especially red dirt." She tried to sit straight, but her back was too stiff and sore. "Do you realize, Mr. Kern Yager, that you've never seen me clean?"

He reached over to slap her knee, but seeing her grit her teeth in anticipation, he pulled his hand back. "Do you look different when you're clean?"

"She looks real good all scrubbed up," a voice called out from the back of the wagon.

Christina didn't turn around. "Thank you, Harvey."

A naive, cheerful "You're welcome" came floating back.

Kern pointed to the wagon rolling along the western edge of the property. "He must be a persistent salesman to drive way back up there."

"Mother sent me a return letter!" Christina pushed her uncle's floppy hat to the back of her head and shaded her eyes with her hand. "That's it. She got my note yesterday, like I said, and sent me a letter in return."

"Don't you two ever use the U.S. Mail?" Kern chided.

"Not until they have home rural delivery. Who wants to drive two hours to town to pick up mail when we can have it fetched right to our barn by a nice man who is thrilled to do us a favor." She tilted her head and batted her dusty eyelashes.

He brushed a dirty hand across his lips. "Is flirting a family characteristic?"

She elbowed him and felt as if she had hit her arm on a door post. "Mr. Yager, there is no way a woman wearing filthy clothes bathed in sweat and covered with dirt can be called a flirt."

He elbowed her back, and she quickly leaned forward to evade it. "You dodged my question."

Christina started to lick her lips but stopped when she lapped up a tongueful of dirt. "Coquettishness seems to be a trait of all the women in my family. Grandma Alena is the very best at it."

"Christina's grandma is real handsome!" the voice from the rocks proclaimed.

"Harvey!" Christina scolded.

"Well, for an old lady, that is."

Kern began to laugh.

"What's so funny?" Christina demanded.

"I've never been around a gal like you before. If I don't watch myself, I'll end up in a whole family of 'em."

"You know, Kern," Harvey called out, "if

you're havin' second thoughts, I'll always be around to take your place if you need me."

"Thank you, Harvey. I'll keep that in mind," Kern called back.

"You do, Kern Yager, and I'll shoot you myself," Christina mumbled without moving her lips.

Kern stopped the wagon at the barbed-wire fence between his place and hers. All three climbed in back and tossed out pieces of rock onto a pile already stacked in a twenty-foot circle about four feet high.

Many of the rocks that Harvey and Christina had to struggle to get into the wagon, Kern slung out with the flip of one hand. "Looks like the drummer's leavin'. Either Joshua sent him on his way, or you got your letter from Mama."

They had just emptied the wagon when someone shouted from halfway down the hill. A man galloped toward them on a gray horse, waving his hand and yelling. His black sombrero flew behind his head, attached to his neck by a stampede string.

"Joshua!" Christina exclaimed. "He must be in a terrible hurry. He's ridin' General Lee bareback." Christina hunted for a clean corner of her handkerchief and wiped some of the dirt out of her eyes.

Kern pulled off his hat. A carefully etched dirt line crossed his forehead. He slapped his hat on his trousers, creating a fine red fog. "He's an old *vaquero*. He's got to let the wolf howl once in a while."

"Look," Harvey shouted. "He's going to try to jump the fence!"

Christina's mouth dropped open as white-haired man and big gray horse flew up in the air and over the top wire of the fence.

"I didn't know that old man could jump like that!" Harvey exclaimed.

"I didn't know General Lee could jump like that," Kern added.

As he galloped toward the wagon, Slashpipe shouted, *"Parar en todo! Parar en todo!"*

"Looks like he has some surprising news. Maybe the settlement has been changed," Kern suggested.

Joshua yanked the horse's mane, and General Lee skidded to a stop in the soft dirt. He leaped over the horse's head and landed on his feet, running toward the wagon.

"Can you do that, Kern?" Harvey gasped. "I can't, and I'm forty years younger than him."

Christina noticed that Joshua wore his teeth.

"Heaven has smiled and blessed an old man today. It is the most glorious day of my miserable life!" he shouted.

"What is it, Joshua?" Kern asked.

"She's here! She's here at this very ranch. She has come to visit me! It's like springtime in my heart. It's better than spring!"

Christina glanced at Kern, then back at the man wearing the sombrero. "Your wife? Your daughter? Your girlfriend?" she asked.

"No . . . no, La Dueña, it's better than all that. It is Doña Alena Louisa — *La Paloma Roja de Monterey!* She is right here on the Proud Quail Ranch. She has come to see me!"

"Grandma?" Christina gasped. "Grandma Alena is at the ranch?"

"She's the one I told you about," Harvey piped up. "Has red hair just like Christina. Not one speck of gray. It's amazin'."

It's called hair dye, Harvey, but I'm not going to burst your bubble. With Kern's help, Christina climbed down out of the wagon. "Is she by herself?"

"Your mother is here, too. She is quite handsome also — for a woman with brown hair."

"Mother and Grandmother are here at the ranch?"

"Yes! It's so exciting! They might stay several days."

"I'm sure they will want to stay at the boardinghouse in Visalia," Christina said.

Slashpipe rubbed his chin. "I need to shave. You did not remind me to shave, La Dueña."

"I never remind you to shave."

"You see, you are as forgetful as me. I will put on my good shirt, and . . . Oh, it's like a visit from an angel from heaven. *La Paloma Roja de Monterey* at my humble *casa*."

"House? There is no house. You sleep under the wagon," Christina reminded him.

Joshua Slashpipe ignored her reply. "Kern, do you play the fiddle?"

Kern leaped off the wagon, and Christina could feel the ground shake when he landed. "Nope."

"I can play the guitar — if I had one. We must find a guitar and a fiddle player," Joshua insisted.

"Why?" Harvey asked, as he jumped off the wagon and stumbled to his knees.

"For a fandango, of course. We will have a fandango. Your grandmother still dances in the dreams of *vaqueros* all over the state of California."

"Only in the dreams of old *vaqueros*," Christina reminded him.

"Yes," he grinned, "very old *vaqueros!*"

"You got yourself a pair of nice teeth there, Joshua," Harvey remarked.

"Yes, I believe I will wear them for a few days."

"Is it just me, or does this old *hombre* look about twenty years younger?" Kern grinned.

Slashpipe held up his finger. "Never underestimate the power of a beautiful woman's smile."

"I can't believe they showed up with me looking like this," Christina moaned. "I thought I would at least have until this afternoon. Well, I suppose we all should go meet them."

"Oh, no," Kern objected. "They love you, no matter what you look like. But they will inspect me like a cattle judge at the county fair. I'm going to clean up first."

"I think I'll wash up, too," Harvey added.

"Christina's mama and my mama are neighbors. She might take back a slovenly report."

"Then come on, La Dueña." Joshua grabbed her arm. "We will both ride General Lee back to the barn."

Her long skirt prevented her from straddling the horse. Christina let her legs flop over the left side. She clutched Slashpipe's bony midsection, which was no larger than her own.

No saddle, no bridal, no stirrups. How does this man stay on this horse? How do I stay on?

"Hang on, La Dueña," Joshua called out and kicked the big horse to a gallop.

"You are not going to jump this horse," she hollered. "He can't make it over with both of us . . . I mean it . . . Joshua, stop this horse immediately!"

The word *immediately* was screamed in terror while Christina's only connection with the mount was her hands clutching Joshua's Slashpipe's stomach. It felt as if her entire body was flagged out behind the horse. When she glanced down, she could see the top barbed wire of the fence.

General Lee staggered down to his front knees when he crashed into the hillside, but quickly jumped up and continued to gallop up the hill. Joshua rode with stiff, straight back. Whenever she felt herself start to slip off the horse, a quick jab of his elbow corrected her position. She bounced and bobbled all the way up the hill.

Her fingers locked together around his midsection were beginning to lose their grip as they approached the water tank. She spotted her mother wringing out a small white towel. Joshua turned the horse quickly to the right without warning. Christina flew off the horse about twenty feet below the women. She had to hit the ground running in order to keep from falling on her face. She finally was able to stop her forward momentum about three feet in front of the stock tank.

"My, that was quite a ride!" Grandma Alena greeted her. The shoulder-length auburn hair was pulled smoothly behind her ears. Dangling silver earrings caught the light of the diffused sun. Christina could not see a speck of dust on her deep blue satin dress with black lace trim.

"You taught her to ride that way, Mother," Martina reminded her. Martina's blue-and-white-striped cotton dress was designed with white lace yoke that accented her very narrow waist. Her long brown hair flowed straight down her back to her waist. Dual soft blue ribbons encircled her head. She, too, seemed immune to dirt. "Here, dear." She handed Christina the damp towel. "You seem to have a smudge on your face."

I just about died riding up this hill. I'm covered from foot to toe with sweat and dirt, and you think I have a smudge on my face? "Mother! I — I wasn't expecting you . . . so soon!"

"It was your intriguing letter. Grandmother came down to keep me company because Loop needed to go to Carson City this week." Martina's smile was poised, under complete control. "So we both thought how delightful it would be to visit our girl out on her ranch."

"Nonsense," Grandma Alena interjected. Her smile was spontaneous, like a toddler who had just discovered a kitten in her closet. "We came to spy out the man of your dreams. Where is he?" She stared off down the hill.

"Mother! There were other reasons why we came," Martina insisted.

"Yes . . . yes . . . of course there were." Alena waved off the comment and stared east. "Is that his place over there? I can't see the buildings from here. Is he coming up to meet us?"

"Yes, he and Harvey Jackson will be up shortly. Mother, did you tell Harvey where the ranch is? He just showed up yesterday."

"I might have mentioned something. When I stop by his mother's for tea, I can't refuse to talk to him."

"Well, Kern and Harvey wanted to clean up before joining us," Christina stated.

"That might not be a bad idea for you," her mother lectured.

"I know I look frightful."

"Let's just say that any man who will marry you after seeing you look like this is a real gem," her mother replied.

"Joshua," Grandma Alena called out to the corrals where Slashpipe tended to General Lee. "Would you please warm up some water for

Christina so she can clean up?"

"Of course, Doña Alena."

Alena scooted close to her granddaughter. "Where did you find a *vaquero* of the old school? Do you know that this man knew me and your great-grandfather back in the old days of Monterey?"

"So he told me. He also said having a visit from *La Paloma Roja de Monterey* was like having an angel visit from heaven. Uncle Joey hired his son, but the son left before I got here, and Joshua inherited the job," Christina explained.

Alena stared down the slope toward the Antelope Valley road. "Ladies, those were the days. Every woman in California was a queen, and every man a chivalrous knight."

"No more Californio stories, Mother. We have a young woman to get scrubbed up before a certain gentleman comes calling," Martina insisted.

"I really can't do much, Mother. I don't even have a clean dress."

"We brought several things in the trunk. I'm sure one of them will fit you."

Christina hung her hat on the corral post and wiped her face with the wet towel. "You brought the trunk?"

Her mother took the towel and scrubbed behind Christina's ears. "Yes, we intend to stay for a couple of weeks."

"Here?" Christina raised up, the wet towel wrapped around her neck. "I reserved a room in a boardinghouse in Visalia."

"Nonsense. Why would we want to stay in Visalia?" Grandma Alena objected.

"Your grandmother's right," Martina insisted. "I stayed in Visalia once when Loop bought those two new saddles. I don't imagine it has changed much. We will stay here."

"But — but I'm sleeping in the barn loft! We haven't built our house yet."

"*Our* house?" Martina's mouth dropped open, and her sweeping brown eyebrows raised. "My goodness, dearest, have you married the man already?"

"I meant our *houses,* Mother. Of course we're not married. Kern and I both need to build houses right away to try to keep the railroad from taking our lieu land," Christina explained.

"We'll have time to discuss all of that later," her mother insisted. "Right now we simply must get you cleaned up and presentable."

"Presentable to whom? Everyone here has already seen me dirty. I'm dirty every day."

"Then we will present you clean. That will be different," Martina announced.

"Joshua," Alena called out as she brushed her auburn bangs that parted in the middle. "Rest up the horses and feed the gray one a little grain. We will need you to hitch them up and drive us to town after lunch."

"*Sí,* Doña Alena, I will have the team ready." He squatted on his haunches next to the fire. A huge pot of water hung from an iron hook.

Alena clutched her ring-encircled fingers in front of her still narrow waist. "Please, Joshua, you do not have to call me Doña."

He pulled off his sombrero and held it in front of him. "I know, Señora Merced, I know . . . but if it does not offend you, it reminds me of when I was young, and my bones were not tired."

"Yes, it reminds me as well, Joshua. They will never understand our California, will they? To be honored by a *vaquero* of the old school is the highest honor any lady can receive. Thank you for your politeness."

"You are welcome, Doña Alena Louisa."

She stepped closer to the fire where Joshua stood, hat in hand. "Did I see that Mr. Yager has a wagon?"

"Yes, he does." Joshua nodded his white head.

"Would you please inform him that we will need to take that wagon to town as well," she announced.

"Grandma Alena," Christina protested, "you can't just appropriate a man's wagon."

Alena Merced turned around. The age creases near her still-fiery green eyes were hardly discernible as the three generations of California women gathered by the springs halfway up the side of Stokes Mountain. "I already appropriated it, dear."

"Where do you want the hot water?" Joshua called out.

"In the barn. Christina will be bathing, so I will expect you to stay far away from it. If you approach the barn, I will, by honor, be forced to shoot you," Grandma Alena informed him with her widest smile.

"Yes, of course. That is to be expected. I will remain by the oven and keep all gentlemen far from the barn, sacrificing my life, if need be."

"Yes, of course." Alena nodded. "That is to be expected."

Mother and grandmother marched Christina into the barn. They didn't climb the loft but waited just inside the doorless structure until Joshua packed in a steaming kettle of boiling water and two buckets of cold water. When he was gone, Martina turned to her daughter. "Now, dear, remove all your clothes."

"What?" Christina ran her ringless fingers through her dirty, greasy hair. "You want me to . . ."

Martina turned to Alena. "She's still a modest thing, isn't she?"

Grandma Alena raised her thick, arching eyebrows. "You taught her that, dear."

Martina turned back to her daughter. "I will not meet a prospective son-in-law with my only child caked with dirt. Either you remove the clothing, or your grandmother and I will."

Christina's panicked eyes searched for sympathy. "Mother, I am twenty-four years old!"

"What a luxury. You have two gracious bath attendants. Even the expensive health spas don't offer that service," Grandma Alena announced. "You may disrobe now, Miss Swan."

By the time Christina joined the others for lunch around the makeshift table, Kern Yager and Harvey Jackson, both wearing fresh white shirts buttoned at the neck and sporting clean faces, had already joined them.

The men stood as Christina approached. The only similarity to her previous attire was the pair of dusty black lace-up boots. The peach-colored dress she had borrowed from her grandmother had puffy shoulders and lace overlaid on the arms and yoke. Her hair, still damp, was combed back over her ears. Genuine emerald earrings pierced her lobes. A small white enamel poppy was pinned to the third button of her collar, which was the first one fastened. She felt clean for the first time in two weeks.

Christina watched Kern's expression.

He scratched the back of his neatly combed hair. "You were right, Harvey. She does scrub up real purdy."

Harvey kept staring at the food spread out on the table. "Yep. Some of them ain't bad when they're cleaned up."

Martina Swan patted the empty stool next to her. "Darling, we've had a delightful visit with Mr. Yager about his plan to hurry and transplant the citrus trees. It reminds me of that fall when I worked so hard to save the store."

Christina sat down next to her mother. Kern sat on the other side of the table, and she caught his nodding approval. When she turned back, she saw a tear slide out of the corner of her mother's eye. "Of course, I lost the store to fire and your father to a barrage of bullets. So I don't want to make that particular comparison with your present situation."

Christina slid a hand under the table to clutch her mother's. She noticed that Grandma Alena held her mother's other hand.

"Joshua, did you know we are going to stay here and help save this ranch?" Alena announced.

"God has surely blessed me today."

"Why, Joshua," Christina challenged, "I thought you didn't need any help from the Lord."

"I changed my mind. How can I deny such an obvious miracle?"

"And have you made up your mind about Jesus?" Alena questioned.

"Grandmother!" Christina protested.

"Darling, Joshua and I are much too old to worry about niceties. We are getting close to the finish line, aren't we, Señor Slashpipe?"

A wide, tooth-filled grin broke across his face. "You are correct, Doña Alena. There are days when the finish line seems very close."

"You avoided my question about Jesus," she pointed out.

"Am I going to have three women nag me into the kingdom?"

"You will have as many as it takes." Alena nodded graciously. "But it's Martina that you will have to worry about most. If she corners you, you will end up giving all your earthly possessions to the poor and volunteering for missionary service in Africa."

"That's not true," Martina protested. Then she turned to Kern Yager. "Of course, dear Kern, we will have to hear your testimony of coming to Christ."

Christina dropped her mother's hand and covered her mouth. *Mother, what are you doing? This is not an inquisition.*

Kern Yager blushed and mumbled, "Now?"

"Of course not," Grandma Alena replied. "Please go ahead. Swallow that bite first."

He swallowed.

And talked.

And swallowed some more.

They finished the meal of salt pork, stewed apples, black beans, and cinnamon-and-sugar-fried tortillas. Finally Busca left to take a nap in the shade of the water tank, and Harvey Jackson pushed himself back from the table.

"Here's the plan for this afternoon," Christina's mother began.

Christina surveyed the eyes of the three men who sat across from her, especially the steel-gray eyes of Kern Yager. *What do you mean, the plan? Mother, this is my ranch to run. I make the decisions.*

"We are all going to town," Martina announced.

"Did you and Grandma decide to stay in

Visalia after all?" Christina queried.

"Heavens no. We need to buy a few things and visit a person or two. Joshua will drive your wagon and take Grandma Alena and Harvey with him."

Alena pulled a piece of folded white paper from the sleeve of her sapphire-blue satin and black lace dress. "I have a list of supplies," she announced.

"I know every store in Visalia!" Joshua beamed.

"I must have my morning cup of chocolate." She winked at the old man. "Is there a shop with good chocolate?"

"Doña Alena, it is a sad generation that does not greet the California sunrise with a cup of chocolate in their hands."

"I simply couldn't agree more," Alena added.

Martina held up her hands to get everyone's attention. Christina admired her mother's long white fingers. "Kern will drive Christina and me to town in the other rig. Honey, is there a decent dry goods store in town?"

"Mother, I haven't really been shopping since I got here."

"That's obvious, dear. I'm sure I can find some store that meets our standards."

Soon they were rolling south in a two-wagon caravan, a beaming Joshua Slashpipe driving the lead wagon. Perched between him and Harvey Jackson was Doña Alena Louisa Tipton Merced,

La Paloma Roja de Monterey.

In the second wagon Christina was squeezed between her mother and Kern Yager. It wasn't until a break in the conversation just beyond Cottonwood Creek that she dared to venture, "Mother, you did read the other part of my letter?"

"About the young man named Billy?"

"Yes."

"I read it. I'm sorry you are troubled. I'm sure there are other Billy Hayses in the world. I once met a dentist in Oakland named William H. Swan, Jr. It was startling the first time I saw it on the door."

Christina fidgeted with her fingers in the lap of her peach-colored dress. "What troubles me most was the dream," she admitted.

Martina patted her daughter's hands. "I can assure you, my dear, you are my only child. That is something a mother doesn't forget even when middle aged."

"Middle aged?" Kern broke in. "Your mother looks thirty and your grandmother no more than forty."

"Oh! What a delightful man!" Martina laughed. "We are definitely going to keep this one, dear."

Christina pressed on. "I found out a few more things about this Billy Hays I thought you might be curious about."

"Darling, I am much more interested in this strong, intriguing Christian man you are riding

250

next to. I would much rather hear from him than about a thief and murderer named Billy Hays. Mr. Yager, did you have a good experience at the university?"

"Mother, don't change the subject on me," Christina demanded.

"Now, dear, I don't —"

"There are some things that have troubled me, and I just want to tell you once. Then I can relax about all of it. Please, Mother."

"Certainly, dear. Go right ahead. That's what a mother's for."

"One reason this man's image haunts me is that he has Daddy's eyes."

"He has what?"

"The only picture I have of you and Daddy is your wedding picture. His thick eyebrows and the way they tilt up at the ends is identical to this man's."

"That is an interesting coincidence, but I . . ."

Christina noticed her mother's lips and hands begin to quiver. "Mother, are you all right?" she asked.

Martina leaned back and allowed her long, straight brown hair to flow down the back of the wagon seat. She took a deep breath and put her hands to her mouth. "I'm afraid, angel. I'm afraid, that's all."

"Afraid of what? I don't understand."

"I have been living with the fear of a possible conversation like this for many years. Now I am ready. 'Oh, Lamb of God, who taketh away the sins of the world, have mercy on us.' " She braced her arms on the wagon seat. "Go ahead, darling. Tell me all about this boy. I'm ready now."

"Ready for what? I don't understand."

"I'm ready for whatever you're going to tell me."

Kern reached over and slipped his big hand into Christina's and gently squeezed it. "I don't know what all of this means," Christina continued, "but here's what I know. Besides the fact that he's a murderer and will surely be hung if he's not lynched first and that he showed up in a crazy dream of mine about having a brother, his name is Billy Hays. He's about a year younger than I am. He was born in the Carson Range, above Carson City, and . . ."

Kern nodded at her mother. Christina glanced over and saw that her mother's eyes were closed, and yet tears streamed down her cheeks. "Go on. . . . Honey, please go on."

"Anyway, this Billy claims his father left his mother before he was born. He was told that his father ran off to Sacramento with a dance hall girl who took him away at the point of a gun. His mother is Indian. He has dark skin but funny big ears and those arching eyebrows. He grew up in the mountains at some kind of logging camp until his mother died when he was twelve. I think he's probably been a thief and footpad ever since. Normally, he's the type I'd absolutely avoid and never want to see again. He started running with Cole Travis, and they are in big trouble. There's just something peculiar about Billy. I can't explain it."

Tears still flowed down her mother's cheeks; her fists were clenched white. "Mother, what's wrong? What do you know? What does all this mean?"

Kern Yager stopped the empty wagon in the middle of the road.

Christina heard her mother murmur, "Was his mother's name Carmela?"

Christina felt a shudder of icy terror in the bright San Joaquin Valley sun. Both women's eyes met, and as if orchestrated, they clutched each other and began to sob.

There was no crowd of men around the jail when they arrived.

"Are you sure you don't want me to come in with you?" Kern asked after he lifted both women to the sidewalk.

"It's a family matter, Kern, and we'll need someone to drive who is clear-headed and dry-eyed. But thank you for your kindness," Martina said.

Christina held her mother's hand as they walked up the stairs. "Why didn't you tell me all this about Daddy before?"

"How could I tell the delight of my life that her daddy had deserted wife and daughter, squandered our money, and ended up a derelict living with various women in Nevada? Even now I have to force every word out of my mouth with great pain to my heart. Twenty-three years is not long enough to heal the hurt I feel. I'm sorry, darling. I just couldn't. That's all. . . . I just couldn't."

The deputy led them back down the hot, stuffy, dank hallway to where another guard watched the cell.

"But Daddy did come home and save us in the fire from the attack of the outlaws, didn't he?" Christina whispered.

"You've seen the newspaper clippings. Every word is true. Your daddy had made some bad choices, and he was too proud to admit them and come home. He wanted to, honey. I know he did. When I brought him back, he saved us . . . and he loved us."

"But this Billy could actually be my brother?"

"Your half-brother. At the time Carmela had several . . . admirers. I don't know if we can be sure."

Suddenly Billy Hays sauntered up to the other side of the iron grate. Martina froze when she saw his eyes.

"He is, isn't he?" Christina asked.

Martina nodded.

"I am what?" Billy asked. "What do you women want with me?"

Christina clutched her mother's shoulders. "Are you all right, Mother?"

Martina brushed the tears back and folded her arms under her chest. "Billy, sit down on the bunk because I have some rather shocking news for you."

"I ain't got to do what you say."

"Billy, I said, sit down!" Martina demanded.

He sat.

"I met your mother, Carmela, on only one occasion, but I want to talk to you about your father," Martina began, "and your sister."

"I ain't got no sister!" he fumed.

Martina took a deep breath and then let it out slowly. "I told you it would be shocking news."

It was after dark when they drove back to Stokes Mountain. The back of the wagon was stocked with groceries, dry goods, and a sleeping black-and-white dog. The front seat contained two weepy women and a very quiet Kern Yager.

"Mother, my head is still spinning. I found out things about my father I never knew. I discover at age twenty-four that I have a half-brother. Not only that, but he is a killer about to be hung. What am I supposed to do now? I don't even know how I'm supposed to think and feel about all of this."

"I don't know either, darling." Martina sat up straight, running a wide comb through her long hair. "I'm not much help to you today. I have been a disappointment to you, and for that I apologize."

"Treat him like a brother," Kern blurted out.

"What? He's strange. He's a killer. He leered at me in a suggestive manner when I first met

him. Now I should treat him like a brother?"
Christina complained.

"Being a brother does not depend on exemplary behavior. It depends on bloodlines. What if he was a whole brother instead of a half-brother? What if you had known him all his life, and now he murdered someone and was awaiting trial? What would you do in that case?"

"And he was guilty?"

"Yep," he said.

"Then I guess I'd pray for him, visit him, encourage him. I'd probably attend the trial. Pray for justice. Help him to prepare to meet the Lord. I don't know," she rambled.

Kern's voice was so low it seemed to roll like a river. "That about sums it up, doesn't it?"

"He — he doesn't deserve to have someone treat him that way," she argued.

"Who does?"

Martina patted her daughter's knee. "Kern's right, dear."

"I know it. I just wish I didn't know all this. What if they had gone to Badger instead of stopping at my place? Then I wouldn't know any of this."

"It must be the Lord's doing," Martina offered.

"You've got to help me, Mama."

"Honey, I'll do what I can. Let me say something that sounds cold, but I don't intend it that way. Billy isn't related to me. Only to you. What I mean is, I'm the woman who took his father away from his mother at gunpoint. But you, you are flesh and blood. He is not going to want to see me."

"I don't think he wants to see me either."

"As the days go by, he will," Kern suggested. "As family goes, you're all he's got. And when he figures that out . . . and that he can't escape hanging, he'll need you."

When they rolled up the driveway, bright lights were blazing from the barn. They could see Joshua Slashpipe sitting in the stock tank in long underwear, still wearing his sombrero.

"Joshua," Kern called out, "you beat us home."

"A fact I greatly regret. Harvey went back to your place. He was too tired to wait up for you. I'm going to bed now, too, if I can drag my weary bones out of this tank."

"There you are!" Grandma Alena called out from in front of the barn, which now sported a heavy canvas curtain for a door. "Kern, you unload the wagon. I have something to show my granddaughter." She stopped to stare at Christina and Martina. "Well, you two look like you were hog-tied to the back of the wagon and drug all the way home."

"Does she know about Daddy?" Christina whispered.

"I'll have to tell her later," Martina replied. "At the moment my eyes and my heart need a rest."

"Come in here," Grandma Alena insisted.

Inside the well-lit barn, four sheets hung like curtains around a white enamel bathtub with claw feet surrounding crystal globes.

"A bathtub! You bought a real bathtub, and I don't even have a house?" Christina exclaimed.

"A woman does have her priorities," Martina asserted.

"The men refused to carry it up to the loft," Alena explained. "Now come on up the ladder. I'll show you our rooms."

"Our rooms?" Christina gasped.

The loft was cleared of hay and straw. Sheets were nailed to the barn walls to add privacy. Blankets clothespinned to stretched ropes divided the loft into three rooms.

"Your mother and I will take this bed." Alena pointed to a brass-framed bed with green comforter and feather pillows.

"You bought beds and carried them up here?" Christina gasped.

"Joshua and Harvey carried them up here." Alena led them to another partitioned area. "And this will be your room, honey."

"A four-poster oak bed with a feather mattress!"

"Think of it as a pre-marriage present from Grandma," Alena offered. "Then this room with the sofa is the drawing room."

"Grandma, I can't believe you did this."

"My sweet *Palomita Roja* needs a bed to sleep in and dream about strong men with breathtaking smiles. I just bought what was on the list."

"Mother, did you know about this?" Christina demanded.

"Of course," Martina replied. "It was my list."

Eight

Christina eyed her mother sitting on the love seat in the blanket-partitioned sitting room of the loft. Martina's long brown hair hung neatly combed and tied back with purple ribbons. She looked as if she could have been sitting in the parlor of some fancy New York hotel. *Culture for dear Mama is not an option. It's a necessity she chooses each day of her life. Her lace collar is crisp and fastened high up on her neck. Her posture perfect. Her open Bible lies lightly in her lap. Her eyes search each word.* When Martina looked up and saw her daughter, her smile was warm, sincere.

"I slept in," Christina admitted.

Martina marked her place with a scarlet ribbon and slowly closed the Bible on her lap. "How's the new bed?"

"Absolutely wonderful." Christina stopped to gaze in the little mirror hanging on the gigantic wooden post. "I feel spoiled rotten, of course, but it feels so good to be clean, to wear a nightgown and have fresh sheets. How are you doing, Mother?"

"With your loft? Or with the discovery of Billy Hays?"

"Both."

"Honey, your living in a loft doesn't bother

me. If you're still living here a year from now, that would cause some concern. But it's Billy that I've been talking to the Lord about."

"Billy Swan or Billy Hays?"

"Both, I suppose. Actually, darling, I am doing well. I feel relieved. From the day your daddy died, I knew that someday I would have to tell you more about him."

Christina walked over and began rubbing her mother's shoulders and neck. "Do you ever wish you had never married Daddy? That you had found someone more faithful? Maybe that you had met Loop earlier?"

Her mother's reply was instant and firm. "Never."

"Never?"

"First, I was madly in love with your father. I could never regret that feeling. As I'm sure you know, it is one of the most wonderful feelings in the world. And second, you are the joy and delight of my life. And there would have been no Christina Swan without a William Hays Swan, Jr. Honey, we don't get to select the turmoil in our lives, but we do get to choose how to react to it."

Christina ran her fingers through her mother's long hair, a childhood habit that neither saw fit to change. "That's what our life on this earth's about, isn't it? The Lord puts us into various situations and then sees how we will react."

"That's one way of putting it. He hopes we will learn, grow . . . change."

"How do you like Kern, Mother?"

"I've never in my life seen such a strong man . . . with such a tender spirit. You found a keeper, Miss Swan." Martina took her daughter's hand and kissed the long, blistered fingers. "Mother is already praying that your first child will be a redheaded girl."

"She is? Then Grandma Alena approves of Kern?"

"Any man who could sit there so peaceful while the two of us grilled him over his faith like we did yesterday is quite a patient man."

Christina sat down next to her mother. "I think he was mainly stunned."

Martina grinned. "You might be right."

"Where's Grandma?"

"She's out riding, of course."

"Do you think she'll ever give that up?"

"Never." Martina reached over and picked some lint off her daughter's dress. "Riding fast horses is her passion, her only passion since your grandfather died."

"I don't have any fast horses for her, although General Lee surprised me yesterday."

"She and Joshua took Cole's and Billy's horses since they have not been claimed yet. They decided to ride up to the top of Stokes Mountain and see how many wild, unbranded cattle they could round up and drive back. The railroad will take over much of that undeveloped land. They didn't think the railroad needed those cows. Besides, the more developed this place looks, the more convincing it will be to the commission. Mother is convinced that when they show up, we should present an industrious working farm and ranch."

"Joshua will be in heaven riding with his *La Paloma Roja*."

"Yes, and Mother enjoys the attention. Sometimes she stays up at Rancho Alazan too much. She has Uncle Walt and Aunt Andrea and the kids with her, but her role is so different now. She likes being the queen, you know."

"I know. When Joshua called her La Doña, I thought we would lose her to her memories."

Martina stood up and then reached back and brushed a wild strand of red hair from Christina's eyes. "Are you ready to have breakfast and get to work?"

"I believe so. From the explosions, I assume that Kern and Harvey are busy blasting."

"Quite a strange geography, isn't it? It takes dynamite to get to the good soil."

"I will change into my old clothes after breakfast so that I can go help them," Christina announced.

"Nonsense. You and I have to go to town," her mother countered.

"Again?"

"Your brother goes before the judge for arraignment today. I think you should be there. And I have a few more things to purchase in Visalia."

"Joshua is busy with Grandma. Does that

mean Kern or Harvey will drive us?"

"Since when do you or I ever need a man to drive a rig for us? Your grandma is not the only woman in the family who likes running horses fast. Besides, Kern and Harvey are going over to Mr. Atwood's farm to start digging those two-year-old trees."

"Not without me, they aren't!" Christina fumed.

"Oh?"

"Mother, that Lucy Atwood follows Kern around like a dog with its tongue hanging out. And she's — she's — you know, she fills out her dress quite well."

"That's wonderful!"

"What's wonderful about it?"

"Honey, if Kern's the type who falls for all that when he has you around, it's better that you find out about it now."

"He's not that type."

"I believe you're right. In which case, you have nothing to worry about," her mother insisted.

"I'm not worried about Kern. I'm concerned about Lucy. She is definitely that type."

High clouds stacked up against the Sierras as the women drove to Visalia. The air felt heavy. Thunder rolled above their heads as they crossed the bridge at the St. John's River, but it felt too hot to rain. Even though she drove the wagon, Christina arrived at the courthouse not nearly as sweaty and sticky as on previous days.

I believe my mother wills the dust to stay away, and it obeys. She handed the reins to her mother. "Are you sure I should do this alone?"

Martina shifted the lead lines from one hand to the other as she tugged on the cuffs of her gloves. "Billy is right about me. I took his father away from his mother at gunpoint. He was my husband, and I believe I did the right thing, but I do not expect Billy to accept that. I'll be along later. You should introduce yourself to the District Attorney. Perhaps they want more than your written statement."

The courtroom was packed with men. Some wore suits and ties. Some wore white boiled shirts buttoned at the neck, ducking trousers, and suspenders. Some wore Strauss coveralls and flannel shirts. All wore outrage in their eyes and wrath on their lips. They left their guns with the half a dozen sheriff's deputies who guarded the doorways.

As far as she could tell, Christina was the only woman in the room. Whispers and nods followed her down the crowded rows. Several men scooted over to give her room. As she was seated, she spied the District Attorney who had spoken to her previously in the hallway. Finally, the county sheriff and two more deputies led two shackled prisoners into the courtroom.

Christina stared at both their faces. *Lord, what a pitiful sight. In the barn, after the crime, they were so confident, so bold, so arrogant, so invincible, so cavalier about their crime and murder. But now they are no more than frightened rats caught in a trap that they cannot escape, awaiting a worse fate. Lord, have mercy on their souls.*

Several times during the inquiry the judge had to silence the crowd. The general sentiment among the spectators seemed to be that a trial was a waste of money and time, that justice would be better served with a noose thrown over a tree limb.

As the arraignment dragged on with legal detail, the crowd grew more impatient. Christina began to doubt if Cole and Billy would even last the hour. Finally the District Attorney asked her to present herself to the court. Once she was in the witness chair, all eyes focused on her except for Billy and Cole, who stared down at their iron-shackled hands.

After the judge explained the difference between a trial and an arraignment, the District Attorney asked her to make a statement about the capture of Travis and Hays.

She gave a condensed version of the evening they were captured. When she finished, the judge rang his gavel to quiet the crowd that murmured openly of lynching.

"Your Honor, I would like to make one more statement that I think is germane to these men standing for trial," Christina announced.

The gray-haired man in the black robe nodded for her to continue. The crowd hushed.

She took a deep breath and looked straight out at the crowd. Her mouth dropped open when she saw the woman with long brown hair and purple ribbons standing next to the deputies at the back door. Martina held her clutched hand to her lips and nodded at Christina.

I know, Mama. . . . I know. I need to tell them.

"Miss Swan?" the judge prodded.

Christina cleared her throat. "Your Honor, I have explained how my neighbor and I apprehended these two, and I have been honest about what they told me that evening. Mr. Yager, my neighbor, who is also my fiancé, and I brought them to town because we feel strongly about justice. Those who commit crimes should face the penalty of their actions. Justice means that the penalty fits the crime, and I believe these men deserve whatever punishment this court declares is appropriate for their crimes."

"Hang 'em today. That's what they deserve!" someone shouted.

The judge gaveled silence, but the murmurs continued.

"I will certainly say the same things at the trial that I did today. However, some of the comments in the crowd today have not been correct, and they disturb me. Cole Travis and Billy Hays are not rabid dogs that need to be instantly shot to protect society. They are men — men created, like all of us, in the image of God. And, like all of us, they are sinful. They will pay the consequences for their sin, just as you and I will. But they should be treated like men, not animals, even in condemnation and capital punishment, if that be the verdict.

"As I have testified before, Mr. Travis was a previous acquaintance of mine. He was neither a murderer or a thief back then, and I found him a pleasant person to know. I thank him for those amiable memories."

Cole Travis now lifted his head and gazed at her along with all the others. She took another deep breath and glanced back at her mother, who brushed tears from her eyes and nodded once again.

Christina peered up at the judge and then back out to the crowd. "Your Honor, Billy Hays, too, is a man. I have heard shameful remarks murmured in this courtroom about his parentage. I have heard horrible, bigoted words used by men who would be ashamed to have their sons and daughters hear them speak such things. Like Cole, Billy deserves fair punishment for his inexcusable crimes.

"But like every person here, Billy Hays does not exist as an inhuman scourge of society. He is a man with a family."

The entire crowd grew so quiet that Christina could hear her heart pounding in her chest. She stared at Billy as he raised his head. "I am his sister."

The crowd roared.

The judge pounded the gavel. "Would you repeat that, Miss Swan?"

"I said, I am Billy Hays's sister, his half-sister.

It's a fact both of us only recently discovered. As you might imagine, it puts me in emotional turmoil. I have a great desire for God's justice to take place and know I can count on His grace to prevail. I am concerned, however, that many in this room are not concerned with justice."

"Get her off the stand, Judge!" someone shouted. "She's tryin' to protect that half-breed murderer."

Once again the judge quieted the crowd. He looked down at the defendants' table. "Mr. Hays, is this woman indeed your sister?"

Like snow in a frying pan, the fright in Billy Hays's eyes dissipated. There was almost a smile on his lips. "Yes, sir, I reckon she is. We had the same daddy, although our mamas were different."

The judge turned to Christina. "Thank you for your comments. They will be duly recorded and considered. You may be dismissed."

She hurried past the defendants' table without looking at either man. Her eyes were focused on her mother at the back of the room.

Among the mumbling of various blasphemous curses, someone called out, "What are we waiting for? Let's hang 'em both before dinner."

Christina spun around and called out, "Judge!"

"You are out of order." He gaveled loudly.

"No more than most of the men in this room," she shouted. "If I were judge, I would not let any man attend the trial without bringing his wife and children with him. Let his sons and daughters hear his words and see the hatred in his eyes, and understand that the power of revenge easily tramples the power of justice!"

"You are dismissed, Miss Swan!" the judge declared. "Another outburst and you will be held in contempt of court."

As if on cue, the crowd rose up. Christina did not know if they were going to proceed with a lynching or just hurl insults at her. The gavel banged repeatedly on the judge's bench.

As in a blurry dream, Christina saw her mother scurry down the aisle to her. Martina turned to face the crowd beside Christina. Her mother glared at a big man who blocked their path. Then she thundered, "Sit down."

He and half the men immediately sat down.

Her mother surveyed the others left standing. "I said . . . sit down!"

They sat.

Every last man.

The air outside was still hot and sticky, but felt fresh in comparison to that in the courtroom. They didn't say a word to each other until they reached the wagon.

"How long were you in the courtroom?" Christina mumbled.

"Nearly the whole time, honey. I didn't want to interfere, but I couldn't stay away."

"It was not the way I planned it. I didn't know I was going to say those things."

"They had to be said. I was proud of you. A mob like that loses sight of wisdom, justice — of the things that make us human."

"I know they are going to hang, Mother. But I will not see them dragged behind someone's horse and draped over a tree limb. Did I really do all right?"

"Honey, your daddy would have been proud of you."

Christina began to weep.

"And more important, the Lord is proud of you. Now dry your eyes, or you can't read the signs in the back of the wagon."

"What signs?"

"The ones I had your grandmother order the other day." Martina pulled the brown canvas tarp back, revealing dual two-by-ten-foot wooden signs stretched across the wagon bed.

"The 'Proud Quail Ranch' and 'Yager Farms'! Mother, they are beautiful."

"That land commission is going to find developed property when they come to inspect on July 1."

"July 1? Oh, no, Mother. . . . We have until September 1," Christina insisted.

"Not according to that list in the courthouse hallway. It said final inspections would not be completed until September 1, but they would start those inspections on July 1. The very first location would be lieu lands on or around Stokes Mountain."

"But — but we can't possibly get anything

developed by July 1."

"Posh," her mother replied. "A person can accomplish a lot in a couple of weeks. Besides, none of us have anything better to do now, do we?"

At noon the next day Kern Yager and Harvey Jackson returned from the Atwood farm with eighteen two-year-old orange trees, their roots encased in 150-pound balls of burlap-wrapped dirt. They drove up the long drive to the springs near the barn.

"I like the new signs," Kern said as he swung down off the wagon.

"It was Mother's idea," Christina greeted him. "It does make both places seem more permanent. The trees look beautiful."

"Well, it wasn't a happy trip," Harvey groused.

"You and Lucy didn't hit it off?" Christina asked.

"She wasn't even home."

"She's still in San Bernardino," Kern explained.

A wide grin broke across Christina's face. "Why, that's too bad. You two clean up. Mother's got supper ready."

"We aren't havin' beans and tortillas again, are we?" Harvey asked. "I don't think I could eat 'em for one more meal."

"I believe it's beef stew and sourdough biscuits," Christina announced.

"Now that's better," Harvey said, brightening. "At least the day won't be a total waste."

By the time Harvey and Kern strolled to the table, the others had gathered around. Martina served the food. Kern said the blessing. Joshua clicked his white, straight teeth.

They all dove into stew and sourdough biscuits. For the first several moments the conversation centered around the events at the courthouse the previous day.

Kern stabbed another helping of meat. "Where'd we get the beef?"

"We butchered one of the cows."

"Which one?"

"Not Mrs. Manchada, if that's what you were wondering," Christina declared.

"This is the cow with the bad heart," Joshua grinned.

"Bad heart?" Kern asked.

"When I caught her by the horns and dallied the *reata,* she just dropped dead. I think it was a heart attack."

"What do you mean, dropped dead?"

"There is only one way to drop dead. She wasn't used to a rope, and it must have scared her to death."

Christina chewed on the slightly stringy beef. "The meat won't last long in this heat."

"Joshua and I will jerk it all tomorrow," Grandma Alena informed her.

"We have a few cows to brand if we can catch them."

"What's the total count on the herd?" Christina asked.

"Forty-two cows and thirty-six calves," Joshua announced.

"No bull?" she asked.

"Not yet," he replied.

"How can there be no bull?"

"He will come back at the right time."

"But we'll have all the cows fenced in."

"That will not stop him," Joshua grinned.

"It's beginning to look like a cattle ranch up on the hillside, but the farm ground still looks deserted," she said.

"It will have eighteen trees along the road tomorrow," Kern announced. "Harvey and I figure two days of diggin', haulin' and plantin' trees, and then a couple more days waterin' them in and plantin' corn."

"Corn? I thought you wanted to plant tomatoes?"

"Eventually. . . . But I've got fifteen acres already plowed, and corn will grow faster. It's too late for tomatoes this year."

"Kern figures that corn will make this place look settled quicker, provided we can irrigate it this summer, which is unlikely without ditch water," Harvey noted as he smeared honey on his biscuit.

"If we can keep to that schedule of haulin' trees, we'll have two fine little orange groves by the first of August."

"The first of August!" Joshua exclaimed.

"You haven't told him yet?"

Kern looked over at Christina.

She took a deep breath, then looked at her mother, then at her grandmother, and back at Kern Yager.

"When Mother and I were at the courthouse yesterday —"

"You expectin' a salesman?" Harvey interrupted.

"We have someone coming up the drive." Joshua waved a sourdough biscuit in the general direction of the road.

Christina stood and shaded her eyes. "It looks like a carriage. It won't be the land commission. They aren't due until the first of July."

"The first of September, you mean," Kern corrected.

Christina sat back down and slipped her arm into his. "That's what I've been trying to tell you. At the courthouse they posted a note that the land commission would begin their work on July 1. And their first stop is the lieu land on Stokes Mountain."

"July 1!" Kern blurted out. "They can't do that! They said September 1."

"They are going to complete the survey and make recommendations by September first, but assessments will begin July first."

Kern leaped up and stomped away from the table. "We can't do anything by July first — that's two weeks away! They keep changing the rules, and I can't do a thing about it!"

Christina scampered after him. *No . . . no, you don't, Kern Yager. You aren't going to have a bad spell today.* She grabbed his arm and spun him around toward the driveway. "Honey, we have company coming up the drive. We have to go see who it is."

He lumbered along beside her. "I can't do a thing. They are going to take what they want, and I am helpless to stop them!"

"What's wrong with Kern?" Harvey called out.

"We're just going to see who's in the carriage," Christina called back to those at the table.

"I think I'll go with you," Harvey piped up.

"Perhaps someone's brought a note from Loop," Martina said. "I'll walk down with you."

"Well, come on, Señor Slashpipe," Mrs. Merced said, "we might as well make it a parade."

By the time the carriage bounced and rocked its way up the slope of Stokes Mountain to the springs, all six waited by the stock tank.

"My, I didn't know there were so many families up here."

"Only one family," Martina replied.

"One family?" the man stared over at Joshua Slashpipe.

"I'm the black sheep of the family," he grinned.

"Do you work for the county?" Christina asked the man. She still held onto Kern Yager's arm. He was blank-faced, staring off across the field.

"Heavens no! I'm from Chicago. I was over at Mr. Earl's farm earlier in the day, and when he knew I was headed toward Dinuba, he asked me to drop off a message to Mr. Kern Yager and Miss Christina Swan."

"That's us." She tugged at Kern's arm, trying to get him to pay attention. "Is he bringing us our lumber soon?"

"I hate to be bringing you bad news, but the message he wanted to send was that the Antelope Valley Lumber Mill burned to the ground last night. Seems as if lightning hit the sawdust burner. It will take three to six months for them to get back in operation."

"Six months?" Christina gasped.

Kern jerked his arm away from her hand and turned toward the open hillside. "They just won't stop it! It's always like this!" The tone of his voice exploded somewhere between fury and terror. Christina saw her mother step back and her grandmother flinch.

I am not losing him. Lord, You've got to help me do something right now!

Christina ran in front of Kern and jumped up, locking her arms around his neck and smashing her lips into his. Her feet were off the ground as she hung like a rag doll.

"Christina!" her mother called out.

Her eyes clamped shut, her lips pressed against his tight, chapped, unresponsive ones.

"Wait a minute. . . . Leave her be," Grandma Alena cautioned.

"My word, this is unusual," the man in the carriage mumbled.

"Christina, you aren't behavin' proper," Harvey complained.

Kern grabbed her. His big hands encircled her waist.

He's going to throw me to the ground, Lord. Right in front of everyone, he's going to throw me to the ground. Her arms still locked around his neck, she clutched her elbows, tensed her muscles, and forced her lips against his.

He yanked at her waist.

She thought her arms would fall off.

He tried to turn his head.

She kept her lips on his.

"Christina!" her mother hollered.

"This reminds me of the bull and the bear," Joshua mused.

He yanked at her waist again. She could hear her dress tear.

"Mr. Yager, put down my daughter!" her mother yelled.

He dropped his hands from her waist, and she flopped against him, her boots still a foot off the ground. His hands went up to her cheeks, and he forced her face away from his. Still she hung onto his thick neck.

She opened her eyes. Tears streamed down his cheeks. "I love you, Kern Yager, and you can't run away from me," she cried.

She spun her head and bit his thumb. He released her cheeks, and immediately she began kissing him again.

The man in the carriage cleared his throat. "My word . . . I've never . . ."

"I have," Grandma Alena chimed in. "Let them be."

Kern's chest and shoulders began to shudder. She gripped her arms so tight around his neck that she thought she would choke him. His lips began to quiver, but she refused to pull back.

Then his lips relaxed. The tension in his neck seemed to melt away, and his shoulders slumped.

The kiss warmed.

This time his arms encircled her waist and hugged her tight.

Real tight.

She pulled her mouth away and gasped for a breath.

"I love you, too," he whispered. "I'm tired. I need to sleep."

She loosened her grip on his neck and slipped down until her boots came back to the dirt.

"Mother, I'm going to walk Kern back to his place. Please continue with dinner. I will explain later."

"You're goin' to his tent?" Harvey called out as they started to walk across the hillside.

"Mr. Slashpipe, would you please shoot Mr. Jackson for that insulting remark?" Christina called.

"Yes, of course," Joshua replied. "It would be proper."

"Wait!" Harvey called out. "She's just joking. I didn't mean any insult."

"I believe you may spare his life," Grandma Alena pronounced.

"This is strange — this is very strange," the man in the carriage muttered.

About fifty feet from the springs, Yager glanced down at the short brown grass on the hillside. "I need to sleep."

She slipped her fingers into his. "Not yet, honey. Let me walk you to your tent. You don't want to sleep on the dirt."

They continued to stroll.

"I'm tired of this, Christina."

"Of feeling this way?"

"Of other people messing with my life, of losing control, of reliving that day."

"What day, Kern?"

He locked his jaw and clamped his lips tight.

"It's all right, baby — it's all right," Christina cooed. "You don't have to relive it, not for me, not ever. Honey, I love you just the way you are. You don't have to change."

"It's not fair. You deserve better than me."

"Kern Yager, stop your mumbling. You're the best thing that ever came into my life."

"I can't forget, Christina. I pray and I cry and I sleep, but I can't forget."

"You need more good memories to offset the bad ones. That's what I'm here for. We're going to make lots of good memories together."

"I can't make you marry me."

"No, you can't. I'm volunteering."

"You don't know what you're getting."

"I know exactly what I'm getting, Mr. Yager. I've seen you at your worst. But you, on the other hand, have never seen me at my worst. You are the one in for a surprise — not me."

"What do you do in a bad spell?"

"I pout."

"That doesn't sound too serious."

"I pout for days at a time, sometimes for weeks."

"Is there any cure for it?" he murmured.

"You can give in . . . or . . ."

"Or what?"

"Give me the same treatment I just gave you."

"We might never get any work done."

"Yes, but who would care?"

"Your mother will. I just made a fool of myself in front of your mother and grandmother. I feel ashamed."

"I'll explain to them. They'll understand."

"I need to sleep."

"Come on, we're almost to the gate."

Busca barked once when they trudged up to the shed and then slumped back into the shade.

She untied the strings of the white canvas tent and pulled the flaps. He stooped down and entered the tent, still clutching her fingers. He fell facedown on top of the blanket neatly draped across the cot. His feet hung two feet off the end of the small bed. She scurried around and tugged off his dusty brown boots. As she did, she surveyed the contents of the tent.

There were books, journals, maps, spyglass, clothes, India rubber boots, and trunks. Everything was neatly folded or stacked in its place. On a tent pole near where she squatted was an oak-framed picture of a man, a woman, and a child that looked about two.

She started to open her mouth and then clamped it shut. *It must be his mother and father and him. I must ask him . . . some other time.*

When she stood, her head brushed against the roof of the tent. On the canvas floor of the tent was a thick oriental carpet.

He opened one eye and held out his hand.

She took it, and it went limp.

"I've got to sleep," he repeated.

"I know, honey. Go on, get some sleep."

"Will you stay with me?"

Christina felt a sinking feeling in her chest. She rubbed the palm of her hand against his cheek. "I've never wanted to do anything more in my life, but I can't."

"I want you here when I wake up."

"Honey, I'll check on you, but I can't stay. Not inside this tent. Not next to your bed."

"What if I promised to behave?"

"It's not you that I'm worried about. There is no way I could promise you that I'd behave."

She could hear the labored breathing of fitful sleep even before she finished the sentence. She tugged off his hat and laid it alongside the tent post and then stared at the picture. *Daddy's remarried and a lawman in Lordsburg. Mama died when he was young, and yet he hangs her picture still. Mrs. Yager, you know why your boy's this way, don't you? I wish I did.*

Anyway, I think I wish I did.

Christina's mother met her halfway across the hillside. By the time they reached the others, she had explained what she knew about Kern Yager's bad days. All the rest, including the man from the carriage, sat at the rustic table finishing the stew.

"How's your man?" Grandma Alena quizzed.

"He needs to rest. He'll be fine."

"That was quite a treatment you gave him."

"I wasn't sure what to do."

Her grandmother raised her eyebrows. "It looked like fun."

"It wasn't. I mean, it's scary when he starts withdrawing like that."

"It reminds me of your Grandpa."

"What do you mean?" Christina quizzed.

"He didn't withdraw like that, but he had an experience in the past that changed his character and almost prevented us from ever getting together. I never did explain to you why he wouldn't enter any building with more than one story, did I?"

Martina folded her arms across her chest. "Mother, this is something you've never even told me."

"Nor will I now. All I'm saying is, the consistent love of a good woman can soothe a lot of pain from the past."

"What I want to know," Harvey blurted out, "is whether his technique works with all women. I reckon it's something I could learn."

"Christina," Martina said, turning toward the man from the carriage, "let me introduce you to Mr. Aristus Albany. He's a salesman who has a very interesting product."

"Miss Swan, I'm indeed sorry that I was the bearer of such bad news."

"What do you sell, Mr. Albany?"

"I am the western region representative for Lyman Bridges Ready-made Homes."

"What do you mean, ready-made homes?"

"My company based in Chicago sells houses that are mostly built. The walls are finished in sections with doors and windows hung, trusses are built, and the floor is in sections. All you need to do is secure the floor to your own foundation, raise the walls, secure the trusses, and roof it. Four men can put up a house in a week to ten days."

"You ship it from Chicago?"

"Precisely. I can only ship it to the rail station at Goshen. The rest of the transportation is up to the buyer."

"They would be expensive, no doubt."

"Much more reasonable than you might think. Here is our brochure and price list. You'll see that the basic cabin, with only one room, starts at $275. It goes up to our two-story, eight-room house selling for $5,250. That excludes shipping, of course."

"Shipping from Chicago must be expensive," she continued to probe.

"Because this is a new territory for the company, I have been authorized to offer shipping at a 50 percent reduction."

"Four men can build it in a week?" Christina questioned.

"How about three women and three men?" Grandma Alena inquired.

The salesman glanced at all three women, one at a time. "I have a strong feeling that you women can accomplish most anything you set your minds to."

"He's a very perceptive man," Alena replied.

Christina leafed through the brochure and pointed to a page. "I like this model."

"Number 25? Your daughter has a good eye for houses. That is one of our best-selling models. For merely $1,800 you get one bedroom, kitchen, living room, bathing room, screened back porch, and full-veranda front porch. It so happens that number 25 is my demonstration home. You may stop by our Visalia location soon and inspect it for quality. I think you will find that Lyman Bridges Ready-made Homes are the finest in the entire country."

"You have one put up in Visalia?"

"It's still at the depot in Goshen. It will take a little time to construct it."

"Just how long will it take to send a ready-made house out from Chicago?"

"That is the most extraordinary news. I can guarantee that you will have it at the station in Goshen in merely four to six weeks," he said.

"By August?" Christina gasped.

"Yes. Isn't that incredible?"

"It's horrible!"

"What?"

"I need it now. I'll buy the one at Goshen from you," Christina offered.

"I'm sorry, but it's not for sale. It's my model home. I cannot sell it; it's against company policy."

"Mr. Albany, you could sell it to Christina and immediately order another for your demonstration model," her mother suggested.

"Yes, and anyone who wanted to see it could come out here to the Proud Quail Ranch and take a look for themselves," Grandma Alena added.

"Happy, satisfied customers are a very persuasive selling tool," Martina insisted.

"I'm sorry, ladies. I have to follow company policy."

"Mr. Albany, I need a house standing on this property, as does Mr. Yager on his. It could make the difference between keeping our land or losing it. I appreciate your difficult position, but I hope you appreciate mine. I know you have only one house, but at least that's a start."

"You know, Martina," Grandma Alena began, "I just don't think Mr. Albany has a vision of what his model home would look like at the base of Stokes Mountain. Mr. Albany, would you mind taking a short stroll with us?"

"I certainly wouldn't turn down two lovely ladies for a stroll, but the model house is not for sale."

Alena slipped her hand into the man's arm. "I know, but perhaps if you can envision what we want to do, you'll have a selling point for others."

Martina captured the salesman's other arm. "Mr. Albany, with these muscles, you haven't always been a drummer."

"Most of my life I've been a carpenter. But the sales job opened up, and I wanted to see California and . . ."

The three ambled away from the table. "A salesman's life must be quite lonely, being away from your wife and family," Alena added.

"Actually, I'm not married."

"No!" Alena exclaimed. "That might explain your hesitation to provide a home for our Christina and her family."

"She has a family already?"

"Oh, you know how young people are. It won't be all that long," Martina replied. "And your ready-built homes are just the type I always hoped my grandchildren could be raised in."

The voices faded out, leaving Joshua Slashpipe and Harvey Jackson huddled across the table from Christina.

"I don't reckon that old boy has a chance in

the world," Harvey blurted out.

"I predict that he will not only sell to you, but at his cost," Joshua added.

Kern Yager sat in the rocking chair on his shed porch and looked over the brochure. "They have this ready-made waiting in Visalia?"

"Yes, and he claims four men can build it in seven to ten days," Christina explained.

He handed her back the brochure. "Good. Then we'll build it on your place, of course."

"No, we won't."

"Of course we will. We will save the Proud Quail Ranch first."

"We will do no such thing. Mother, Grandmother, and I decided that the barn is looking increasingly like a house, so it is your farm that is without a structure."

He pulled his wide-brimmed hat off and spun it in his hands. "What did your mother and grandmother decide about me?"

"Grandmother Alena said you reminded her of Grandpa. He had something horrible in his past that he had to overcome. But she wouldn't tell us what."

"What cured him of his problem?"

"A redheaded, strong-spirited wife and the challenge of a wild, unsettled land."

"You wouldn't know where I could find —"

"A redheaded, strong-spirited wife? I just happen to —"

"Oh, no," he interrupted, "I didn't have any

trouble finding one of those. What I need is a wild, unsettled land."

Christina punched him in the ribs, then clutched her knuckles, looking down to see if they were bruised.

"How about your mother? What did she say?" he persisted.

"She was shocked with my method of treatment. Public displays of affection are not my mother's strong suit. But she was quite relieved that you had a spell."

"Relieved?"

"For a while she was afraid I'd found the perfect man."

"Why did that bother her?"

"Because she knows all too well that I am not the perfect woman. She was afraid you would wake up someday and think you'd made a huge mistake. She's convinced that our own imperfections keep us more tolerant of other's imperfections."

"Well, in that case, I should be an extremely tolerant man."

"Good, because we're going to build this ready-made on Yager Farms."

"No, we aren't."

"Of course we are. If you don't agree, I'll have Grandma and Mother latch onto each arm and take you out for a little walk and talk. By the time they finish with you, you will have agreed to call your first son Wilson and send him to Grandma to raise. So what's it going to be, Yager? Will you build the house here, or do I sic Grandma and Mother on you?"

"Was there ever a time in your family history when the woman didn't get her way?"

"Not that any of us can recall."

"Then I have no choice in the matter."

"Of course you have a choice." She bowed her head and batted her eyelids. "You can choose to agree with us."

Christina drove the tree wagon.

Kern dug out the holes and planted.

Harvey dug a trough around each orange tree.

Grandma Alena drove the water wagon, while Joshua Slashpipe held the India rubber hose and watered in the transplanted tree.

The trunks of the orange trees were no thicker than two inches. The tops had been pruned back to an eighteen-inch globe. A few actually had small green oranges hanging on them.

It turned out to be another incredibly hot, sticky day. Only the conversation made the time pass quickly. The sun had just sunk behind the coast range when a black carriage rumbled up the Yager Farms driveway. It pulled out into the field behind the water wagon.

"Kern Yager," a woman's voice called out, "what do you mean by buying trees from Father and not even saying hello to me?"

Kern lifted the last 150-pound tree out of the wagon and knelt down to place it gently in the hole. Harvey leaned on his shovel and gawked.

Christina watched from forty-four feet across the field.

"A little south, Kern darlin'," she called out.

"How's that?" he called back, ignoring the woman in the carriage.

"Perfect. Just like you, honey dove," Christina drawled.

"Kern Yager, I'm speaking to you." Lucy Atwood lifted her skirt and hiked over the loose soil. She ignored Alena and carefully stepped over Joshua's water hose as she stormed toward the kneeling Yager.

"Lucy! What a surprise." Kern waved toward the rear wagon parked twenty-two feet away. "Let me introduce the woman you just hurried past. She is *La Paloma Roja de Monterey*."

Lucy tucked her black hair under her ostrich-plumed white straw hat and called out, "Hello, Mrs. Rojas." Then she turned back to Kern and whispered, "Lapaloma is a strange first name. But I really didn't come over here to discuss the hired help."

"Uh, hum . . ." Harvey, standing with shovel in hand, cleared his throat.

"Lucy, this is Harvey Jackson. We had a mutual friend in college."

"You must be a graduate student," she noted.

Harvey nodded vigorously. "I figure a man can never learn too much."

"My sentiments exactly. Kern, wait until I tell you what I saw in San Bernardino. There is a tree that grows lemons and grapefruit and

291

oranges — all on the same tree. Isn't that amazing?" Lucy bubbled.

Yager cut the twine at the top of the burlap sack and pulled it back to expose the dirt. "Your daddy has one just like it."

"Really?"

"Yep. Harvey here spotted it first. He's got a very quick mind," Kern reported.

"Is that right?" She gave a quick glance Harvey's way.

"Yep." Harvey warmed. "I said to myself, Harvey Jackson, that's too big to be a lemon. Sure enough, it was grapefruit."

Christina strolled over and flopped down on her knees beside Kern. She rubbed a dirt line across her sweaty forehead with the back of her blistered hand and then held onto his arm. "Howdy, Miss Atwood. Did Kern darlin' tell you the news?"

Lucy tried to brush road dust off of her white gloves. "Eh, what news?"

"He's goin' to make an honest woman out of me."

"He's what?"

"He's goin' to marry me. Ain't that right, Kern?"

"That's right." Kern squeezed her tight, and Christina fought for a breath. When he noticed her consternation, he quickly released her. "Are you all right, sugar plum?"

"I reckon," she gasped. "My heart almost stops beatin' when you hold me tight." *I know my lungs stop working. If I don't train you to be more gentle, I'll have cracked ribs on our wedding night.*

"That's her grandma on the water wagon." Kern pointed.

Lucy's mouth dropped open. "Mrs. Rojas is her grandmother? But that means that she's . . . she's a . . . she's not completely . . ."

"She's 100 percent Californio. Did you know her mama was born in an adobe hut north of Sutter's Fort before the gold rush?" Kern added.

"Eh, I . . . but . . . no. There were no white women who gave birth to . . . I mean, besides the renowned Alena Tipton Merced . . . and she was in . . ." Lucy spun around and stared at the older red-haired woman driving the water wagon. "What did you call her when I first walked up?"

"*La Paloma Roja de Monterey,*" Yager reported.

"Does *paloma* mean dove?"

"Yep."

"My word, you mean that woman is the legendary Red Dove of Monterey?"

"That's my grandma," Christina beamed.

"I . . . I own a copy of her journal. I've almost got the whole thing memorized," Lucy gasped. "I cry every time when I read . . ."

Christina stood up and brushed the dirt off her brown dress. "When you get to the place where Grandpa kills the grizzly and then hugs the panicked little Indian girl?"

Lucy took out a starched white linen handkerchief and brushed the corners of her eyes.

"Yes, that's the place."

"So do I," Christina concurred.

"You know how to read?"

"Lucy, I'm going to have to ask your forgiveness."

"You seem to have lost your accent."

"Yes, well, it started out as a little game, but I had no intention of letting it go this far. I manage the ranch over there next to Kern's, and we're working on a few projects together. Before I moved down to Tulare County, I was a schoolteacher, and before that I graduated from the University of California, majoring in mathematics. That's where Kern and I first met."

"What? What are you saying?"

"They've been playactin' with you," Harvey explained.

"You mean it was all a charade? But . . . why?"

"It's my fault, Lucy. I lost my heart to Christina years ago, and I didn't know quite how to tell you."

"Years ago?" Lucy challenged.

Christina folded her arms across her chest. *This is news to me, Kern Yager.*

"I was too bashful to visit with her in college. But when I went into the courthouse to study the survey maps of available land, I spied this piece owned by one of the Merced sons. So I picked this place out just in case."

"You're not making this up?" Lucy challenged.

"I've never heard this story before," Christina

admitted. "You mean, you've been, that all of this isn't . . . I don't know what to say."

"Say you'll marry me when we get the house built."

"Of course I'll marry you, but I want to know right now, are there any other secrets you're holding back on me?"

"Just one." His eyes dropped toward the dirt.

"My, oh my," Lucy purred. "Hasn't this been an informative afternoon?"

"Can you ever forgive us for the acting?" Christina asked.

"Most definitely! I am relieved actually."

"How's that?"

"Well, to lose out on dear Kern to the granddaughter of Alena Merced — well, that is acceptable. To lose out to an ignorant farm girl — that would certainly crush my spirit."

"I reckon I know just how you feel," Harvey sympathized.

"You do?"

"Yep. Those are my sentiments exactly. Isn't that right, Christina?"

"Harvey did say something very similar just recently."

"I simply must visit with your grandmother. My word, I once wrote an epic poem about her life."

"You did?" Christina reached over and placed her dirty hand on Lucy's white-gloved one. "May I read it sometime?"

"It was horrid. Trust me." Lucy squeezed

Christina's hand. "I threw it away."

"This is our last tree. Would you like to stay for supper?" Christina asked.

"Yes, and I promise to behave myself."

"And I promise no more acting," Christina added.

Harvey Jackson scooted over next to Lucy. "You know, Miss Atwood, I've known Christina's grandma and mama since I was just a lad."

"Oh?" She quickly studied the man's face.

"Our families are very close. You mentioned that story about the bear and the little Indian girl."

"Yes."

"One time when I was a kid, Christina let me wear that bear claw necklace the little girl made for her grandpa."

Lucy turned back to Christina. "You still have that necklace?"

"It's at the barn."

"You have to let me try it on. It would be like trying on the crown jewels!" Lucy swooned.

"Now who's playing the actress?" Christina chided.

Harvey stepped in between the two women and looked straight at Lucy Atwood. "I believe I've seen you before."

"Really? Where?" Lucy quizzed.

"At Crawford's Opera House in Topeka, Kansas. I saw a Saturday performance of the *Pirates of Penzance*, and you played Mabel. I'm sure it was you. Oh, you had on some makeup to soften your natural beauty, but it was you."

"I'm not an actress, and I've never been to Topeka," Lucy insisted.

"Well, that is truly a loss for mankind," Harvey droned.

"Just exactly what kind of business are you in, Mr. Jackson?"

"Harvey came to visit Christina, but agreed to help us out for a few weeks," Kern interrupted. "What he's really good at is scientific experimentation."

"Really? That sounds interesting. My father is good at that, too."

"Tell her about your theory to rid the old cabin of skunks. If it works, Harvey could make a fortune."

Harvey dropped his shovel and held out his arm to Lucy Atwood. "If you have a moment, I'd like to walk you over to that stone corral while I explain to you my secret theory." He glanced at the others. "I wouldn't want just anyone to hear this."

"I'd be delighted, Mr. Jackson." Lucy clutched his arm.

Christina's mother had supper ready when they all straggled up to the barn. The table had been extended with some creative carpentry, but the seating was still stumps and stools and homemade benches.

Lucy Atwood sat between Christina and Grandma Alena, but the conversation was subdued until everyone had their fill of beef dumplings and apple-raisin pie.

"I can't believe that I'm having supper with Alena Merced and holding in my hand the famous bear claw necklace," Lucy said.

"That is half the necklace," Alena corrected.

"Yes. The other half went to the little Indian girl. Whatever happened to it, do you suppose?" Lucy asked.

"We never saw them again," Alena admitted. "Joshua, did you ever hear anything about that Indian family?"

He pushed back his black sombrero. "Many people have grizzly claw necklaces."

"Yes, but not with these special silver beads," Alena reminded him.

"That's true. I did hear French Jean at Firebaugh's Ferry say he had won such a necklace in a poker game at Volcano . . . but he lost it again on a hand with three queens. He was also the one who told me the South would win the war, so I don't believe much that he says."

"Nonetheless," Lucy insisted, "this is quite a historic event, getting to visit with the Red Dove of Monterey."

Grandma Alena chuckled. "I haven't known many people who actually read my little journal. I believe there were only 500 copies printed."

"And many of those are in my attic," Martina added.

"My father gave me a copy on my sixteenth birthday. I still read it at least once a year. My, what romantic times those were," Lucy remarked.

Alena glanced across the makeshift table at Joshua Slashpipe. "Were they romantic times, Joshua?"

"I believe in the history of the earth there have been three truly romantic times," Slashpipe answered grinning, his false teeth shining.

"And, pray tell, what were those three times?" Christina asked.

"When Adam first met Eve in the Garden of Eden."

Martina laughed out loud, then covered her mouth. "Oh, my, I didn't mean to interrupt, but that truly must have been a romantic moment indeed."

Joshua waited. "And the second were the days of King Arthur — all those damsels in distress."

"I do believe Mr. Slashpipe is more well read than he appears," Christina remarked.

"I couldn't agree with him more," Lucy concurred. "What would be more romantic than a handsome knight on a white horse riding up to save me?"

"Were all those knight fellas handsome?" Harvey asked.

"Yes," Lucy mused, "a man had to be handsome, brave, loyal, and honest to be a knight."

"I reckon all the ladies in distress were beautiful," Harvey quizzed.

"That's obvious," Lucy replied. "Please continue, Mr. Slashpipe."

"And the third time was the Californio days," he triumphed.

"And I missed all three," Lucy moaned. "Do you suppose there will be a fourth?"

"Not for a thousand years," Joshua proclaimed.

"Oh, I don't know . . ." Harvey drawled. "Here we are surrounded by a bevy of beautiful forms of feminine loveliness."

Now Grandma Alena laughed out loud. "Harvey, I didn't know you were such a smooth-talking man!"

"Miss Lucy seems to bring it out of me," Harvey replied.

"I do?" she said.

"Not only that, but Lucy's inspired me to go ahead with my scientific experiment."

"Are you going to try out your formula on Mrs. Mofeta and her brood?" Kern asked.

Harvey leaped up. "Yep. I'll just slip down there by moonlight and apply the distraction."

Lucy leaned over to Alena. "You know, I heard that if this works, Harvey could make a fortune."

"I don't suppose any of you would like to hike down there with me?" he called out.

Lucy pushed away from the table. "I certainly would."

"I think the rest of us should stay here, Harvey," Kern responded as he scraped his knife across the empty tin pie plate. "Too many folks could upset the experiment."

"We've got to hike over to Kern's shed to pick up my concoction. Maybe we ought to tote one of the lanterns."

"Oh, posh, Harvey," Lucy said. "There's enough moonlight for us to see. I'll just hold onto your arm so I won't stumble."

Like a child at a stick candy display, Harvey Jackson faded into the evening shadows of Stokes Mountain with Lucy in tow.

"I can't believe what I'm seeing," Christina said to her mother. "She really seems interested in Harvey."

"He is a handsome boy," Martina replied.

"He's twenty-four. That's not exactly a boy," Grandma Alena reminded them.

"I think they make a perfect pair," Kern grinned. "Lucy needs a man she can easily manipulate, and Harvey needs someone to push him through life."

"How about you, Mr. Yager?" Martina quizzed. "What kind of woman do you need?"

"Mother!" Christina chided.

Kern didn't hesitate. "I need one strong enough to tell me when I'm wrong and tender enough to hold me when I hurt."

"And when you don't hurt and aren't wrong?" Martina probed.

"Then I want one with a spunky spirit and soft . . ."

"Soft what, Mr. Yager?" Martina pressed.

"Mother, this is getting embarrassing!"

"I certainly hope so," Grandma Alena responded.

"Lips," Kern finished.

"I think we should change the subject," Christina insisted.

"And I think we should clean up these dishes," her mother added.

Grandma Alena and Martina had adjourned to the loft apartment. Joshua had pulled out his teeth and was braiding a horsehair belt by lantern light next to the corrals. Christina, still wearing the bear claw necklace, took Kern's hand and walked south, away from the barn.

"What do you think is taking Harvey and Lucy so long?" she asked.

"Maybe they got lost," Kern suggested.

"A person can't get lost with this much moonlight."

"Would you like to try?" he teased.

"Yes, I would. Come on." She tugged him away from the lantern light.

"Wait . . . wait," he cautioned.

"Oh, what a liar you are, Kern Yager. You said —"

"I asked you if you'd like to try to get lost. I didn't say *I* wanted to get lost."

"Oh, so that's the deal? You just want to tease me."

"What I want to do is marry you."

"When?"

"Yesterday."

"Mother says we have to get the house built and then invite down all her brothers and their families."

"That's fair enough."

"Are we going for a moonlight walk?"

"Do you trust me?" he asked.

"Do you trust me?" she replied.

"I don't trust either one of us after dark."

"Neither do I," she replied. "Come on, let's check on Harvey's experiment."

"First, let me grab a gun," Kern said.

"What for?" she quizzed.

"If I see a skunk running at me with sweet potatoes and garlic all over its face, I intend to shoot it."

They had not hiked fifty feet down the hill before they met a charging Harvey Jackson and breathless Lucy Atwood, hand in hand.

"Are the skunks chasing you?" Christina guessed.

"No, me and Miss Atwood was out by the gate a visitin' when someone galloped up to the stone corral and dove inside," Harvey reported. "His pony just kept on running up the road."

"Then a dozen riders came galloping up the Visalia road and turned and followed the pony toward Antelope Valley," Lucy added.

"You think they were chasing the man in the corral?" Kern asked.

"I reckon."

"Could you see who they were?" Christina inquired.

"Nope."

Lucy fought to catch her breath. "Isn't this exciting?"

"Is he still in our corral?" Christina asked.

"As far as I know, unless he ran away while we were comin' up the drive."

"Let's go check it out," Kern insisted.

"Tonight?" Harvey gulped.

"It sounds so exciting," Lucy added.

"It does?" Harvey said.

"Yes. Christina and I get to come along, don't we?"

"Would either of you stay here if I told you to?" Kern replied.

"No," Christina and Lucy replied in unison.

Suddenly gunfire erupted. It was so rapid it sounded like Chinese firecrackers on the Fourth of July.

"They came back," Harvey shouted.

"They're shooting!" Christina grabbed Kern's arm.

"How exhilarating," Lucy giggled.

"This isn't a game," Yager admonished her. "Get back to the barn."

Joshua Slashpipe trotted down the hill toting a shotgun. "What is it?"

"There's shooting at the stone corral," Christina reported.

"Joshua, take them back and look after them. Harvey and I will check it out," Kern announced.

"I don't even have a gun," Harvey gulped.

"You may take this one." Joshua shoved the shotgun into his hands.

"Harvey, you be careful," Lucy cautioned.

"Sometimes I reckon I'm just too brave for my own good," he mumbled.

As both men scurried down the hill into the darkness, the shooting stopped.

Nine

Christina, her mother, her grandmother, and Lucy paced the open doorway at the front of the barn where Joshua Slashpipe stood guard with a lever-action carbine. There was a flicker of light by the corrals but no more gunfire.

A distant shout brought all of them out into the yard. "Christina . . . Christina!" Harvey clutched his lungs as he stumbled into the lantern light.

"Where's Kern?" she cried.

"He's okay. He sent me for you. Bring a lantern and your Bible."

Christina clutched her hands together. "What? What happened?"

"It's that half-brother of yours, Billy Hays. He's down in the stone corral dyin'," Harvey reported.

"But h-he's in jail," Christina stammered.

"Not anymore. They escaped," Harvey panted. "The deputies shot him nine times."

"And he's still alive?" she said.

"He wants to see you."

"How about Cole?"

"Cole's dead," Harvey related.

By the time Christina had scurried up to the

loft to retrieve her Bible and a lantern, Joshua had the team harnessed and parked in front of the barn.

"We're all going," Martina insisted.

The wagon rumbled down the slope of the hill. The two lanterns illuminated each person's face. No one said a word.

Lord, I've known I had a brother for one week. One week. And now he's down in the rock corral dying. This has been absolutely the worst week in my entire life.

She wished at that moment she could hold Kern Yager's massive hand.

Okay . . . it's been the very best week of my life, too. But why? Why bring Billy into my life if You're just going to take him out again?

Kern met her at the gate of the stone corral. A dozen shadowy, bearded faces huddled nearby. He plucked her off the wagon and set her down next to one of the deputies.

"Are you his half-sister?" the man asked.

"Yes, I'm his sister."

"He wants to talk to you. You ain't carryin' no gun, are you?"

"Of course not."

"The rest of you folks stay back. We've got a dangerous killer in the corral."

Martina climbed down off the wagon. "You have a dying man with nine bullet holes in him," she insisted.

"Twelve." The deputy sounded almost apologetic. "He jist wouldn't give up."

"We brought down some coffee and leftover pie," Martina announced. "If you boys will build a fire, you can have a bite before you ride back to town."

"We got to get this old boy to the sheriff," someone called out.

"Dead or alive?" she challenged.

"It don't matter."

"And it doesn't matter if he dies here with his sister or along the trail back to town, does it?"

"I reckon it don't," someone acknowledged.

Christina's mother continued to give the orders. "Then build me that fire. Mother and Lucy, serve these men some pie."

Her voice faded as Kern carried one of the lanterns and led Christina to the far side of the stone corral. Billy Hays was propped up under the watchful eye of a very tall, thin deputy with the bayonet pulled out on his .45-70 Springfield trapdoor musket.

"How many holes do you intend to make in him?" she asked.

"Jist as many as needed," the guard boasted.

Christina knelt down in the dirt by Billy's side.

"I'll watch him," Kern said to the deputy. "You go on and get some coffee."

"I'd better wait."

"We can watch him die as easy as you. There's no need for you to miss out on the pie."

"What kind is it?"

"Apple-raisin."

"Well, I reckon he ain't goin' to move." The

tall man ambled off toward the others.

Kern stayed back of the lantern.

"Billy, it's me — Christina." Blood was oozing out so many places that it stained even the heavy canvas tarp the posse had draped over him. She could see no wounds on his head as she brushed the hair out of his face.

He opened his weak brown eyes and stared at her without speaking.

Lord, a few days ago when we captured him in the barn, I thought him to be the most vile murderer on earth, and I wished him dead. Now that he's dying, he looks like a child. Lord, I don't know how I should feel. I don't know what You need from me. I don't know what Billy needs from me. Lord, help me.

"Billy, it's me — Christina. Kern said you were calling for me."

His voice was so weak, she had to lean within inches of his mouth. "I was just studying your face," he managed to say. "I always figured if I had a sister, she would be beautiful like you."

"Thank you, Billy."

"Course, I expected her to look like my mama. But then you do look like your mama."

"Not really. She has brown hair and —"

"Your eyes. I noticed in the jail the other day that your eyes was identical to your mama's."

"And yours are just like our daddy's." Christina began to sob.

"That's what my mama always said. He was our daddy, wasn't he?"

"He was, and he didn't live long enough to know either one of us."

"I'm glad I found that out. And I'm glad I found you. I wish I would have found you when I was twelve."

She stroked his knotted, grimy hair. "So do I, Billy. . . . So do I."

"Things would have been different. I've never been sorry for anything I ever done. I ain't got no soul. But when I look into your eyes, I'm sorry for ever'thin'. Sorry for robbin' them trains, sorry for killin' that land agent, and most of all sorry for disappointin' you. A man needs kin, Christina. He needs somebody to live for. I never had nobody to live decent for."

Christina hugged the dirty, bloody, dying man and sobbed.

Kern scooted over and held her shoulders. Gently.

She sat back up and dabbed her eyes on the sleeve of her dress. Billy looked right at Kern Yager. "You take real good care of my sister," he whispered.

"I promise you I will, Billy," Kern replied.

"Good." He turned his head toward her. "I was ridin' out here to see you. I guess I knowed they would find me and kill me. But I had to see you one more time."

"Why did you try to escape, Billy? What were you and Cole thinking?"

"The judge ruled that the trial would stay in Visalia, and the sheriff said he wasn't going to waste good money for courtroom guards. They would have lynched us for sure."

"Billy, Cole's dead, and you're dying. This isn't much better than a lynching."

"I got to see you, didn't I?"

"I believe the Lord brought you into my life for a reason right before you die. I believe you need to make your peace with Jesus and accept Him as your Savior."

Billy mumbled something. She leaned close to his mouth. His eyes gazed off into the summer night sky.

"It wouldn't be fair," she heard him say.

"What wouldn't be fair?" she replied.

"For Him to save me. I don't deserve it."

"Nobody deserves to be saved. We are all sinners. Kern, me, Grandma, Mama — all of us! But God delights in saving sinners."

Again his voice trailed off.

This time when she pressed her ear to his lips, her necklace banged against his chin. His eyes shot open. This time they were clear and focused. She pulled her head back.

"Where did you get Mama's necklace?" he demanded.

"What? The necklace? This belonged to my grandfather. Did your mother have a bear claw necklace?"

"That's my mama's necklace. It had ten claws and the same silver beads."

A shudder went down Christina's back. "What?"

"I buried my mama in that necklace," Billy declared.

"Kern, go get Grandma and Mother," she ordered.

He stood up and then glanced back at her.

"Now!" she barked. She turned to the injured man. "Billy, can you hear me?"

"Barely," he whispered.

She leaned her mouth to his dirty, sweaty ear and surprised herself, and him, by kissing it. "Billy, listen to me. Did your mother tell you where she got the necklace?"

"Over at one of the missions," he mumbled. His voice was a little louder than before.

Christina didn't turn around, but she knew that her mother and grandmother were standing in the lantern light behind her. "Billy, did your mother make a necklace for a white man who saved her life from a bear, and then he broke it in two and gave half of it back to her?"

His voice was so deep and clear it brought goose bumps down Christina's neck. "At old San Juan Bautista on the day the old priest died."

"Oh, my word!" Grandma Alena gasped. She fell to her knees beside Christina. "His mother was the little Indian girl!"

"That ain't my mama's necklace?"

"My grandfather was the one who saved your mother."

Billy's head slumped back against the stone wall of the corral. His eyes blinked closed.

312

"Then maybe the Lord had His hand in this after all."

She stroked his cheek. "Yes, He has, Billy. And you need to let Jesus be your . . ." She grabbed his lifeless head in her arms and rocked him against her chest.

"Oh, Mama," she sobbed. "Oh, Mama, do something. Please, do something. Don't let him die. I don't even know if he believed. Oh, Lord, please, I just want another minute . . . please . . ."

Martina squatted down beside her sobbing daughter and slipped her arm around her. "Baby, I can't do anything. I'm so sorry. The Lord is fair and just. You'll just have to trust Him now."

"But, Mama, he didn't say he believed. We were talking about the necklace, and he never said it."

Grandma Alena scooted over to the other side of Christina. "Your mama's right, *Palomita*. We have to trust the Lord now." Alena tugged the necklace over Christina's head and gently slipped it around Billy's neck. "I believe your grandfather would want Billy buried with this necklace."

Christina and Kern drove the wagon to town with Billy's body. The posse trailed behind. They waited until the sheriff and the coroner wrote up the death certificates. Cole Travis was shipped north to his father. They took Billy straight back to the Proud Quail Ranch.

He was buried at daybreak in a casket made out of a bathtub shipping crate, exactly fifty steps north of the barn.

He wore a new flannel shirt.

And a very old bear claw necklace.

Christina read the Bible over him.

Her mother painted words on a piece of barn board that served as a marker. It read: "Billy Hays. He loved his mama. He missed his daddy."

After the service Christina promptly went to bed and slept until past noon, when Joshua sprinted to the open barn door and shouted, "The house is here! The ready-made house is here!"

By the time Christina had pulled on her clothes, tried to comb her hair, and jogged across the ranch to Kern's tent, everyone else was staring at two huge freight wagons piled high with walls and windows.

"Who brought it?" she called out as she approached.

Kern pointed to a smiling Lucy Atwood.

"I told Daddy all about last night and about the ready-made house you bought. He insisted that I take his crew and his wagons and deliver it for you."

A big man in Strauss coveralls tipped his hat. "I put this very same model together for a man in Billings, Montana, a couple years back."

"That's wonderful!" Christina exclaimed. "Maybe you could —"

"Miss Lucy already promised us to stay until it's fastened together. I don't need two purdy women battin' their eyelashes at me."

Christina danced around the wagons. "This is so exciting. Look, Mother, it's just like a big dollhouse."

Martina studied the piles of wood. "It does have some potential. However, I don't see how it all fits together."

"Won't it be marvelous to watch them put it together?" Christina said. "How long will it take you?"

"If you four ladies stand right there and watch us, it will take four weeks. But if you go busy yourselves somewhere else, it will take four days. It don't make no difference to me, lady. The choice is up to you."

In four days and two hours, Lyman Bridges's number 25 ready-made house stood ready to paint next to the well at Yager Farms. Christina tugged her mother and grandmother from room to room. "Can't you just see how beautiful it will look with rugs and curtains and . . ."

"And furniture?" her mother questioned.

"Oh, yes! Kern said we're going to have furniture right away and —"

"And how about a wedding?" Martina asked her daughter.

"A week from Saturday. How does that sound?"

"It sounds quick," her mother replied.

315

"It doesn't to me," Grandma Alena replied. "I once took a rowboat out to a ship in the harbor to look for Echo Jack and Alexandria and came back hours later married to your grandpa."

"You two redheads always stick together," Martina sighed.

"Is that all right, Mama?"

"Okay, a week from Saturday. But Mother and I have to go home and get a few things ready. Then we'll return on Friday next with your uncles and their families."

"My, that ought to be a whole trainload!" Grandma Alena exclaimed.

Kern met them at the front door. "What do you ladies think? Does it make a good first home?"

"My first home had adobe walls, a dirt floor, and a kitchen out in the yard. This is like a mansion," Grandma Alena declared.

"How about you, Mrs. Swan?" he asked Christina's mother.

"It's lovely, Kern. By the way, did you know that you are marrying my daughter right here a week from Saturday?"

"I hadn't heard the exact date, but it doesn't matter." He grinned and gave Christina a bone-jarring hug. "I'd marry this girl any hour of any day."

"Well," Martina mused, "try to wait until a week from Saturday. I'd hate to disappoint her uncles."

The next day Joshua Slashpipe drove Mrs. Hackett and Mrs. Merced to the train depot in Goshen. Kern and Harvey headed to the Atwood ranch for another load of trees.

And Christina spent the entire morning wandering around a stark, empty house mentally decorating, furnishing, and rearranging each room.

In the next seven days they planted 102 more trees.

On the eighth day Harvey Jackson sprinted up the drive to the barn screaming, "They're gone! They're gone!"

Christina pulled on her robe and hiked down the ladder. "What are you saying, Harvey?"

"Mrs. Mofeta marched her brood of seven right out under the front gate and then east past Kern's along the base of the mountain. The skunks are gone. I did it, Christina! I really did it."

Joshua rode General Lee up next to Harvey. "He's right, La Dueña. The skunks are gone. I also saw them with my own eyes."

"Harvey, I'm really proud of you."

"I bet my sweet Lucy will be proud, too. Say, do you reckon I can borrow a horse and ride over to her place and tell her? I feel like celebrating!"

"That's a very good idea. The land commission will be here tomorrow. We've done all we can. The wedding is not until Saturday. I believe we should all celebrate," Christina announced.

"I'm glad to hear you say that." Joshua flashed a wide, toothless grin. "I think I will ride to Visalia. I will celebrate a little myself."

"And I will pray the Lord keeps you from temptation," Christina lectured.

"La Dueña, pray that He will only keep it a little distance from me. I would at least like to see what it is I am so faithfully avoiding."

Christina hiked across Kern's plowed field to his tent and little shed. He was shaking out blankets.

"Are you taking down the tent?"

"I figure it won't impress the land commission much. I'll sleep under the wagon tonight."

"You've got a beautiful house right over there, Kern Yager."

"I told you, I'm not going to spend one night in it until we can live in there as husband and wife."

"But you don't need to sleep under the wagon. Everyone's gone over at my place. Why don't you . . ." She could feel her face blush.

"Like I said, I'll sleep over here under the wagon."

"Yes, well . . . it's only for a few more days. I brought these for the house."

"Sheets?"

"Think of them as temporary curtains. I don't want that land commission to glance in there and see an empty home. I'll drape these around the window, and it will give it a lived-in look. Do you want to come help me?"

"Christina, you know I won't go in there with you until we're married."

"My, you certainly have a lot of do's and don'ts. Come on, Busca, you can help me."

The black-and-white dog barked and trotted along beside her.

Kern scooted to catch up with her. "I did do something to make the place a little more homey."

"What's that?"

"I put the rocker on the front porch last evenin' and sat there gazing out across the valley."

She hiked around the front of the unpainted house that sat on the red-dirt hillside without tree or flower in the yard. "I love it! How was it?"

"A little lonesome, to tell you the truth."

"Good. I mean . . . I hope you were missing me. I was certainly missing you. Since Mother and Grandma Alena went home, the loft seems large and empty. Let's sit in the rocker," she suggested. "Or is that against the rules?"

"Christina!"

She grabbed his hand and tugged him up on the uncovered front porch.

Busca beat them to the rocker.

Kern nodded to the porch.

Busca whined and curled up in the rocker.

"He doesn't share well," Kern admitted. "I've discussed the matter with him at length, but he won't listen."

"Well, your buddy days in the rocker are numbered," Christina scolded. "So go ahead and sit down. I'll sit on the . . ."

Kern scooped up the dog with one hand and tugged Christina to the rocker where they sat side by side, hip by hip. He cuddled the dog in his lap and scratched Busca's ears. "See, there's enough room for three. Besides, I need to keep my hands busy."

She watched him gently stroke the dog. *After we're married, I'm going to town and get a lady dog.* "What are you thinking about, Kern Yager?"

"About this land. It's hot. It's barren. It's hard to work. There will always be problems with water. Sometimes the mosquitoes are thick. And the food spoils. And I've never felt more at home in my life."

"That was the way I felt after one day," she admitted. "It was as if I had come home. I can't explain it any other way. With 76 Land and Water settled with the railroad, perhaps they'll finish the ditch over to our places."

"If they are still our places after tomorrow."

"They will be. I just know it, Kern. I know that sometimes you feel trapped into thinking you can't do anything. But this is one time we've been working day and night, and we've done it! I wouldn't have buried Billy up there if I didn't know in my soul that we would keep these places." She took a deep breath and brushed the corners of her eyes.

"You thinkin' about Billy still?"

"I suppose."

"Darlin', you told him about the Lord. That's all you could do. A man has to make up his own mind."

"I know . . . I know . . . but that's not the only thing I was thinking. I was wondering why I'm so upset about Billy's death when I've only known him such a short time. I mean, I've known Cole for years . . . and we were close at one time . . . but his death came as no shock. I had warned him for two years where this lifestyle would lead, and he refused to listen. It's like I resigned myself to his fate long ago."

"But Billy's different?"

"He was dirty, vulgar, threatening, a thief, and once a heartless murderer. But for a few days it was as if the Lord pulled back a veil and let me see him the way Jesus sees him. I've never had that happen before with a stranger. It's changed me. I'll never look at some despicable, lawless person without wondering if there's a Billy Hays underneath." She let out a deep sigh. "This talk is so heavy. I do look forward to lighter conversations in this rocker."

"And I look forward to no conversations at all." He patted her knee, then brought his hand quickly back to the dog.

Christina put on one of the new dresses her grandmother had left and tucked her clean auburn hair back in combs before the sun broke over the Sierra peaks. She followed the scent of Joshua Slashpipe frying salt pork in a big black skillet.

"La Dueña, you are up early and looking more beautiful than ever."

"I couldn't sleep. I have no idea when the commission will be here."

"I think it will not be until almost lunch. No one seems to work around the courthouse until ten o'clock. By the time they ride out here, it will be noon. Shall we have a meal for them? Or do you want to hear their verdict before you invite them to stay?"

"We will definitely invite them to lunch, no matter what. Judging from the time in the middle of the night you returned, I would say you did plenty of celebrating."

He managed a toothless grin. "I rode all the way to Springville."

"Why?"

"My good friend Tracero Gomez runs cattle for the Double P back in the mountains."

"How was Tracero?"

"Very happy to see me. He offered me a job."

Christina felt her shoulders stiffen. "You already have a job. I presume you told him that."

"I told him I would take his job after the wedding."

"You're goin' to quit me?"

"La Dueña, when you marry Kern Yager, my work is complete."

"But I don't want you to quit. I want you to

stay on the ranch."

"La Dueña, with some water you can have a very nice farm. But it will never be a great rancho. Perhaps some hillside pasture, but that's all. I've spent more time with a shovel in my hand than a *reata* . . . more time on the wagon seat than the saddle. This is not good for my soul, La Dueña. I am a *vaquero,* an old *vaquero.* I must ride. I must rope. I must dance the fandango. It's in my blood. I can't help myself."

"Joshua, where is your home?"

"La Dueña?"

"Everyone needs a place to come home to. I will not let you quit me unless you promise me that this is your home."

He pulled off his sombrero and brushed the corners of his eyes. "I would like that, La Dueña. Perhaps someday I could be buried next to your brother."

"This will be your home, but I don't want to talk about sad things today. This is a great day. A glorious day! The land commission is about to free up our land."

"You sound very confident."

"I am. Let's bake them a pie."

Joshua shoved the sombrero back on his head. "Let's bake them two pies!"

The black carriage of the land commission pulled to the front of the ranches just past three o'clock. Four men dressed in black suits and black hats, with sweat pouring through the collars of white shirts, piled out.

Kern Yager and Christina Swan, in his wagon, met them at the roadway. Avery McClain, a court recorder who was along as a clerk of the commission, introduced them all.

"There is shade by the barn, and I've fixed lunch for all of you. Please, come on up. Then you can do your inspections."

"That's very kind of you, Miss Swan." McClain wiped his forehead. "That's so much better than the last place we stopped."

"I thought perhaps this was your first stop."

"We had to visit a small parcel east of here — just a twenty-acre parcel, and there is nothing on it but a tent. When we arrived, a man ran out of the tent and began to curse us. When we tried to calm him down, he fired several shots at us with his shotgun."

"I believe he was aiming over our heads," one of the commissioners added.

"He wasn't aiming over our heads when he pelted the carriage with buckshot," McClain maintained. "And here is the strange thing. The only shady spot on the entire acreage is a patch of tall prickly pear cactus that housed a bunch of skunks."

"Skunks?" Kern quizzed.

The railroad representative shuddered. "It was a horrid, foul place. The man said they just moved in recently. Our railroad wants no part of such land. But we couldn't get close enough to tell him that."

"You're making decisions right on the spot?" Kern asked.

"I believe that was the exception. For the most part, we need to review an entire area and then select which land would be equitable. That decision won't be made until September."

"But you'll have a pretty good idea before you leave a place?" Kern inquired.

"All three of us will have an opinion, but that doesn't mean we all agree. That's why they appointed three. At least two of us have to agree one way or the other," the ditch company representative said.

"Please, gentlemen, there is no reason to remain out here on the roadside. It's much too warm. Come on up," Christina invited.

"Maybe they want to take a look at both places before they eat," Kern suggested. He pointed to the Yager Farms sign above his driveway. "You might as well take a look at my place first."

"That won't be necessary," the third commissioner stated. He turned to Christina. "Miss Swan, we will take you up on your hospitality. It's been rather nerve-wracking, and we've just started the survey."

"What do you mean, you don't need to look at my place?" Kern interrupted.

"We already know what you have there. We jotted it down as we drove up. Miss Swan, is your uncle at the barn? We had hoped to talk to the owner, Mr. Joseph Merced, whom we understand is your uncle."

"He owns the ranch, but he has given me complete authority to run the place."

"I take it he has other holdings, and this one is of small consequence to him."

Christina glared at the man. "It is of tremendous consequence to me!"

"Well, yes, I suppose so . . ."

"Why don't we talk business later. I'd like a little shade and something to eat," McClain said.

Kern swung into the wagon next to Christina, and they led the carriage up to the barn. She could hear his teeth grind.

"They have already made up their minds, Christina."

"Nonsense, they just got here. No matter what they are thinking at the moment, we have plenty of time to convince them otherwise."

"They are going to take these places away from us, and we can't do anything about it."

"Kern, don't start that again. We've worked too hard to give up."

"I don't give up, Christina. But I can't win if I'm not even given a chance to fight."

"Kern, we've got to trust the Lord in this."

"Sometimes that doesn't work," he fumed.

"Of course it does. You're just upset." She waved her hand to the right. "Pull over there to the corral, and let them park their carriage in the shade. And promise me we'll never own a black leather carriage in this kind of heat."

"All of our work didn't mean a thing," he grumbled.

Christina tugged him over to the table in the shade where Joshua had the food spread out.

After cleaning up with spring water, the men sat down to a feast of beef chops, fried onions, canned tomatoes, and sweet potato casserole, followed by apple pie and blackberry pie.

The conversation during the meal was somewhat strained, limited to the topics of weather and the upcoming November election for president. Kern had not spoken six words since he sat down.

With pie plates empty and coffee cups in their hands, most of the visitors loosened their ties and pushed back from the makeshift outdoor table.

Finally Kern erupted. "Gentlemen, I really must know. If you have already appraised my property without even investigating it, I deserve to know your recommendation."

"Like we said, Mr. Yager, we will let you know in —"

"Gentlemen, do you see my house down there?"

"Yes."

"On Saturday I intend to marry this beautiful woman in that house, and we will make it our home. I want to know before the wedding if you are going to kick us out in September."

"We understand your situation, and I hope you will understand ours."

Kern's big fist slammed into the makeshift table. Some of the dishes flew two feet in the air. "Don't drag me around on this. I've been workin' my hands raw for months. I want to know where I stand."

"We have all been working very long hours." Christina tried to soothe him. "Kern's a little nervous about the wedding and everything."

"All right, Mr. Yager. We understand your being worried about starting a family and all. We list your place as one section of undeveloped land," the representative of the railroad declared.

"Undeveloped?" Christina gasped. "It has a house, plowed ground, a well, and two-year-old orange trees!"

Kern sat in silence and stared down at his large hands, now folded on the table.

"I must admit, Mr. Yager, that you are a very hard-working man. Quite ingenious, too. But we know those two-year-old trees were transplanted from Mr. Atwood's farm."

"But the settlement just said two-year-old trees," Christina protested.

"I don't believe transplanting was the intention of the agreement. Besides, the well is hand-dug and could not sustain an orchard, not that sixty trees represent an orange grove. It's our most knowledgeable opinion that this land is too far west to grow citrus. They will all surely freeze this winter."

"What about the plowed ground?" she asked.

"There is no water to farm it, or it would be planted right now," Avery McClain replied.

"And the house?"

The commissioner representing 76 Land and Water Company spoke up. "It's Lyman Bridges's number 25 ready-made that until a week ago was sitting at the siding in Goshen. I know. I tried to buy it from the salesman, and he refused, saying it was only a demonstration model. I have no idea how you talked him out of it. The reason you have sheets hanging over the windows is because it's unfurnished on the inside. The truth is, Yager Farms is a charade. Therefore, we deem it undeveloped land according to the settlement."

"But you can't just take it away like that," Christina protested. "Kern worked so hard."

"He will be compensated for what he paid for the land. There is some fine property over by Venice Hill that could make a citrus farm. Perhaps he'd like to purchase some of that. The house can be disassembled and moved to any location you choose. Or I would personally be happy to purchase the home at the retail price and move it myself. Either way, you do not have to surrender the property until September."

When Kern Yager stood up quickly, all four men flinched. But Yager just marched off across the hillside toward his place.

Christina ran to catch up. "Kern, wait. . . . Don't do this to me . . . not now . . . Please wait. . . . We'll talk it out."

She clutched his fingers, but he continued to take long strides. He didn't clutch back. "Kern, I have to talk to these men. I can't come with you now, darling. Kern!" She stopped scampering and dropped his hand.

"It's always going to be this way. I can't win. I'm tired. Very, very tired," he droned.

"Kern, honey, go lay down and take a rest. As soon as I talk to these men about my place, I'll be over and rub your shoulders. We'll sit in the rocking chair and figure this out. The Lord will provide, Kern Yager, the Lord will provide."

"Not always, Christina. Not always." He stomped on across the mountainside.

Lord, I don't know what's in his mind when he gets like this. I need to be with him. But I need to talk to the commission. Jesus, this would be a good time for me to wake up from a bad dream. Perhaps I'm still teaching school at Willow Bend after all.

All the men were standing next to the table and nervously holding their hats when she returned.

"I do hope Mr. Yager hasn't gone to fetch his shotgun," one of the commissioners said.

"La Dueña is the one with the shotgun," Joshua maintained. "It's her you should fear."

"Yes, her capture of the murderous outlaws made the newspapers up and down the state."

"Mr. Yager is a bit frustrated at the moment, as you can imagine. He likes to be alone at such times. Now I do not yet have a shotgun in my hand, but I would like to know how you will list my place."

"You mean, your uncle's place?"

"I mean," she barked, "my place!"

"Well, Miss Swan, your generous hospitality and graciousness aside, I must tell you that these three sections will be listed as undeveloped as well. I think we have explained the situation with the transplanted trees."

"But we have natural spring water," Joshua objected.

"Yes, you will be able to keep your fifty-six trees alive with a water wagon, at least until they freeze."

"And the cattle?" Christina asked.

"Until a few weeks ago most were running wild atop Stokes Mountain. If they are unbranded, they are yours to sell or dispose of as you wish. But we stated clearly in the settlement that grazing land would be considered undeveloped property."

"She has a house," Joshua proclaimed.

"It's an old barn."

"Have you ever seen a barn with two bedrooms in the loft and a bathtub in one of the stalls?" Joshua asked.

"A bathtub?"

"Yes, come and look at it if you like. You can even take a bath. I will warm up the water," Joshua offered.

"That is not necessary. We believe you. We also believe that such furnishings can be moved out as easily as they were moved in."

"I assure you," Joshua retorted, "they were not easy to move in."

"The fact remains that this will be listed as undeveloped land with a spring."

"And a graveyard," Joshua added.

"A what?" the railroad commissioner gasped.

"Yes," Christina pursued, "we have a family grave site here on the ranch. My brother is buried here."

"But that's not on our maps!" the clerk exclaimed.

"Show them the grave site, Joshua. If you'll excuse me, gentlemen, it is too painful for me to hike up and look."

"You actually have family buried on this property?" a commissioner asked.

"I'm his only known relative, so naturally I would bury him here," she stated.

"Why didn't you use a public cemetery?" one of the men asked her.

"I believe that will be obvious when you see the marker. Take the shovel with you, Joshua. They will not believe Billy is buried there, and you will have to dig up the coffin and show them his poor, bullet-riddled, decaying body."

"Miss Swan, we are not heartless!" McClain sputtered.

"That remains to be seen."

Joshua carried the shovel, but he and the four black-suited men quickly returned.

"Billy Hays was your half-brother? I hadn't

heard that," the clerk commented.

"I'm ashamed of the life he lived, but he was my half-brother, and all men deserve a place to be buried."

"I must concur with you there," the third commissioner said.

"No fraternal cemetery would accept him, of course. So we buried him at the ranch. I will hold the railroad liable for protecting the grave site from vandals. Once they find out Billy Hays was buried here, they will want to desecrate the grave site."

"We aren't in the business of protecting cemeteries. You will have to move the body."

"Move it where, Mr. Commissioners?"

"Wait a minute. We must talk this through. We will have to discuss the matter and get back to you," the railroad representative said.

"Yes, we'll have a final decision by September."

Christina pulled herself up into full Merced form. She felt the spirit of her mother and grandmother. "You will need to do better than that. I'm supposed to live here, guarding my brother's grave site for two months, and then you force me to move and to drag out his decaying bones? I wonder what a Tulare County jury would say to that?"

"If we might have a moment . . ." McClain requested.

"Joshua and I will take a short walk." Christina slipped her hand into the old man's arm and waltzed him down the slope of the hill.

"Can you believe your brother just might save the ranch?" Joshua whispered.

"I thought all along that the Lord brought me into his life to help him in some way. Perhaps Billy was brought into my life to help me instead."

"It's too bad Mr. Yager had no relatives to bury."

"He has a lot in the past to bury, Joshua." She stared off across the hillside. "Go tell him what the commissioners are discussing. Perhaps he wants to return."

"I don't think he wants to talk to me."

"Please tell him. If he's sleeping, leave him be. If not, tell him I need to see him."

"I will go," Joshua reported. "But I will keep a safe distance."

When she returned to the barn, the commissioners were climbing into their carriage. "What did you decide?" she demanded.

"I presume you can get two witnesses besides yourself to sign a statement that your brother is buried in that grave," Avery McClain stated.

"There were seven of us here that day."

"We will need two testimonies in our files."

"Does this mean I get to keep the Proud Quail Ranch?"

"Miss Swan, you may inform your uncle, Joseph Merced, that this property will not be considered in the lieu land settlement. We will list it as developed with a family grave site. The railroad is acutely aware of growing hostilities since the Mussel Slough tragedy. We have no intention of letting the newspapers proclaim that we are desecrating family grave sites."

The Tulare County representative pulled a white handkerchief out of his suit pocket and wiped his forehead. "And we will certainly pass a county ordinance immediately forbidding any burials on other lieu lands until after September 1. If word of this gets out, we will have a rash of new graveyards."

Christina watched the black carriage descend the long drive.

I knew it, Lord. I knew You were going to do it! This is my place. I didn't know how You would do it, but You did. Thank You, Jesus! Now we have a ranch . . . a farm . . . both of us — me and Kern.

She glanced across the ranch at the ready-made house and then broke into a trot. Halfway across the dry grass hillside, she slowed to a walk. Sweat dripped from her chin, her nose, her earlobes, her eyebrows, her fingertips.

She stopped to catch her breath and felt dizzy. *Lord, I can't faint right now. I just don't have time. Perhaps later when it cools off after dark.*

She was still bent over at the waist, trying to catch her breath, when Joshua Slashpipe rode up on General Lee.

"What did Kern say?" she asked. "Is he coming over?"

"He's gone."

335

"What do you mean, gone? Maybe he's sleeping in the house. Did you look in the house?"

"I looked. But he, Busca, and the big sorrel horse are gone."

"Where did he go?"

Joshua pointed northeast to a distant rider on the brown barren slopes of the mountain. "I think he's riding to the top of Stokes Mountain. Perhaps he needs time to think. Every man needs to get away and think at times."

"When is he coming back?"

"Perhaps he's not coming back."

"Of course he is. I have to tell him about the Proud Quail. They said they will not impound it! We do have a ranch. Perhaps not as big as we wanted, but it's a very nice place. He will certainly be back by the wedding on Saturday."

"Perhaps."

"Why do you keep saying perhaps?"

"He packed his bedroll and left you a letter. Whenever I do that, it means I'm not coming back."

"That's ridiculous. I love him dearly. We're getting married on Saturday. He wouldn't just ride off. What does the letter say?"

He handed her the letter. "I did not read it, of course. Would you like to ride with me back to the barn?"

"No, I'll walk back. Perhaps there are times a woman needs some time to think."

"Yes, perhaps there are." Joshua rode slowly up toward the barn.

Christina shaded her eyes from the glare of the sun with her hand and studied the rider ascending Stokes Mountain. "You are not riding out of my life, Kern Yager."

Then she tore open the letter.

Dearest Christina,

I don't know the outcome of the commission concerning the Proud Quail, but I assume we are in the same predicament. I love you dearly, as you well know. It takes every ounce of discipline to ride away from you. But I must go before I make your life even worse. My unpredictable melancholy spells prevent me from ever being the kind of husband you need and deserve. I have tried for over twenty years to contain them, but I must be honest and admit defeat.

You are the first, besides my father, to hear this story. I promised to tell you someday, and I'm a man of my word. When I was four years old, my father was marshal at Rough-and-Ready. He arrested three cutthroat killers and threw them in jail.

While he was tracking down a fourth, the three escaped and came to our house looking to kill him. No one was home but my mother and myself. They were drunk and intent on revenge. When they couldn't find Daddy, they decided to take it out on my mother and me.

They tied me in a chair and made me watch as they held my mother down and . . .

I screamed and yelled, but they wouldn't stop.

My mother cried for help, and I couldn't do a thing. When they were finished with her, they rode off. After a while she wrapped a blanket around herself and came over to where I was still tied in the chair. Her face was covered with dried tears and blood where they beat her. I thought she was going to untie me, but she just hugged me and kissed my face and told me she loved me.

I was crying and trying to get free, but I was still helpless. She went to the kitchen and retrieved her small revolver. Then dragging the blanket, she walked out into our front yard.

I heard the shot, but I couldn't do a thing until neighbors found me. I slept for two solid weeks after that and prayed every time I woke that I would die and go be with my mother.

Every time I think I'm in a helpless situation, I become that four-year-old boy tied to the chair, and scenes of my poor, dear mother flood my mind.

Christina, I don't think I'll ever get over that. It scares me to think that you and our children might have to put up with such dangerous behavior. I think the Lord wants me to live my life alone.

I'm glad for this day for one reason. At least one other person on earth knows why I am the way I am. You are, indeed, the only woman I have loved, and I do not intend to ever change that status. Forgive me for making your life so complicated.

Affectionately yours, Kern Yager

Tears streaming down her face, she shoved the letter into the pocket of her dress and sprinted toward the barn. "Joshua," she yelled, "leave General Lee saddled up."

"You are going after him?"

"Yes, I am."

A wide, toothless grin broke across Joshua Slashpipe's face. "That is good. That is very good. Do you want me to put on the side-saddle?"

"No, I want you to close your eyes and promise you will never tell a living soul about this, especially my mother."

Joshua turned his head and looked toward the barn.

Christina hiked her skirt and her petticoats up to her hips and climbed up on General Lee, straddling the saddle. She brushed down her skirt the best she could and cantered to the east.

When she came within fifty feet of the barbed-wire fence, she kicked her heels into the General's flanks and whooped as he galloped toward the wire barrier. When General Lee left the ground, she closed her eyes and braced herself. Upon landing, he stumbled. But she locked her knees against the wide buck-and-roll pommel and held tight to the huge Mexican saddle horn.

The General responded by righting himself, snorted, and resumed the gallop up the hillside. His gray neck stretched forward, muscles taut, ears pitched forward as if he fully understood the urgency of the matter.

Somewhere near the crest of the treeless, brown-grass-covered mountain, Kern Yager must have heard her yelling. She saw him turn back to watch her approach. He climbed off the sorrel and stood next to the barking black-and- white dog.

Christina didn't slow down but dove toward Yager's arms. The impact knocked him flat on his back, and she found herself sitting on his chest, which reminded her of sitting on a park bench.

"Don't you move, Kern Yager, until I'm through talking to you."

The dog barked wildly as she caught her breath. She shouted, "Busca, sit down and be quiet!"

The dog whimpered once and then lay down beside Yager.

"Did you read my letter?" he asked.

"I read it. And until the day I die, I will shed tears every time I think of it. But I want to shed those tears with you, Kern Yager. Nobody has to cry all alone. That little four-year-old boy had to cry by himself, but you don't have to. Never again."

"But I can't change."

"Good. That means you're still a man of your word. You have to keep your promises, right?"

"I suppose so."

"Well, you promised me that after the house was built, and after you told me what happened to you long ago, you'd marry me. Well, here I am, so marry me."

"Right now?"

"You can wait until Saturday."

"Can I sit up?"

She climbed off him and sat down on the dirt. "Only if you promise not to run away. We need to talk."

He sat up. "I can't believe you still want to put up with me."

"Those are exactly the last words my mother said the other day about you. She said, 'I still can't believe Mr. Yager wants to put up with you, dear.' "

"She said that?"

"Mother is very forthright." Christina slipped her hand into his and squeezed.

This time he squeezed back.

Gently.

"I learned something from my brother as he lay dying. He said that a person needs someone else to live for. I need you to live for, and you need me. If you ride off, who will you live for, Kern Yager?"

His shoulders slumped. "Billy was right."

"Besides, you'll never believe what the land commission did. They were going to rule the Proud Quail undeveloped, and then Joshua told them about Billy's grave. They got all worried about the publicity of confiscating family burial sites —"

"They're going to let you keep your ranch?" he blurted out.

"They are going to let us keep our ranch. It's for you and me."

"Oh, sure, I failed, so you're going to bail me out. Is that a pattern for our relationship?"

"Kern Yager, you are the most stubborn and strongest man I've ever known. I'd punch you in the nose for that remark, but I'd probably bust every finger in my hand. We'll buy the ranch from Uncle Joey. Who cares if we buy it from the railroad or the 76 Land and Water or Mr. Joseph Merced from Mariposa? It's plenty big for us . . . and our family."

"I want boys, lots of sons to take care of their mother if I'm not there," he announced.

"Good. I trust from that remark that the wedding is back on."

Kern slipped his arm around her and hugged her tight. "At least you know what you're getting."

"I'm going to get a separated shoulder if you don't learn to be gentle," she gasped.

He immediately pulled his arm back.

"I didn't say to do that. Why must everything be in extremes with you?" She tugged his arm back to her shoulders. "Just lay your arm gently here."

His arm barely grazed her back. "Like this?"

"You can be a little more enthusiastic than that!"

"I've got a lot to learn."

"It's a good thing you're marrying a teacher."

For several minutes they sat on the hillside

and stared south.

"I've never looked at our places from up here," Christina said. "They look small from a distance."

"The house looks tiny from here."

"We can move it over to the barn."

"And we'll dig up the trees and move them as well," he added.

"Do you really think they will freeze this winter?"

"I don't know. Maybe we'll build a bonfire next to each one and keep them warm."

"They said we don't have enough water for citrus. What do you think?"

"We'll just have to try digging some wells," he offered. "That is, as soon as we make enough money."

"Uncle Joey or Grandma Alena will loan us the —"

"Christina!"

"Yes, Mother," she teased. "You're right. We have to pay our own way." She gazed off to the west. "What is that line over there beyond the Proud Quail's western fence?"

"That's how far the ditch came when they started litigation and halted progress."

"But now that it's settled, won't the railroad insist that the ditch be completed?"

"Only to their land," Kern said.

"Do you see that farm with that ready-made house?" she announced. "As of September, that will belong to the railroad."

All of a sudden he burst out in a deep, uncontrolled laugh.

She grabbed his arm. "What's the matter?"

"Because they confiscated my farm, they will dig the ditch clear over to it . . . right across our place. We will have ditch water to irrigate, Christina Swan!"

"And if they hadn't taken your place, we would never have gotten the ditch!"

He lay on his back and stared up at the hot, blue July sky. "The Lord has been incredibly good to me!" he shouted. Then he suddenly got quiet. A tear slid out of one eye.

"Is something wrong?" she ventured.

"I just realized that I've never said those words before in my life."

"I've said them lots of times," she admitted, "but I've never meant them as much as I do today."

She rolled over on the hillside and kissed his lips. When she pulled back, he was smiling. "Are we married yet?" he asked.

"Just two more days, Kern Yager."

He stood up and plucked her off the hillside as if he were picking a poppy. "They'll be the longest two days of my life." He set her down on her feet. "Are you ready to ride back?"

"I'm sorry, Mr. Yager, but since neither horse has a sidesaddle, we'll have to walk back. I don't straddle a horse, you know."

They had led their horses about fifty yards when Christina stopped and slipped her hand in his. He started to squeeze. "Remember," she cautioned, "gentle . . . but enthusiastic."

He pulled her hand to his lips and kissed her fingers.

"How was that?"

"Very nice."

"Are we married yet?" he repeated.

"Am I going to have to listen to that for two solid days?"

"Probably."

She pointed across the hillside. "What do you see when you look out there, Kern?"

"Lots of potential and hard work, I suppose. How about you?"

Christina kissed his large fingers. "I see the fulfillment of prophecy. 'I will open rivers in high places, and fountains in the midst of the valleys: I will make the wilderness a pool of water, and the dry land springs of water.' "

"Do you always quote Scripture to change the subject when faced with temptation?" he teased.

"Only for two more days," she replied.